THE SURVIVORS OF THE CROSSING

ALSO BY AUSTIN C. CLARKE

Novels

Amongst Thistles and Thorns
The Meeting Point
Storm of Fortune
The Bigger Light
The Prime Minister
Proud Empires
The Origin of Waves
The Question
The Polished Hoe
More

Short Stories

When He Was Free and Young and He Used to Wear Silks
When Women Rule
Nine Men Who Laughed
In this City
There Are No Elders
Choosing His Coffin

Memoirs

Growing Up Stupid Under the Union Jack: A Memoir
Public Enemies: Police Violence and Black Youth
A Passage Back Home: A Personal Reminiscence of Samuel Selvon
Pigtails 'n' Breadfruit: The Rituals of Slave Food, A Barbadian Memoir

P E E P A L   T R E E

INTRODUCTION BY AARON KAMUGISHA

THE SURVIVORS OF THE CROSSING

AUSTIN C. CLARKE

First published by William Heinemann Ltd
in Great Britain in 1964
This new edition published in 2011 by
Peepal Tree Press Ltd
17 King's Avenue
Leeds LS6 1QS
England

ISBN13: 9781845231668

Supported by
ARTS COUNCIL
ENGLAND

To my mother, and Fitz Herbert Luke, a man among men. And in memory of Ken Lovell, who died violently.

AARON KAMUGISHA

THE SURVIVORS OF THE CROSSING
AND THE IMPOSSIBILITY OF LATE COLONIAL REVOLT

Towards the beginning of Austin Clarke's *The Survivors of the Crossing*, a group of disgruntled sugarcane plantation workers are meeting and becoming more and more boisterous with the rum that has been in heavy supply that night. Their self-appointed leader, Rufus, has just circumscribed the range of their actions – he doesn't want armed confrontation and bloodshed, but a civil meeting, as men, with the plantation owners. At this point, a worker named Mango exclaims: 'Sit down with them!... Be-Christ, if you ask me, we should jump down in their backsides! This is 1961!' (p. 56). However, immediately another worker, Jo-Jo, cautions: 'But this is Barbados, though' and this simple statement is enough to take "the argument out of Mango's sails", leaving the men to brood, and the moment to pass.

This phrase, 'But this is Barbados though', is repeated once verbatim, and elsewhere in almost identical form (see pp. 34, 56, 144) as a jocular but grim reminder of the strength of the colonial state in Barbados. Its implications pervade *The Survivors of the Crossing*, Austin Clarke's first, much misunderstood novel, which was first published in 1964, two years before Barbadian independence.

On the surface, the narrative of *The Survivors of the Crossing* is structured around a tragi-comic attempt at revolution on a plantation, and the humour, vices, passive-aggressiveness and violence that characterize the tensions between accommodation and resistance to the late colonial state and its power. However, in its focus on this very specific phase – the last couple of years before formal independence – it is also a tale with much to tell us about the survival of coloniality in the Caribbean today, and the possibility of human freedom beyond it.

A critical reflection on *The Survivors of the Crossing* inevitably means considering the image of Barbados in the Caribbean imagination. Barbados, still occasionally referred to by the derisory term 'little England', conjures in many Caribbean people's minds a place with the most unmediated and unbroken contact with its colonizer of all the Anglophone Caribbean. On the surface, there is nothing strange about this. Colonialism's power has always been stronger in some places than in others, the possibilities of revolt correspondingly more or less attenuated. In the twentieth century, apartheid South Africa and the U.S. South have been considered almost talismanic sites of extraordinary oppression, places where the racial state has exacted a particularly high psycho-existential price on the lives of people of African descent. Barbados, at points in its history, can be seen as their corollary in the Caribbean. Of all the sugar islands, continuing plantation control of the land in the post-emancipation period meant that there was less scope for alternatives to estate labour for African Barbadians than for the former enslaved in, say, Trinidad, Guyana or Jamaica. Yet Barbados has been perceived very differently from those other sites of oppression. Rather than a space which captured the attention of the African diasporic world as a rallying point for activism against white supremacy, and a place where the memory of oppression still makes one shudder, Barbados is presented as a key example of colonialism's persistence – but one that attracts little sympathy, because its residents' complicity in their subordination is assumed without question. The attraction of this way of seeing Barbados spans from ideas in the popular imagination to scholarly musings. In a startlingly Eurocentric essay in the *New World Quarterly* Barbados Independence issue, full of uncritically received stereotypes, the Jamaican writer John Hearne mused that for the wider Caribbean community, 'the Barbadian is a "problem".'[1] For Hearne, the presence of a large number of English settlers in colonial Barbados had produced a civilizing effect on the island, leading to the creation of a sense of 'public manners'.[2] The Barbadian's 'obstinate "Englishness" ' is, apparently a 'source of real psychic strength', because it is responsible for the greater sense of social order and 'more civil and socially responsible behaviour' allegedly to be found in that country than in its Caribbean neighbours.[3] For Hearne, the extent of civility in an Anglophone Caribbean territory evidently increased with the longevity and pervasiveness of British rule, and in a standard colonial trope, he reckoned that colonization begets civilization. Ronald Segal, in his survey of the Black diaspora, quoted a Trinidadian confidant who told him that, 'Barbados, well, Barbados is the one place where apartheid works.'[4] Writing twenty years later, Paul Gilroy, the acclaimed black British cultural critic, did not attempt as lengthy an explanation of 'Barbadian-ness' as Hearne or Segal; for him, Barbados is simply 'a Caribbean island still known as Little England, an island that remains perversely and ironically more English than England itself.'[5]

It is not merely what we know about the traditions of rebellion and counter-hegemonic popular culture in Barbados, extensively chronicled by Hilary Beckles and Curwen Best respectively, that should give us pause here.[6] Rather, it is the manner in which Barbados has come to serve as a trope of civility, order, and the legacy of Britishness in a post-independence Caribbean, a trope created largely to serve the interests of a Caribbean-wide creole, bourgeois nationalist project. A genuine revolutionary like Stokely Carmichael saw through all of this with the greatest of ease. In dismissing an ahistorical tale about the reasons for the 'courtliness, restraint, and civility' of Barbadians, he shrewdly noted that the major and bloody slave insurrections Barbados experienced during slavery gave the lie to this stereotype[7] – and he could have added the insurrectionary role of workers in the labour rebellions of 1937.

The power of this colonial image of Barbados is the key to making sense of the quite astonishing misreadings of *The Survivors of the Crossing* by two of the region's most distinguished scholars, readings that reveal much about their strange fascination, veering between contempt and admiration, of the island. In his highly influential *The Growth of the Modern West Indies*, the classic sociopolitical study of the transition from semi-feudal pre-1930s Caribbean society to the modern order of nationalist politics on the cusp of independence, Gordon Lewis declares his position on Barbados early. 'It is difficult to speak of Barbados except in mockingly derisory terms,' states Lewis, and 'almost every coloured West Indian one meets elsewhere has a half-bitter, half-hilarious story of what happened to him when he visited "Bimshire".'[8] In Lewis's reckoning, Barbadians are a people who possess 'a smug self-satisfaction so pervasive as almost to constitute a national spirit.' While Lewis seeks an explanation for the social phenomena he claims to track, candidly attributing it to a 'white plantocracy proverbial for its reactionary conceit', it is impossible to escape the aversion he feels for the place, and the sense that black Barbadians quite simply should have done better against the array of forces against them. Barbadians are, for Lewis, a peculiarity, a real anachronism in a decolonizing Caribbean, but 'deprived of the British protective umbrella… [they] will learn to fend for themselves under the Caribbean sun.'[9] Lewis lumps Clarke's *The Survivors of the Crossing* within his critique of Barbadian backwardness, charging that the novel's assumption that a wildcat strike could be quelled so easily by a plantation owner was 'dangerously anachronistic'. Of course, the strike is not quelled simply by the plantation owner, but by the old alliance that brings together the employers, the state in the form of the police and the magistracy, the church as a form of ideological power, and petit bourgeois business interests. It is, indeed, the duplicitous shopkeeper, Biscombe, with his control over credit, who more than anyone ensures that the strike fails. I will argue that Clarke is far from 'anachronistic' in his portrayal and that the novel, beyond its turbulent humour, offers an incisive and radical portrayal of why the strike fails that takes in not only the power of the late colonial state and the shortcomings of worker ideology, but also the role of those who are absent from the novel's surface: those who are on the brink of inheriting the colonial state.

The other major misreading of *The Survivors of the Crossing* – which also points to Clarke's originality – is that by C.L.R. James, arguably the twentieth-century Anglophone Caribbean's most distinguished man of letters. Barbados fascinated James throughout his life, for reasons both idiosyncratic and shared by a wider Caribbean community. For James, Barbadians had to negotiate such a predatory colonial order that he would not condemn, though could not ignore, the conservative turn of a politician such as Grantley Adams, whom James couldn't help but admire, despite his anti-socialist politics and support for British colonialism in the 1950s. Yet far from reproducing the standard stereotype of the conservative Bajan, James's admiration for the island's legendary cricket culture, sutured as this was to a disciplinary coloniality, meant he never thought of them as less than quintessentially West Indian. James gave a number of lectures in the 1960s praising the work of the new Caribbean novelists, particularly George Lamming, Wilson Harris, V.S. Naipaul, Earl Lovelace and Michael Anthony, whom he saw as harbingers of a new Caribbean identity emerging at the moment of independence. In his essay 'A New View of West Indian History', he is fulsome in his praise of these writers, but when he turns to Austin Clarke, his criticism is hostile and, as I shall argue, misplaced.[10] James quotes a long excerpt from *Survivors* in which one of its principal characters, Stella, talks with great candour about her behaviour towards her current lover, the shopkeeper Biscombe, and her neglect of her common-law husband, Rufus, now in jail (p. 142). James thundered that this passage was a product of 'Clarke's own dirty mind', that it was indicative of the 'strain of cruelty, strain of contempt' that some educated West Indians have for 'the mass of the population'. Never had James 'heard any West Indian, either directly or indirectly speak in this way'. It was a 'horrible book', to be dismissed and forgotten. It is painfully obvious that what James couldn't stand was the calculated cynicism and wit about sexual relations, and in particular the failings of men as perceived by Stella, and Clarke's very honest treatment of the contradictions between class and gender with respect to power.

Both points picked up by Lewis and James – on the apparent lack of agency of the plantation workers, and the explicit sexual agency of women – demonstrate areas where Clarke has clearly hit a nerve, and are exactly what I wish to explore further in this introduction. One of the qualities of *The Survivors of the Crossing* is precisely that it doesn't conform to being an anti-colonial treatise. Its characters are not solemn, dignified anti-colonial actors, nor the precursors of a future society free of coloniality that we may yearn for. Rather, they are people living human lives with all the passion, wit and vices that their survival demands. The novel tells a story which is key to comprehending the post-independence moment, and to do so we must reflect on the very moment where Clarke begins – in the late colonial state.

THE IMPOSSIBILITY OF LATE COLONIAL REVOLT

In *The Wretched of the Earth*, Frantz Fanon noted that with the coming of independence, the nationalist party 'sinks into an extraordinary lethargy'.[11] Considering this observation in a Caribbean context, we are reminded of how quickly the radical moment of the 1935-1938 revolts passed, and how, despite a series of impressive gains – the formation of modern trade unions and political parties, universal adult suffrage, (failed) federation and independence, all within twenty-five years – the old colonial order lingered. It also shows how quickly the new elites, the brown/black West Indian middle classes, became satisfied with what Fanon called their "historic mission: that of intermediary" in the reproduction of coloniality in their societies. The dilemmas that this would cause for the post-colonial state were seen clearly by C.L.R. James at the moment of independence. In his essay 'The West Indian Middle Classes', James noted that this class 'for centuries… [has] had it as an unshakeable principle that they are in status, education, morals, and manners separate and distinct from the masses of the people.'[12] James's lament concerned the role of this class as a facilitator of colonial governmentality, its lack of a historical imagination and capacity to come up with ideas of its own, or indeed *anything* beyond a desire for acceptance by the ruling elites.

This narrative of neo-colonial dominance, which though it stresses the power of imperial encirclement and comprador complicity does not deny or foreclose the reality of resistance, has been key to efforts to comprehend the nature of the Caribbean post-colonial state. However, I would suggest here that what *The*

Survivors of the Crossing shows most clearly is that the problem is not the impossibility of anti-colonial revolt, but that of *late* colonial revolt. What avenues of protest, what language of revolt remain open when independence has all but been "won", but the elites who will lead us there are revealing themselves to be dour, vacuous, uninspiring, corrupt – and complicit with the colonial office? What does it mean to speak or act counter-hegemonically when nationalism is mobilized not for true sovereignty, but for a balkanized independence, and appears to be the *only* game in town?

In the aftermath of the 1937 labour rebellion, Barbados, like its neighbours, underwent significant transformations which included the passage of legislation that secured the legitimacy of trade unions, the creation of political parties, and, by 1951, universal adult suffrage. These genuine advances were constrained both by the class politics of the colony, and the Cold War politics of the time. The colonial middle classes had established power bases in the unions and political parties after the 1930s rebellions, and the social and cultural capital they possessed facilitated their ascendancy in the nationalist movements. In Percy Hintzen's reading, 'by the time adult suffrage was introduced […] the lower class was firmly organized into political and labor bureaucracies dominated by middle-class leadership. Where they were not, Britain showed extreme reluctance to move the constitutional process along to full independence.'[13] The post-colonial state was, in part, a gift of the British to the Caribbean middle class, who were seen as possessing the social and cultural capital that made them fit to rule. In Barbados, the major political party and trade union, closely linked and emerging out of the same movement, according to Nigel Bolland, 'imagined nothing more radical than a Fabian colonial socialism, and so failed to challenge the dominant structures of this classic plantation society.'[14] At best this meant a liberal democracy predicated on glacially slow welfare reform, and by the 1950s parties like the People's National Party (PNP) in Jamaica and the Barbados Labour Party (BLP) in Barbados had purged themselves of their radical elements, both a reflection of Cold War politics and part of a performance given for the benefit of colonial officials, demonstrating their responsibility and right to rule. In 1961, the region was shaken by Fidel Castro's Cuban revolution, but it is not a promise of a different radical Caribbean that stirs Rufus, the protagonist of *The Survivors of the Crossing*, into action. Rather, it is a letter from a friend in Canada, boasting (and as we see later, exaggerating) the benefits of life outside Barbados, and the promise of humane, dignified work conditions, respect and material comforts beyond the life of a rural cane-field worker.

Clarke's title suggests that he wanted to think about a people who had endured much since the Middle Passage, and to reflect on the relationship between that past and their current condition. The scene he presents is wedded to the social structure that has become one of the most utilized models for theorizing contemporary Caribbean social realities: the plantation. The plantation is where Caribbean social theory begins, linking the social dynamics of the region to the plantation sphere in the Americas, stretching from the U.S. South to north-eastern Brazil. It is a theory that links productive capacities and particular forms of labour organization with the wider social structure and social and cultural ideologies. *The Survivors of the Crossing* predates George Beckford's classic treatment of plantation society in the Anglophone Caribbean by almost a decade, and there is much in the novel that is supportive of Beckford's claim of the plantation as a 'total social institution', 'omnipotent and omnipresent in the lives of those living within its confines'.[15] In this respect it connects to other works of fiction focusing on the sugar estate, such as Peter Lauchmonen Kempadoo's *Guiana Boy* (1960; 2002) and Rooplall Monar's short story collection, *Backdam People* (1986), both of which are written by authors who grew up on sugar estates, who are both very clear about just how omnipresent an institution it was.[16] The image of the plantation as a total institution that generates particular mentalities both with respect to worker-manager relations and intra-worker relations has been subjected to intense criticism, particularly in its alleged denial of human agency to those dispossessed by its power; and as noted above, *Survivors* has been accused by Gordon Lewis and others of falling into that trap.[17] My view is that, very far from denying agency, Clarke (like Kempadoo and Monar) sees worker agency within a setting whose oppressive reality cannot be wished away. A starting point towards understanding this dynamic can be found in Lloyd Brown's more nuanced critical appraisal of the novel, which he reads as a 'realistic satire of ingrained social attitudes', and one which recognizes that power encourages an exaggerated belief in its reach, a misapprehension that has bedevilled many movements for social change.[18]

My view is that many things are colliding in Clarke's novel: shrewd assessments of social and political forces; frenetic scenes of intrigue in which people are often not what they seem (the excited discovery of a young novelist of what can be done with narrative and plot); and an engagement with Barbadian nation-language constituted by performative hyperbolic expressions that render literal readings problematic. There is, too, the irony of a radical awakening provoked by the supposed virtues of Canada. This no doubt arose from the fact that Clarke was writing this novel in 1962-63 while on the dole in Ontario. Yet it exemplifies so much about a novel in which chance, attitudes based on ignorance of reality, and the double-cross have as much importance as the more weighty concerns of race, class and colonial power.

The story of *Survivors* centres around the cane-cutter, Rufus, and his attempt to encourage his fellow workers to demand better wages and treatment from the plantation. Stimulated by a letter from his friend Jackson in Canada, who describes an idyllic life there and scoffs at what he has left behind, Rufus repeatedly tries to organize the plantation workers. In the process he undergoes significant transformations – from reformer, to maroon, to rebel, seemingly with hardly a cause – and inevitably, by novel's end, the "martyrdom" of lengthy imprisonment.

The dismissal of *Survivors* by Edward Baugh as 'propagandizing, over-ambitious, and somewhat strident in its angry, implausible narrative'[19] misses the aching humour in the language and characterization that fill this text, and his charge of 'propagandizing' is strange given that there is no tragically suffering, morally upright hero in sight. Even so, Baugh's charge, taken with Lewis's opposite accusation that this is a novel complicit in coloniality, suggests a failure, from both directions, to attend to Clarke's satirical tone. The stridency noticed by Baugh (and he is at least right in detecting anger) is perhaps better read as the coming together of the hyperbole that satires often engender and the eruptive violence of Barbadian nation-language that Clarke more than any Barbadian writer has managed to capture.

The characters of *Survivors* all show deep traces of the legacy of the plantation and its pervasive impact on late colonial society. Biscombe's betrayal of the workers' cause is attributed not just to his class position and interest in perpetuating the colonial order of things, but because he is a "two-tone" man (p. 127, 135), with all the supposed treachery embodied by persons of his skin colour. Whippetts the schoolmaster is a more ambivalent case. He is at first firmly identified with power, and in response to Biscombe's growl that he is "on the side o' power… the white man side", Whippetts says he is "on the side o' British justice" (p. 135). Later, struck by the ferocity of the plantation, he changes his mind without ever throwing in his lot fully with the workers, only to be branded a sympathizer and faced with unemployment.

The one interest not explicitly reflected in the novel is that of the official agricultural workers' trade union and the politicians gearing up for the spoils of independence in Bridgetown, but I suspect that Whippetts substitutes for that absence. It is clear that the sugar workers embarrass Whippetts in their proletarian otherness from the adopted British culture that gives him his precarious status, particularly because he knows that the white manager and clergyman see him with the same contempt as they see the black workers. Unfortunately, little has been published from an independent perspective about the actual balance of bargaining power on the agricultural estates in the 1950s and 1960s, but one can read between the lines in Francis Mark's *History of the Barbados Workers' Union* (1966)[20], to see in its criticism of the indiscipline of the sugar workers in involving themselves in "wild-cat" strikes the view that the function of the workers was simply to be unionized as part of the vote bank for the conservative Barbados Labour Party to which the union was affiliated. Neither union nor party was committed to challenging the power of the largely white business and agricultural oligarchy, but rather to accommodating a split between political and economic power.

If there was embarrassment on the side of the black reformist politicians and trade union bureaucrats over the undisciplined antics of workers such as Rufus, I also suspect that Clarke was very far from exaggerating the extent to which the union and the governing party in waiting abandoned the workers on the estates to the still unreconstructed power of the white oligarchy. It was not an exaggeration, I think, to portray the ruthless beating a poor Barbadian like Rufus suffers, given the pervasive power of the white elite in the highest ranks of the police force, which only declined in the decade after independence.

From a very different class position, Boysie, Rufus's first reluctant comrade in the fields, is similarly susceptible to seeing which way the wind blows. His moods range from apathy: 'I is a young man who only want a piece o' pussy when the night come, and a rum to drink' (p. 95) to a narrow economic self-interest "Well, let Rufus think o' the people, man! I thinking 'bout Boysie, because Boysie is people too!" (p. 126). When a fire threatens to engulf the plantation towards the novel's end, Boysie is ready to mobilize and march a platoon of workers to save it. Whether it is the spectacle of meetings of agitators that end with the singing of the British national anthem, or the colour picture of Queen Elizabeth II hanging from a tall cane stalk in the hut occupied by Boysie and Mango, *Survivors* is full of tragi-comic scenes that are a continual reminder of a colonial power that is hegemonic, though not completely dominant.

In Rufus, *Survivors'* central character, we see dramatized for the first time in Clarke's writings the problem of leadership and its implications for the post-colonial state. This theme has been central to Clarke's oeuvre over the last half-century, and can be traced through *Survivors* to his 1980s novels *The Prime Minister* and *Proud Empires*, the hilarious Grenada secret files, and the short story 'The Funeral of a Political Yard-Fowl'. Rufus certainly does not meet the criterion of leadership in the late colonial state – he is a poor, illiterate man whose very nominal association with the ruling party cannot save him from being beaten by a policeman on the accusation of being a communist. In the world outside the novel, as has been suggested, none of the dominant political parties would have been interested in protecting Rufus, an untutored violent man at their margins. But Rufus's story is not merely one of tragic disempowerment, because in him we see the conundrums of West Indian political leadership, described so well by Archie Singham in his classic text *The Hero and the Crowd*.[21] For Singham, a decisive feature of a charismatic leader is their 'ability to politicize and mobilize the mass, not merely to propagandize them'.[22] The illiteracy of the masses in the immediate post-1930s period made the seductions of 'demagoguery and propagandizing the mass' difficult for leaders to resist, leading to a hero-crowd relationship between leader and masses, soon to be institutionalized as ruler and ruled.[23] Singham in this formulation places the burden for the phenomenon on the lack of education of the masses, rather than the authoritarianism of the trade union and nationalist movement. On the one hand, Rufus's attempt at leadership is driven by his frustration over the failure of the mainly middle-class political elite to address the realities of exploitation that were a crucial part of colonialism; on the other he has no access to (or at least he cannot see) any other models of leadership than those of the controlling 'heroes' – and his attempt to play this kind of role founders on the fact that he possesses neither the cultural capital nor the charismatic authority of the educated middle classes.

The one villager with proven leadership skills is the preacher, Clementina, and Clarke makes it sadly clear that Rufus cannot conceive of the possibility of female co-leadership or having a woman even as his "second-in-command", preferring the already confirmed treachery of Boysie. And in response to his raging and preaching about the need for solidarity and commitment, the tyranny of the plantation and hopes for a different future, the crowd of villagers seem not so much disbelieving as resigned. They know all too well that this is the future that post-colonial leadership offers them – and they are expected to be silent, as their dreams and opinions are secondary to the knowledge emanating from the speaker's platform.

In the characterization of Clementina and Stella, two initially minor characters who become major, and who forecast the more fully developed female characters in Clarke's later fiction, one sees the absurdity of C.L.R. James's allegation of an ungentlemanly strain of cruelty in this novel. Clementina's ability to verbally attack the overseer and to use her deep religious faith to maintain the villagers' interest in collective action against the plantation suggests a capacity for leadership beyond Rufus's dreams. The elaborate description of her pudding and souse sales is an early sign of Clarke's abiding interest in working-class women's economic autonomy and capacity to survive – which we see again in the depictions of domestic work by women in Barbados and Toronto in his subsequent works, *Amongst Thistles and Thorns* and *The Meeting Point*.

Stella is even more intricately drawn, arguably the most memorable character in the novel. Her sexual exploitation by men such as Rufus, Biscombe and the overseer is a searing reminder of the vulnerability that colonialism engenders and neo-colonialism perpetuates in the lives of black women, and here we see perhaps an early sketch of Mary-Mathilda from Clarke's acclaimed later novel, *The Polished Hoe* (2002). Stella's tenacity, will to survive, and shrewd assessment of what she might wrest from a sexist and racist society is well seen in her speech on the power of pussy (p. 142). Her comments to Clementina here were one of the passages that drew C.L.R. James's ire, as the roughness of her words and harshness of her portrayal of women's power in intimate relationships was entirely too much for him. James misreads Clarke's depiction of Stella as emanating from a superior middle-class perspective filled with contempt for the Caribbean masses. Rather, Clarke's critique is better understood as a de-romanticizing of the folk, and an unsparing reflection on the coloniality of the intimate lives of many of his characters. Stella's intimate interactions with men are not merely based on a calculus of needs and ability to pay; and early in *Survivors*, in his description of her relationship with Rufus, Clarke beautifully describes a relationship charged with dissatisfaction, abandoned dreams, and abuse. They both yearn for an intimacy they can barely trace the contours of, and neither possesses the communicative resources to convey what they long for. The theme of survival in Clarke's title again becomes profound here – and the question of the limits of an existence without the promise, or even seeming potential, of the freedom to shape its direction is posed acutely. Mere survival may be an achievement under conditions in which people of African descent are targeted for non-existence, but *The Survivors of the Crossing* goes beyond this to ask how we should regard this mere existence at the moment of political independence. It is a sobering question.

In its dramatization of a failed and never-nearly successful rebellion against the plantation, *The Survivors of the Crossing* examines the question of the possibility/impossibility of late colonial revolt against a system which, on the cusp of independence, had shown so clearly that the immediate future would be neo-colonial.

But Anglophone Caribbean independence was not just a transfer from the colonial office to the West Indian middle classes; it represented the genuine aspirations for self-determination held by so many Caribbean people. While the limited character of that independence and conservative nature of the new governing elites was clear, independence was something Caribbean people could not *not* want. And after years of uncertainty about its meaning, and as its limitations became clearer, Caribbean people would strike out more forcefully than was possible in the late colonial state against the absurdities and tyranny of their new 'independence', in radical organizations from black power to Marxist political parties, from Rastafarianism to the literary and social journals such as *Savacou* and *New World Quarterly*. At the beginning of the second decade of the twenty-first century, almost a half-century after independence, and in the midst of a conjuncture presented by neoliberal globalization that insists that no other future is possible, we might do well to remember the way the late colonial state similarly seemed to attenuate even the possibility of *imagining* radical change. And recall that its power over our imaginations was broken.

ENDNOTES

1. John Hearne, 'What the Barbadian Means to Me', *New World Quarterly* 3, Nos. 1 & 2, Barbados Independence Issue (1967): p. 6. For a response to Hearne, see Linden Lewis, 'The Contestation of Race in Barbadian Society and the Camouflage of Conservatism', in Brian Meeks and Folke Lindahl eds, *New Caribbean Thought* (Jamaica: University of the West Indies Press, 2001).

2. Ibid.

3. Ibid., p. 7.

4. Ronald Segal, *The Black Diaspora* (London: Faber, 1995), p. 304. This unnamed confidant has since revealed himself to me, and is one of Trinidad's most accomplished academics of the last thirty years.

5. Paul Gilroy, 'On the Beach: David A. Bailey', in *Small Acts: Thoughts on the Politics of Black Cultures* (London: Serpent's Tale, 1993), p.147.

6. Hilary Beckles, *Black Rebellion in Barbados: The Struggle Against Slavery, 1627-1838* (Bridgetown, Barbados: Carib Research and Publications, 1987), *A History of Barbados* (Cambridge, 1990); Curwen Best, *Roots to Popular Culture: Barbadian Aesthetics, Kamau Brathwaite to Hardcore Styles* (London: Macmillan, 2001).

7. Stokely Carmichael, *Ready For Revolution: The Life and Struggles of Stokeley Carmichael* (New York: Scribner, 2003), p. 16.

8. Gordon K. Lewis, *The Growth of the Modern West Indies* (New York & London: Monthly Review Press, 1968), p. 226.

9. Ibid., p. 256.

10. C.L.R. James, 'A New View of West Indian History', *Caribbean Quarterly* 35, 4 (1989), pp. 49-70. This lecture was delivered at the University of the West Indies, Mona Campus on 3, June 1965.

11. Frantz Fanon, *The Wretched of the Earth*, translated by Constance Farrington (Penguin, 1967), p. 137.

12. C.L.R. James, 'The West Indian Middle Classes', in *Party Politics in the West Indies* (San Juan, Trinidad: Vedic Enterprises, 1962).

13. Percy Hintzen, 'Afro-Creole Nationalism as Elite Domination: the English-speaking West Indies', in Charles P. Henry, ed., *Foreign Policy and the Black (Inter)National Interest* (New York: State University of New York Press, 2000), p. 17.
14. O. Nigel Bolland, *The Politics of Labour in the British Caribbean* (Kingston, Jamaica: Ian Randle, 2001), p. 462.
15. George Beckford, "Plantation Society," *Savacou* 5 (June 1971): p. 8.
16. *Guiana Boy* (Crawley, Sussex: New Literature, 1960), and as *Guyana Boy* (Leeds: Peepal Tree Press, 2002); and *Backdam People* (Leeds: Peepal Tree Press, 1986).
17. Gordon Lewis reads the novel far too literally. By the mid-1950s, Barbadian sugar workers had certainly been organized by the Barbados Workers Union, but the fact that sugar workers staged a 1958 wildcat strike (which was criticized in the union's official history) suggests that the workers perceived the limitation of the union's support. In any case, it would be absurd to suggest that the social and economic power of the plantation had substantially diminished. For a fascinating account of this power in the late 1980s, see Hilary Beckles, *Corporate Power in Barbados, The Mutual Affair: Economic Injustice in a Political Democracy* (Bridgetown, Barbados: Lighthouse Publications, 1989).
18. Lloyd W. Brown, *El Dorado and Paradise: Canada and the Caribbean in Austin Clarke's Fiction* (Parkersburg, Iowa: Caribbean Books, 1989), p. 34.
19. Edward Baugh, 'The Sixties and Seventies', in Bruce King ed., *West Indian Literature* (London: Macmillan, 1995), p. 65.
20. Francis Mark, *History of the Barbados Workers' Union*, (Bridgetown: Barbados Worker's Union, 1966), pp. 157-159.
21. Archie Singham, *The Hero and the Crowd in a Colonial Polity* (New Haven and London: Yale University Press, 1968).
22. Ibid., p. 311.
23. Ibid.

Aaron Kamugisha is a lecturer in Cultural Studies at the University of the West Indies, Cave Hill Campus.

PART ONE

THE CIRCUMSTANCE

1

Rufus looked up from the ocean of young green sugarcane plants and saw the threat of rain, painted grey and black in the skies. Remembering the amount of work still to be done, he rubbed his hands, soiled with the loamy earth, over the front of his trousers. The trousers were musty and smelly, and thoughtlessly he scratched long and with determination.

'Jesus, Jesus!' he said to the skies.

But he raised the four-pronged agricultural fork high above his head and plunged it into the passive earth, and with a choking bitterness in his heart grunted. 'Yahh!' Again and again he raised the fork in the air, and each time the explosiveness within him choked the word from his mouth, as if he were breaking his heart. He was thinking of payday on Saturday – five days away – and of the twenty shillings he would get for ploughing the three acres of cane field that surrounded him like the Atlantic Ocean.

'Rain coming, and all this damn land still lef' back to work,' he complained.

And in a spasm of disgust, he let the fork rest idle in the ground, while he passed his forearm over the streams of perspiration that were rushing down his forehead and his brow. But the nearness of the rain installed a curious momentum in his tired hands. He grabbed the fork once more. Frustration placed some kind of demon mechanism in the iron-wrought fork, and he drove it into the gluey soil, and raised it again, and grunted, 'Yahh!' as if he was overjoyed to teach this piece of recalcitrant earth a damn good lesson. The fork rammed into the blackness at his feet. Again and again. Then, exhausted, he had to pause. He reached into his pocket and took out a red, white and blue envelope which he had been carrying unopened since last Saturday afternoon.

'Heh-heh-heh!' he giggled, as he broke the seal of the soft crackling envelope. 'Heh-heh-heh-heh!'

He followed the mountains and valleys of the handwriting, bold and mysterious and unidentifiable. His eyes could not believe the silence of the words. His eyes could not understand the message of the words. But a feeling of pride gathered deep in his heart: to think that he was the recipient of this important-looking airmail letter from overseas! From a large continent, sent to him on this small island! And it had come from so many miles across the seas, and had landed right here, in the correct place, in the correct village!

'Lord, Lord, Lord! This is a funny thing!' he said, when he had placed the letter safely back into his hip pocket.

He looked to his right towards the sea, the same sea which separated him from the origin of the letter, and he saw the tall buildings of clouds like grey skyscrapers closing in on him, and preventing him from finishing his morning's ploughing. But he did not abuse the clouds this time. Now he was glad that the clouds were there. They were attached to the sea. And he felt that this joining of the sea and the clouds and the land far away in which his friend lived was a good relationship. He had to laugh. The sea meant the presence, the existence, the absence of a land beyond, a land in which his friend was living. This letter had crossed that sea. The letter and the sea and the friend were as close to him now as the ocean of canes in which he was anchored by hard work.

He began to think of that afternoon when the postman dropped the letter in front of him, and how the eyes of his companions in the rum shop scrutinized the letter, and then Rufus; and how Boysie, his friend, raised his glass and drank a toast to him, the first man in the village to get such an important letter from overseas.

'Rufus, man,' the postman had said, 'you living real big as arse these days, man! Look, I have a letter for you! Big, big registered first-class airmail thing from up in Canada!'

The eyes in the shop had pity on Rufus, as he searched the envelope in vain for some indication of its sender. For an embarrassing second he had actually held the letter upside-down. The men in the shop looked away, and left him alone in his confusion.

But he remembered in time that the postman had said Canada.

'Oh, Jesus Christ, man! The letter from Jackson! From Jackson!' And immediately the men, most of whom, like Rufus, could neither read nor write, began to voice their opinions about Canada, about Jackson and about the letter, saying what they would give for a chance to leave the plantation and the island. Yes, the letter was indeed from Jackson. Jackson had left the island six months ago to join his woman, Girlie. She had gone on before with a batch of women who were chosen to work in Canada as domestics. Girlie was working with a rich doctor's family. But before Jackson had immigrated, he and Rufus used to attend political meetings held by the Bridgetown Labour Party in the Lower Green. They had joined the party, though they had never got around to paying their dues. But they would spend long hours arguing with the young, educated party leaders, talking about the low wages of labourers, about the conditions of work on the plantation on which they worked, and about the dependency of their entire village on the plantation. The young, educated leaders, and Jackson too, promised to solve the situation. Rufus and Jackson would sit in a bunch of canes after work, and drink rum and talk about these solutions. But when the first door of opportunity to improve himself cracked open, Jackson pushed it farther open and squeezed through, and left for Canada. Rufus was abandoned to face the problem and find the solution.

This was the first letter in six months. But he was glad to hear from Jackson. And though he could not read it himself, and keep the contents secret, he pushed it into his pocket, convinced that it contained some solution to the unbearable existence in the village, which Jackson had worked out all by himself.

Yes, the letter was from his friend. And it made him happy. He returned to his drinking, and even bought two rounds of rum for Boysie. In the morning, when they were alone, he would get Boysie to read the letter. But the weekend went, and still the onion-skin envelope remained unopened in his pocket. Now it was Monday morning.

Rufus looked to his left towards the South Field where Boysie was working. In the distance Boysie looked like a black dot, a black bird picking at worms in the ground.

The plantation had laid off more than sixty men last Saturday. He and Boysie were kept on. Rufus could not understand why. He was an old man; younger men had been laid off and yet the overseer had selected him, a fifty-year-old. Boysie thought he knew the reason. The overseer was living with Rufus's woman on the sly. Rufus knew this. But he never discussed it with Boysie, and so Boysie never let on that he knew.

Rufus cupped his hands round his mouth and shouted like thunder, over the waves of canes, for Boysie. And while Boysie's small figure grew larger as he came tumbling over the tricky soil, Rufus took the letter from his pocket and folded and re-folded it, to give it the appearance of being read. But he caught himself and was sorry that he had tried to deceive his best friend.

'Now why I do that for?' he repented. 'Why I do that? 'Course, Boysie know the situation – '

He turned his attention to Boysie, coming closer and closer over the horizon. It began to drizzle. Rufus left his fork standing and went to meet Boysie. The rain came down harder and Rufus threw his old black jacket over his head to keep the gutters of water from drowning him. They were sheltering beneath a low-hanging banana bunch. The rain poured off the brim of Boysie's old felt hat and ran down on to his chest.

'Rain, rain, rain! Rain, rain, rain!' he said disgustedly.

'Twenty shilling' a week, rain falling, falling like hell, and the plantation laid off fifty-odd mens!'

They watched the rain coming down all around them, like sheets of lead. It was so heavy, they could not see about them. Rufus waited for the right time to ask Boysie to read the letter. He must be patient. Boysie was a rough-tempered sort of man who resented being told what to do. He was not a favourite on the plantation.

'I hear' the fact'ry closing down half way in the crop season, Boysie.'

'How you mean?'

'You know the interpretation o' that in terms o' socialism?'

Boysie spat noisily on a leaf. The green substance took its time to slide off and mix with the mud at their feet. Rufus waited until it had disappeared in a small lake before he spoke again. Then he said, 'What interpretations you see in that, Boysie?'

'If the fact'ry closing down, the fact'ry closing-to-hell-down! You didn' say so?'

'Jesus Christ, Boysie! It mean' more than that, man! It mean' sufferation, starvation, a plague! It mean' all them things, and them is things that me and Jackson always telling you idiots in the village!'

'You mean a plague like what nearly mash' up England' backside in the old-time days?'

'The very said thing!'

Boysie took a small green bottle from his hip pocket, drank some of the contents and then handed it to Rufus. Rufus kept the bottle to his lips a long time, while Boysie's eyes were pinned anxiously on him. But Rufus drained the bottle, and then tossed it into the guts of a nearby cane field. Like small boys, they waited to see if it would ever hit the ground. When it did, the tension on their faces relaxed.

'And the Jockey get a twenty-shilling increase in wage!'

Boysie said nothing to this. Perhaps he was still thinking about the distance the bottle had travelled.

'How you see that, now, Boysie?'

'I gets credit from Miss Gertrude' Food Store for what the plantation pays me. I ain't no blasted socialist, man! And without that twenty shilling' on a Sa'rday, I can't get my salt-fish and rice, yuh!'

'That ain't progress, though, Boysie! Jesus God, man, that is backwardness you talking!' Rufus wanted to beat his head against the ground until he saw some sense coming out. He wanted to drown Boysie in the mud lake that formed around them. But he knew he had to ask him to read the letter, and so he suffered through this display of complacency until the right moment should present itself when he could ask him the favour. But Boysie went on grumbling about the rain falling all the time, and how he should be doing the plantation's work and not idling.

'If the blasted overseer was to come – '

'Look, Boysie! I have the letter. The letter from Jackson – and I asking you please, please read it for me, man – 'cause I feel strong that something in that letter basic and vital to the situation here.'

Boysie was unwilling. He wanted to go back to work. But Rufus prevailed upon him. He took the letter and read it to himself, holding his jacket over it to prevent the rain from soaking it.

'What you see in that letter, Boysie? You don't see some tinklings o' progress and advancement in that letter?'

'Not one blasted word 'bout progress!' And he gave the letter back to Rufus.

But Rufus was not satisfied. He was certain that any letter from Jackson was bound to have some message, some suggestion of a solution to the problems in the village and on the plantation. He wanted to rip the letter in a thousand bits and throw them into the mud pools in which they were standing. But he could not do that. Instead, he tore his heart with grief because he was powerless without Boysie's help. For the first time he realized his own dependence on Boysie, on any person who could read. Tears welled in his eyes.

'Good Jesus Christ, man! Me and you is pals a long time! Jesus Christ, I asking you to read this thing for me – out 'loud, 'cause I want to hear the noise them words making. Please, Boysie. And then you could go back to the work – but oh, God, man, bail me out, man!'

'If that fucking Jockey catch me – Rufus, it mean' two-three shillings taken off my wage on Sa'rday and, be-Christ, as I jus tol' you, that is my cod-fish and rice I playing with!'

'Read the blasted thing!'

And Boysie had pity on him, and he took the letter from his hands again and read it aloud.

'*Dear Rufus,*

'*Boy, life cool as arse up here in Canada, man.*'

'How them words hitting you? You don't see a tinkling o' progress and striking like they hiding somewheres in them thoughts?'

'The man talking 'bout living a life o' ease, Rufus! If I know Jackson, he talking 'bout the womens he screwing right and left, up there in Canada.'

'Oh, Christ, Boysie, that ain't the interpretation at all. Some kind of symbols hidden 'way inside them words, man. But you read on, please.'

'*Up here, they makes you work only forty hours a week. Any time, even* a half-minute, over that time is overtime. And that means you getting time-and-a-half or double-time for that extra work. Even if you sit down on your backside as some of these Canadian fellars does, talking 'bout hockey and baseball, it mean you still getting that overtime. We gets Sardays and Sundays off, as usual. And the money nice, nice. A man could become a millionaire in a year. Sixty-seventy dollars a week is the pay. And if that man is a hustling kind of man like you, Rufus, maybe he could even take home a hundred dollars a week. And it have a union-thing in which I is a member. And this union says every man is a man. No damn nonsense like back there in the island.

'Special shoes, special kind of shoes you wears on your foot so that if one of them two-ton barrels of paint ever was to fall on your blasted petties, it can't turn you into a invaleed and make you a lifetime cripple.'

'You don't have to tip your hat to the boss. You and the boss calls one another by their first names. Canada is a real first-class place! I tried once to look up the meaning of the word Canada once, in a enclyclopediar-thing, but I couldn't spend enough time looking it up, because the book belongst to a nice Canadian piece of skin I used to date. But I sure, sure that the word Canada mean something like progessiveness! As I was saying. First names is the thing here, man. One morning the boss come round. He smoking this big goddamn cigar, big, big as a two-pound piece of Polish sausage, and – '

'What he mean by that word, Boysie?'

'Sausage, sausage!' Boysie explained exasperatedly. 'You never seen Polish sausage yet! Polish sausage is what we calls black pudding and souse!'

'Oh, Jesus Christ! And I didn' tell you that Jackson is a big man, a new man! He even have new names for simple things like black pudding! Notice he not calling black pudding, black pudding no more. He have a new Canadian name for it! Boysie, that is living for so!'

' – as a two-pound piece of Polish sausage, and gorblummuh, Rufus, he put his big hand round my neck and say in this big, big voice, like how you see a Merican talks, "Jackson," he says, "you is a damn good man! We glad to have you with us." You hear that? Now, that is the manner in which we does things in this advance country. But, betwixt me and you, Rufus, I was scared as hell! Because as you know, no boss in that island ever going to come putting his hand round your neck saving he intend to choke more work out of your backside. So – '

'That part read like a piece o' poetry, though!'

'Progress, Boysie! That is progressive ways!'

'I says, "Thanks, Mister Speegulmann." And as usual, I tip the old hat real nice and crisp to him. Jesus God, Rufus! The man nearly fired me right there and then on the spot! He turn blue as a egg-plant. He say to me, "Oh, God, Jackson, no! We don't do things like that in this country. You is a man. And as a man I talking to you. My name is Sammy." And, be-Christ, from that day he is Sammy to me and I is plain simple Jackson to him! And that is what I call progress. You boys down there on the plantation should be treated in that manner. As men. Progressive. And another thing that different up here. Why the hell nobody down there, not even Mister Whippetts, the schoolmaster, or the Rev, didn't tell me there had so much white people in this Chinee world? Man, wherever the hell you turn, you seeing white people and, be-Christ, more white people! Just like how you see them federations of black people crowd down the Garrison Savannah when the Race Days come, well, multiply that number a hundred times, no, two hundred times, and you still coming only to a fraction of the white tribes that habitate this place call Toronto. Not one blasted black man I don't see. It take me a month and a half to come across a black man. And, be-Christ, when I meet up with one walking down Yonge Street, he turned he face and look off like if I was a piece of shit he happen to stumble on in the street. Well, be-Christ, Rufus!

'Anyhow. If I get my fingers on a piece of overtime change next week, I will send you a real true, true crispy Canadian dollar bill, because I know how deeply in love you is with the Queen, as long as her fissiogomy painted on a piece of currency. And when you get it, I want you to buy a rum in Biscombe Rum Shop with it. And as you hold that glass in your hand, pour two, three drops of the steam on the floor and think of me, Jackson, because it cold, cold, cold as arse up here in Canada. Yours, Jackson.'

'Jesus Christ!' Boysie exclaimed. 'That is letter!'

'Letter for so! And you have to admit that letter address' to both of us, that it saying something basic and vital to me and you. And you will have to agree too that Jackson have that power o' words and ideas in his hand. That letter begging us to do something, Boysie.'

'It read like a piece o' poetry,' Boysie said. He was more impressed by the beauty of the words than by their implication, which Rufus seemed to take so seriously. But Boysie could see nothing in the way of a message, or a call to arms, as Rufus was suggesting. Even if he did see such an interpretation, he would not have informed Rufus; for he had already suffered as a result of some of Rufus's plans, such as the one in which he, Boysie, was supposed to lay in wait for the overseer and put some lashes on him. Only the blackness of the night had saved Boysie from being shot by the overseer. Boysie was not disposed, under these conditions, to see any other meaning in the letter than the obvious one of Canada being a more advanced country than the island. That is why he repeated his impressions of the letter, this time with as much conviction as he could muster. 'It read' just like how the Rev reads from the Book o' God!'

But the letter was already at work on Rufus's brain. There was a message hidden somewhere in it. There had to be. As he knew, Jackson was not the type of man to waste words. If only he could read the letter himself a second time, and find out the germ of the message addressed to him! If only he could find it before it was time to go back to work, before the rain stopped falling. But the words were beginning now to be jumbled in his mind and he could hear their sounds all at the same time.

'Gimme a cigarette, man!' When Boysie produced his last two half-soaked homemades, Rufus lit Boysie's, and then cupped the flaming match in his hands and lit his own.

Rufus threw the burning match into a hole of young canes. His eyes danced as he watched it burn.

'My hand' itching like hell to burn down these plantation canes, you don't know!'

But Boysie only watched him. And the match danced gaily for a short while and then died. Rufus was still chuckling when the last whiff of smoke rose from the match.

'I have a plan!' he shouted, suddenly seeing the meaning of the letter. 'I have a real good plan!'

'If that is a socialist plan, leave me out,' Boysie said. ''Cause I is one fucker who don't have much use for Karl Marks.'

'We going strike! Me and you!'

For a time Boysie laughed it off as a joke. But when he looked at Rufus's face and saw the seriousness there, he tried to control his emotion.

'Me and – ' he stammered. 'Strike? You just said strike? And starve? Gorblummuh, Rufus – looka – '

'If me and you strike, the plantation bound to lis'en. All this bowing down and tipping the hat, just like Jackson mention' is the case up in Canada, all that *done*!'

'But this is Barbados, though!' And when he saw that Rufus was not impressed, he added, 'Besides, there is fifty, sixty mens in the village laid off and willing to grab up we jobs.'

'We will have to talk to them – bring them over to our side – and make them see sense!' And he went on to explain the plan. They were to meet the men tonight in Biscombe's Rum Shop; Boysie would be the chairman; he was to see to it that the men listened. 'They *have* to lis'en,' Rufus threatened. 'Or, be-Christ, if not, Boysie, my big clammy-cherry stick will be ringing hell and brimstones in somebody' backside! And I don't have to tell you how hard that wompuh-stick o' mine could lash a man!'

'You is a cruel man, Rufus!'

'A progressive, socialist-minded man, Boysie!'

Boysie drew deeply on the cigarette to keep it going in the rain. 'Rain, rain, rain,' he lamented. 'Can't make a' honest dollar when the damn rain falling, falling – ' And he turned his back to Rufus and poured urine noisily on the banana leaves.

'Jesus Christ, Boysie! Look!'

But Boysie was enjoying urinating and hearing the water slap the thick, shining leaves.

'Now what the hell happen'?' he asked, without turning.

'The Jockey!'

'The Jockey – !' He buttoned up his trousers before he was finished. 'Lord have His mercy! What I tol' you?'

They were trembling and very confused. Rufus was the first to regain some of his former confidence and spirit, and he told Boysie to hide, that he alone could tackle the Jockey.

'Hey, Rufus,' Boysie said, going into the canes to hide, 'don't forget that man have a blasted gun, eh?'

Both he and Rufus had already stamped their cigarettes out and buried them in the mud.

'You frighten'?' Rufus asked sarcastically. But Boysie was already in the canes and he did not hear.

They waited, each man filled with fear, each man too proud to confess to the other that consternation was working havoc within his heart. Each counted the heavy, dulled hoof-beats of the large, brown horse bringing the mulatto overseer to them. When they saw him first, he was far on the horizon of the South Field, and then suddenly he was on them like a scourge.

'Hey, you!' the overseer shouted when he could make out Rufus in the drizzling rain. 'Hey you! What the hell you think this is? The church picnic?'

'Mister Turnbull – Mister Turnbull, sir – ' Words failed him. They stuck in his throat, where anger and hostility were lodged also. He reached for his hat and dutifully held it in his hand. He nodded twice to the half-white overseer. Just then, as if out of a vengeance which Rufus could not understand, the rain increased and poured on his head. All the time the overseer sat like King Canute on his throne allowing Rufus to stew in the dampness of confusion. All the while Rufus prayed to God that He would not let him catch a cold or perhaps pneumonia, and get sick and die. Rufus prayed to God that none of these things would happen to him.

But in spite of the rain, and the letter he had just heard read, and the loss of wages that would accompany his sickness should he contract pneumonia, custom held his hand with his hat in it, ceremoniously quiet and respectful, at his breast.

'Mister Turn – '

'What the bloody hell!'

'Rain – the rain falling, sir – so I had to shelter a little – '

'Like hell it falling! But you see me shelt'ring?' The superiority of a smirk was playing on the overseer's face. He was enjoying himself. 'And take them blasted foots o' yourn off the white man cane plants, you bastard!'

'Yessuh, yessuh!'

'Where the other bastard?'

'Who, sir?'

The canes behind them rustled gently. Rufus thought he could hear Boysie sniggering.

'You mean Boysie, Mister Turnbull, sir?'

'Yes!' he snapped, 'I mean Boysie, Mister Turnbull, sir!' And without warning he planted the riding whip into the fat of the horse's flanks, and the horse spun round and almost knocked Rufus flat. The overseer rode off. When Rufus got to his feet, he could still hear the overseer laughing. 'Get to work!' he shouted at him.

'Yessuh, yessuh – yessuh.'

But the overseer was long out of hearing. Rufus slapped his dripping hat against his trousers. He ran his hands over the rivers of rain in his hair. And all the time tears came to his eyes, he cursed himself for having been born in the island.

Bent in half, in glee, and holding his stomach, Boysie crept laughing out of the canes. He had heard Rufus's humiliating behaviour.

'Heh-heh-heh-heh! Oh, Jesus, Mister Turnbull, sir!'

'Shut up, Boysie! Shut up!'

'Heh-heh-heh! Lord, Lord, Lord, Mister Rufus, sir! All right, Mister Rufus, sir!'

'Boysie, I say shut up, or, be-Christ, I kill you dead, dead, dead as hell, right now!' He rushed on Boysie, grabbed him by his collar and squeezed it. Boysie's face was beginning to get fat with blood.

'Shut up, shut up, shut up! Shut up, Boysie!'

'All right, all right – all right, Mister Rufus, sir – '

'We meeting tonight!'

'Yessuh yessuh!'

'At Biscombe Rum Shop! And you going attend!'

'Yessuh, yessuh, Mister Rufus, sir!'

And only then did Rufus throw him from him. Boysie wriggled some blood and life back into his neck and buttoned up his shirt. They walked back to their work, not talking, side by side, but not too close.

As they parted ways, and as soon as Boysie was a little distance away, a safe distance, he started laughing again.

'Heh-heh-heh! Yessuh, Mister Rufus, sir!'

2

Unemployment in the village meant few cash sales for Biscombe and much free time on his hands. Always when he had time on his hands, he thought of Stella. She was Rufus's woman. Rufus and Stella lived in a small board-and-shingle two-room house with the children of the common law arrangement, Conradina, twelve years old, and Ezekiel, nine.

Biscombe put his head through the window and screamed for his son, Crappo. Crappo, who was playing marbles in the yard, asked his playmate to wait and he dashed into the house. There were no customers in the shop and Biscombe felt he had an hour of freedom with his own desires.

'Run through the Pasture Lane, down through the alley and see if you see Stella at home,' he told the worried boy. 'Now, if you see that Stella like she is home, but you don't hear Rufus's voice, then you knock soft, soft 'pon the back door, near the kitchen part of the house. Tell Stella I have something to discuss with she. *If*,' and Biscombe stressed the word by rolling his large bloodshot eyes about in his head, trying to give Crappo some indication of the risk involved, '*if*, however, you hear Rufus's voice don't knock. But come right back here and tell me. You understand the message?'

'I understand.'

'Well, lemme hear what I just tol' you, then.'

Crappo considered the message for a long time.

Then he began. ' If – if Stella not home, knock and then come back and tell – '

'Jesus Christ, boy! You is a' nidiot! How the hell you going to call Stella, if Stella not there?' To illustrate his exasperation of his son's stupidity, Biscombe dragged the three-inch-wide leather belt from round his waist and clapped it like thunder on the boy's back. Crappo's skin was toughened to this treatment. He did not even whimper. This made Biscombe more exasperated. 'Boy, why the hell I wasting my money sending you to high school for, if you can't even carry a simple message? Come, come, come, lemme hear what I just tol' you!' The leather belt made a tannery of noise on the anvil of Crappo's backside. Still Crappo could not unravel the complicated message, to make sense of it in his mind.

'If – if she isn' home – '

But Biscombe did not give him time to finish. His heavy hand fell on the boy's back. Crappo screamed louder than the heaviness of the blows warranted. It was his way of attracting the neighbours who came to beg Biscombe and warn him that one fine day he would surely kill the boy with blows. Biscombe would listen to their advice. But the moment they left, the rod of justice was striking hell again on the boy's behind. Now, Crappo was crying – crying real tears.

Then a voice was heard at the front of the shop. It was Stella's.

'Biscombe, Biscombe, Biscombe! Good Jesus Christ in mercy, you killing that boy-child again?'

Biscombe's hand froze above Crappo's head and a smile of embarrassment came to his face. When Stella appeared under the counter and came into the room of torture, Biscombe smiled again and went to her.

'Well, Stella honey, how?'

'Mark my words! One o' these days – '

'I just sending this bastard with a message to you, darling,' he said ignoring her. He put his arm round the fat of her waist and pulled her to him. 'Boy, get outta my damn sight! Go and play!' And when Crappo had left, he flattened Stella against his body and started breathing heavily and suggestively. She forced herself from him.

'You in heat?' The expression on her face changed from feigned disgust to a broad, sensuous smile. 'Take your hands from feeling me up, man! I come to borrow twelve cents – I want twelve cents to buy some pigs' feet from Miss Gertrude for dinner. That man o' mine drink out every damn cent in your rum shop, so I asking you now to give me back some o' the money you robbed Rufus out last Sardee night. Come, Biscombe, I broke.'

'And what you going to give me?'

Stella looked at him with fire in her eyes. Then she smiled. For she knew she could not bring any airs of virginity to him.

'What I going get in return?' he insisted.

'How you mean what I going to give you?'

'I asking you now.'

She felt sad to think that he was asking for his claim to her body. She felt trapped to think that she had to continue selling herself to the Jockey so that he might continue keeping her man, her husband all but in name, working on the plantation. Now Biscombe, who had arranged it in the beginning, was demanding his share. Biscombe knew this. That was why he insisted.

'You whore-man, get outta my way, do!' she snapped. But there was more tears than threat in her voice.

'You have to meet the Jockey again tonight? You meeting the Jockey again tonight, then, eh?'

'That is my business, Biscombe. You lending me the twelve cents or you not giving me the twelve cents, Mister Biscombe? My two children home starving – they need food – the man I lives with – that idiot I wasting my young days living with – if he weren't spending all his strength on this damn backwards socialism-thing, I would have food to put in my children's mouth. And another thing! I been known to you for years and years – me and you been close, more closer than if it was you I living with instead o' Rufus. And in all that time I never had occasions to refuse you. It was a gift. One gift deserve' a next one. But, Jesus God, Biscombe – you forcing me now, Biscombe – you forcing me! And I never thought the day would come when – '

'Come, come, woman, don't preach no religion to me!' he snapped. He was insensitive to her pleading. He knew she was unfaithful to Rufus. He knew she had already taken Boysie, and that now she was taking the overseer, who paid her back by keeping her man Rufus on the job. Stella knew this too. But she had to put up some defence, to draw the line between her precarious chastity and the tendency to appear as the village whore. 'Come, come! You lay down under white man, so you could lay down under me!'

Stella looked at him with eyes of bitterness and frustration. She must have the twelve cents. It meant dinner for her two children, and for Rufus.

'If you still want that twelve cent', well I have to lay down 'pon you,' he reminded her cruelly. 'I don't lay down 'pon you, and you don't get no damn twelve cent'!'

'Oh, Christ, Biscombe!' she whispered. 'You are a blasted Shylock! Good thing you is a' old man and you can't give me a hard time! Come, come, come! Quick! Take off my bloomers, you worthless bitch, and jump on – 'cause I still have to buy them pigs' feet before the shop close'.'

Biscombe took her by the hand and led her like a sheep inside his bedroom at the back of the rum shop. He slammed the bolt shut, locking out Crappo and any customers. He put her on the unmade straw bed. His hands were trembling. He did not have the courage to look her in her eyes. But in two breathless shakes he had reached his limit, and he got off, panting.

Stella crucified him with her eyes. But he was full and contented, and heedless of the shame he had inflicted on her. He went out of the room while she dressed.

Outside in the shop again, he asked her why she would not think of going fifty-fifty with him in this business of selling herself, that the price to a white man or a half-white man should be higher. He reminded her that it was a thriving business – could be a very rewarding business for a beautiful woman like her. 'The onliest thing wrong with you, Stella, is that you poor. But your body could take care o' that. And you will forgive me if I tell you that you throwing 'way your virtues and sustenancies in a pond for nothing.'

'Me and you not in business, Biscombe. I come to borrow twelve cent'!'

'Fifty-fifty,' Biscombe said, ignoring her. 'I get the customers and you look after them.' He began dropping the money into her hand, coin after coin, making them jingle deliberately. 'Fifty-fifty! Or if not – when Rufus, that can't-read idiot o' yourn, come in this shop tonight, I tell him what kind o' cargoes he been carrying in his ship all these months.'

The anger that welled up in her heart for this man standing before her, smiling and making this insidious business transaction, was expressed in tears.

'And let me tell you something, Mister Biscombe, you whore,' she said, trying to make her ineffectual hostility for him sting. 'Neither you, nor the Rufus hasn't put a wedding ring 'pon my finger!' She raised the finger in Biscombe's face. Biscombe closed his eyes. 'It not legal. It ain't legal. I only living with Rufus, not married to him. And my little side-business ain' the same thing as committing fornications. I have to do it, Christ knows, in order to put bread in my starving children's mouth – and – and if Christ vex' with me, well He will have to close His eyes while I do it.'

But Biscombe was laughing. 'Fifty-fifty!' he said, and he placed both his hands on her behind and squeezed the two halves of it. Then he turned and left her standing there.

Stella remained beside the counter with the money in her hand, dumb and stupid and weaponless. When she looked to make sure that he had given her twelve cents, she saw that her tears had polished some rust off the dirty coins.

'Biscombe, boy, how?' Rufus said, patting the proprietor on his round shoulderless back. Biscombe was wearing a sports shirt with a large woman painted on the back and front. The woman was wearing a bikini and Rufus made sure he patted her in the most ticklish place. Biscombe, always ready to laugh, rolled his eyes in glee. 'How?' Rufus repeated.

'Living,' Biscombe said, and returned to washing and polishing his glasses for the night's customers.

'Something turn' up at the plantation.'

Biscombe wheeled round. Was he hearing right? Fifty-odd men laid off, sales dropping like leaves from the apple tree in his backyard, and now what? What could this be! Loss of job? And with a big unpaid liquor bill? What, what, what? All these anxieties were reflected in the movement of his heavy body as he dropped the glasses on the counter and faced Rufus.

'I have something serious to tell you, man,' Rufus told him, patting him on the back, and leading him towards the rear of the shop. They sat on the wooden benches in the special room where the special customers in the village took their drinks, away from the eyes of the story-telling villagers.

'I lis'ning,' Biscombe said, tense as the wire on a telephone pole.

'Something basic and vital turn' up.'

'But you still have a job, though, eh?' Biscombe asked. His consternation was justifiable. Rufus still owed twenty dollars in drinks and biscuits and corned beef. 'You still on the plantation payroll though,' he added, making the statement sound like a question.

Rufus assured him that he was still employed. Biscombe breathed more easily. Then he told Biscombe about this afternoon in the fields, when the Jockey caught Boysie and him sheltering from the rain. They were docked five shillings each for idling and for destroying some young sugarcanes which they had trampled. Biscombe was not very sympathetic. He just wanted to be sure that Rufus was still a working man.

'You get somebody to read the letter for you?' Biscombe asked, trying to turn to a more congenial topic. Rufus shook his head. 'Good,' Biscombe said and began straightening the benches in the room.

'Biscombe, we going to strike. Boysie and me!'

Biscombe struggled for breath like a drowning man. 'Strike?' he spluttered. When he had regained more of his composure, he said, 'But what the hell I hearing, at all? You intends to do what – what you tol' me?'

'Strike, Biscombe, strike!'

'You see this? You see this?' Biscombe asked him. He was holding the little black book of accounts before Rufus. 'But how the hell would you know anyhow?' he added cruelly, realizing that Rufus was illiterate. 'Anyhow, when you strike, if you have enough sense to know how to organize a strike – how the hell – tell me how the hell you going to pay me?'

A heavy pounding on the counter announced the arrival of Mr Whippetts, the schoolmaster. He had come for his nightcap. Biscombe excused himself and went to attend to him. Mr Whippetts was one of his special customers and he was treated with much courtesy.

'I have gentlemens coming for their drinks, man,' he told Rufus. 'You will have to excuse me, man.'

'But I want to talk to you – '

'Come out of this room, Rufus, Whippetts coming. Don't let the gentleman see you hanging round the damn place so, like – like – '

He left Rufus and went to greet the schoolmaster. Mr Whippetts was sweating from the humidity of the afternoon. His white linen suit contrasted beautifully with his jet black colour.

'I say, Biscombe, old chap!' he shouted. There was an obvious ring of the island's broad dialect which could not be concealed beneath the artificial English which the schoolmaster always used in the company of his inferiors.

'How-d'-do? How-d'-do, Mister Whippetts,' Biscombe said, pushing Rufus out of the special room, and at the same time ushering the schoolmaster in. 'The Rev not come yet, but I suppose he won't be too long.'

'In God's time, old chap! In God's time!'

The schoolmaster took his white straw hat off his shining head and placed it on the bench beside him. 'The usual, Biscombe,' he said to the proprietor. And to Rufus he said, 'I say, Rufus! That son of yours, Ezekiel, has a head on his shoulders. Quite a boy! You comprehend of course, old man, that he is entering the competition for a scholarship to high school?' Biscombe was in the main part of the shop fixing the drinks, and the soda biscuits and canned corned beef which the schoolmaster and the Anglican minister always took with their drinks. Rufus took the liberty of sitting beside Mr Whippetts. 'Education these days, Rufus, is a door-opener. You take up the papers any day and see all the smart young lads going to Oxford and Cambridge – London School of Economics. Once upon a time, I tell you, Rufus, you won't see such a thing. But this is a new age, a' age of progress, and that progress coming through education, not through politics, not through independence, not through rabble-rousing. Mark my words, Rufus, son, the biggest breakthrough I seen in my life is coming, and only coming through education.'

The schoolmaster patted his fat belly and looked proud. He knew he was responsible for the minds of all the men in the village. But he was sorry that he was not in a position to take responsibility for Rufus's mind.

'Conradina doing real first class in private lessons, Rufus. Watch that girl. Next month the results from Queen's College entrance examinations going to be published, and I willing to bet you two bottles o' Five Star Special that that girl child o' yours come through real first class. Eh?'

Rufus beamed with a proud smile. However stupid he was, he would see to it that his two children did not grow up in the same darkness.

'Now, that is the said way I sees this predicamunt, Mister Whippetts,' he said, becoming sure of himself in the presence of the schoolmaster. Biscombe was still preparing the drinks. 'I acknowledge the meaning o' learning, 'cause, be-Christ – pardon my language, Mister Whippetts – I know the hardships a man does have to go through when he can't handle a pen, or make head nor tail what write down 'pon a piece o' paper what wipes your backside with. That is why I spending my last cent 'pon them two bastards o' mine. Is education what going to release this village, this island, from the tyrannies o' slavery, and – '

'But slavery abolished, long time!'

'One kind they abolish', but they forget to abolish the next kind,' Rufus said.

At that moment Biscombe entered the room, looking annoyed that Rufus was bothering the schoolmaster.

'Why you don't leave the gentleman in peace? The gentleman come here to relax from the rigours o' life, and, be-Christ you confusing the man' brain. Come, come, come outside.'

Mr Whippetts nodded to Rufus who apologized for having interrupted his siesta. He told Rufus to have patience and hope in the success of his children. Rufus thanked him and closed the door of the special room, leaving the schoolmaster alone with the rejuvenating rum.

Back outside in the privacy of the shop, Rufus tried to reason with Biscombe. He argued that the best thing in the interest of the entire village was to make the plantation understand that the villagers were not entirely dependent upon them. Biscombe asked whom they were dependent on, then, if not the sugarcane and the potato fields.

'But we is mens, though, Biscombe.'

'What kind?'

'You making me 'shame', 'shame', 'shame', now!'

Biscombe did not answer. He only shook the little black book of accounts in Rufus's face.

'I know, I know,' Rufus said. 'You figuring that when the fellars come out on strike, not one blasted soul going to come in this shop and spend a cent in rum. 'Cause rum runs through your blasted veins, Biscombe, not human kindness. And don't tell me that ain't the way you looking at things, 'cause I knows different.'

'Rufus, I is a' old man. You is a' old man. This is a job for younger mens. And if they ain't business, why the hell I should be a martyr? I makes a living selling rum. That is my lifeblood.'

'I know, I know.' Rufus conceded. He had run out of the arguments with which he had hoped to convince Biscombe. Not that he had expected it to be an easy job, for the entire village knew which side Biscombe was on. His father or grandfather had been a manager of the plantation bordering Clapham Hill Plantation for which Rufus worked. It was only two years ago that the cane-cutters had walked out of the canes and left ten lorries half-loaded, and refused to come back on the job until they had received the sixpence increase in wage which the plantation had promised them. Every man, woman and child knew that Biscombe refused to sell rum on credit or serve any labourer who had walked off the job. Biscombe's loyalty was as clear as the public road under the midday sun. But he was Rufus's friend. Had been for almost twenty years. It was because of this friendship that the labourers eventually were able to buy their liquor on trust, and it was also their closeness which got the plantation to face up to its obligations. But now Rufus was suggesting something completely different. Completely revolutionary. This was the first time in the long dark history of the village that anybody – not even Jackson the village socialist had ever suggested it – had come saying he was going to strike against the plantation. It was like refusing to drink the communion wine from the hands of the Anglican minister.

'Rufus! Rufus, I been selling rum and falernum in this said location for nearly thirty years – thirty years running into the thirty-one, thirty-two year'. I been here all that time, and I never,

never, never heard none o' the fellars what make their livelihood offa the plantation talk this kind o' ungrateful, careless talk. Never, never! This is communist talk. And if you think you is some incarnated Karl Marks or something, be-Jesus Christ, Rufus, I tell you that I will have to help the plantation squeeze your balls. 'Cause this is damn nonsense you talking. You thinking 'bout bringing 'struction to this quiet place? Man, not even in the war days, not even when things was really rough with the Marrish and the Parrish, even when Hazel the storm lick'-loose in the whole island and tear down and ripp' up every damn thing, nobody never talk' 'bout strike. I warning you, Rufus.'

'The fellars coming here to meet tonight – '

'Here? In my decent establishmunt?'

'The fellars coming, Biscombe. This is business.'

Biscombe did not consider it worth while to conceal his anger from Rufus. He walked up and down the length of the bar, pounding his fist on the counter. The Anglican minister, the Reverend Richard McKinley, came in the front door to join Mr Whippetts. Biscombe only had time to nod his head to the minister and usher him into the special room. Returning to Rufus, he had a brighter expression. An idea had struck him. He had nothing to lose as long as he played his cards correctly. If Rufus wanted to hold a political meeting in his rum shop, all well and good. He knew that the men would need lots of rum to whet their socialist doctrines and help them shape their resolutions.

When he appeared in front of Rufus smiling and ready to slap Rufus on the back, Rufus miscalculated the changed attitude as his personal, total victory.

'I want you to give me a few bottles o' steam, the special rum, on credit, Biscombe, man. Will pep up the fellars.'

'You's a real son-of-a-bitch,' Biscombe said. The moment he said this, Rufus knew that he was agreeable, as he always was whenever he used this remarkable term of clinching a business deal.

'Thanks. Biscombe, you is a real kiss-me-arse first-class gentleman.' Biscombe chuckled and showed his three gold teeth, two in the bottom and the other in the top, and went straight to the little black book and made a note of the prospective sale. He was the first man in the island to conceive the idea of a sales tax. Any rum sold on credit was increased in price by three per cent, because of the privilege. But Rufus was happy. He did not mind this added expense.

'Well, let we fire a quick rum to seal and sign things, Biscombe, eh?'

'I tell you, Rufus, you can't beat *them* – They is a hundred times more stronger than you. But – ' He did not finish his observations. He went to get a bottle with some Five Star. He poured a little in a glass for Rufus, and he gave himself a couple of drops in the bottom of an enamel cup.

'Till then,' Rufus said, tossing his drink down. 'Seal' and sign', then. Till then, then, Bis boy!'

'Seal' and sign', Rufus,' Biscombe replied without enthusiasm.

'Till then, Biscombe.' Rufus bent under the counter on his way out. He stopped and looked at Biscombe. 'You seen Stella today?' Biscombe almost choked on his drink. Well, if she come round, don't say nothing 'bout this business to her, eh, Bis boy? As men.'

'Seal' and sign', Rufus.'

'I know all the time, Biscombe boy, that you might be a blasted shopkeeper and proprietor, but, be-Christ you is one o' we working men, nevertheless! You is one o' the boys.' Before he jumped down from the door, he looked back and winked at Biscombe, and said, 'Seal' and sign'!'

'Till then, Rufus.'

The moment Rufus left, Biscombe rushed to the telephone. His hands were trembling. He wondered if he was doing the right thing: to inform on the men. Rufus had just confided in him, as he always had – Oh, Christ! it had to be done. A rum shop must sell rum. With a strike, who knows what would happen?

Beads of nervousness started to pour out on his forehead. The red handkerchief in his hand did not seem absorbent enough, for the perspiration was still forming and the kerchief was wet.

'Why the hell he don't answer this damn thing?'

Somebody picked up the phone. Biscombe's body stiffened.

'Mister Turnbull – quick! I want to talk to the overseer!' he said into the phone. And to his own conscience he said, 'No blasted communist going to make me go bankrupt – not at all – '

3

Mr Whippetts could not believe his ears. In all his life, in all the years in which he had shaped and formed the minds of the men, and of the women too, during all the generations of children in this village, he had never heard of such behaviour. A strike! In his village!

The minister too was horrified. He said it was not ordained by God for the people to rise up against their leaders, whether spiritual or temporal. While the discussion ranged across these precarious intellectual precipices, Biscombe nodded his head in agreement, without understanding the technicalities of the arguments. But he knew that these two gentlemen felt the same way as he did. And although they expressed their resentment in terms which he found difficult to follow, he did not really give a damn if they talked above his head.

'I don't pretend to follow all the ins and outs o' your words,' he admitted, after they had talked for about two hours. 'But I know one thing. Strike in this village, mean one thing. People outta work. No work mean' no money. And no money mean' my sales dropping. So you can't be vexed with me if I say again and again that I 'gainst this strike business.'

The schoolmaster nodded in agreement. The minister agreed too. But his reason was slightly different from Biscombe's. He looked at the matter from the point of view of spiritual disobedience. It would mean fewer people coming to church during the crisis. He did not add, however, that smaller congregations meant also smaller collections. Biscombe spotted this gap in his argument and quickly reminded him of it.

'Me and you we arguing the said point then, Rev? 'Cause, if we allow Rufus to go on with this damn nonsense, them collection plates o' yours going to be damn bare next Sundee, and the hundred next Sundees – '

'Respect, Biscombe, respect for the man of God,' the school-master cautioned. But the minister, being also a good-natured human being, smiled and complimented Biscombe on his business acumen.

'The next time that chaplaincy is vacant, Biscombe, remind me to think of offering you the position. We need people like you in the field of Christianity. Can't spread the gospel without funds!'

'We gotta do something!' the schoolmaster said, forgetting his proper English vocabulary. 'Something have to happen. And happen quick!'

And the three of them sat silent, seeking a solution. Biscombe had not disclosed his plan to them. He was waiting to see what solution they could offer.

'If I had knew,' the schoolmaster went on to say, 'I would never enter his son, Ezekiel, for that government scholarship. What would I look like, if people knew I was sponsoring the son of a strike – strike – strike-maker for a government scholarship? You see my position, Mister Minister? As a' employee of the government, I have to be careful. This could ruin my whole career. And I just enter' my application for the headmastership o' that new school in Erdiston. This – this could ruin me for life!'

'What 'bout the police?' Biscombe asked.

'Leave the police outta this, man. The police ain't worth shit in this island. First, the police, then the papers, then the selection committee know', and my chances wash' out in the sea. Leave out the damn police, Biscombe. We could fix this by ourselves.'

'The plantation, then?' the minister suggested. Mr Whippetts jumped to his feet, triumphant.

'Why the hell we didn' think o' that solution long, long time ago? Common sense! The plantation! They intend to strike 'gainst the plantation, so it up to the plantation to look after them. Right?'

'You talking the Gospull, Mister Whippetts.'

'One thing, though,' the minister cautioned. 'How are we to know that they will really come here? How are we to know that they will strike? How sure are we that the men – that Rufus is a communist? We only have what Biscombe said.'

Biscombe was insulted by this attitude, and he struggled hard with himself not to show his annoyance.

'Look, Rev, I don't mean to be indecent, I don't mean to be disrespectful, but I gotta remind you that I born and raised up in this village. I know these people. You is a foreigner – excuse the word – but you been only living in this island for three years. And, be-Christ, they is certain things you would never be able to understand 'bout these people. Well, I know. And Whippetts here, he know' damn good, too. There was a fellar living in this village name' Jackson. Well, he and Rufus was friends. And that's not all, neither. Jackson and Rufus belongst to the Labour Party. And you know as good as a cent, man, that the labour-things those bastards talk 'bout down in the Lower Green ain't no labour problems what going to help the poor people in this country! They talking communist talk! Strike talk! They want to mash up the tranquillities o' this place. But anyhow. Jackson got run out of the island. And he living in Canada now.'

'I thought Jackson left of his free will?' the schoolmaster interjected.

'You thought? Well, you thought wrong, Whippetts. More police and detectives was after Jackson than flies after a dead cat in the road.'

'The letter!' Mr Whippetts exclaimed. 'That letter! The postman bring a letter from Canada last Sa'rday.'

'Oh, Jesus Christ! What I been telling you? Is common sense! Jackson and Rufus in communications with one another. And that is trouble.'

'Infiltration,' the minister pronounced.

'You damn right it is infiltrations,' the schoolmaster agreed. 'Biscombe, call up the plantation!'

Again Biscombe was triumphant. A smile came to his mulatto face and his gold teeth gleamed in the gathering darkness in the room. He lit the two kerosene lamps and put them on the long table.

'The manager coming!' he said.

Mr Whippetts stared at him, wondering, wondering. Then he challenged him.

'Why the manager coming here tonight, Biscombe? I didn't

know he used to take his liquors in your establishment? He don't drink at Goddard's no more?' But Biscombe pretended he was busy cleaning the crumbs from the table and bringing in more biscuits and corned beef. 'You called the manager, Biscombe?'

Biscombe wheeled round, surprised at the question.

'Me? Call them? Oh, Christ, Whippetts, I isn't a traitor! I 'gainst this thing, as I said, 'cause it mean' bad business for my rum shop. But that is all. I not sending nobody in Glendairy for breaking the peace – '

'I hope so, Biscombe.'

'Well, let's forget the whole thing and drink,' the minister suggested. And they did that.

Biscombe sat with them for one round of drinks and then he left to tidy up the shop. While he was there, a large black motor car pulled up in front of the shop. The manager got out. He was furious and excited. Behind him was Turnbull, the overseer. Turnbull entered the shop first.

'Jesus Christ, Biscombe, it is true?' he asked, nervous as if he was going to war. Biscombe noticed the revolver in his pocket. Sweat began to gather on his face again.

'A gun? You bring a gun?'

'Well, what the hell you expects, Biscombe? A strike need' tough talking to. Anyhow, the manager waiting by the car. He want' to talk to you. And, Biscombe, he want' to come in the special room and wait – perhaps a couple o' Five Stars?'

'Lord have His mercy, Turnbull! I only call to put you on your guard. I didn't expect no guns, man.'

'Take it easy, Bis, boy. You is a real kiss-me-arse ally. You is a first-class good boy!' The evening was humid and the overseer had to wipe his forehead every now and then to keep cool. 'And lis'en, Bis, boy. We have Stella outside in the car. It is going to be shit tonight, boy! Fireworks! I have him by his balls, wherever he run'!'

'But the gun, Turnbull! Jesus Christ, I don't like guns, man!'

'Forget the gun, man! Only one little shot – bram! – between his balls, and he run, be-Christ, like a rabbit. And Biscombe, guess what? I catch that same bastard today shelt'ring from the rain under a banana tree! Jesus God! You ever seen such a' arse? Shelt'ring from the rain under a tree – and a banana tree at that?'

'Rufus tol' me what happen'.'

'And the five shilling' he lost for – ?'

'Everything, Turnbull.'

'And 'bout this big communist riot plan' for tonight, too, eh?'

'Every fucking thing, Turnbull! Now you get your informations, now leave me alone!'

'No need to get nasty, Bis, boy! We have everything under control.'

Biscombe went to hear what the manager wanted. As he left, the overseer stopped him. He placed his arms round Biscombe's shoulders and patted him.

'You on our side, Biscombe. The manager promise' to spend money in this rum shop tonight like water. Money like fire! Now go and be a good boy!'

'You said Stella out there, too?'

'Yeah. I going to park the car in a' alley so they won't see it. You go and bring in Stella and the manager in the special room till I come back. When the bastard coming?'

But Biscombe was too worried to answer. He climbed down from the threshold of the front door and walked in the darkness to meet the manager. Stella was in the back seat, proud as a nightingale to be so near to the manager of the plantation. Biscombe saw her and pretended he had never known her before. The overseer came out soon after him.

'Jolly good work, Biscombe,' the manager beamed. 'I suppose my man told you how we intend to pay you for this piece of information. Well!' Without saying any more, he went with Biscombe into the shop, into the special room. Stella waited in the car with the overseer, and they joined the party a few minutes later.

'Good God, Mister Manager!' exclaimed the schoolmaster at the sight of the manager in the village rum shop. 'Is prosperity coming to our humble establishment?' But the manager said nothing. He only smiled. And as he sat down, he shifted something heavy in his hip pocket. Biscombe noticed and looked away. 'Biscombe, another two bottles of steam!'

'No, no, no!' the manager said, holding out a crisp ten-dollar bill. 'Drinks for the gentlemen.' And to the minister he said, 'This seems a pleasant place to hold communion, Mister McKinley, don't you think?'

'All chapels are not churches, Mister Manager.'

The men arrived about thirty minutes later. There were about seventy of them. The moment they entered the rum shop, they began banging their fists on the counter and shouting for Biscombe.

Biscombe was trembling now. He did not know what to expect. He had not planned it this way and he was nervous about the outcome. Stella was present, and this did not make him happier. Not one word had been said in all the time they were drinking in the special room about the impending meeting and strike. This made him even more tense as he was a simple man. If he hated a man, he told him so. If he was expecting Stella to come and share his bed, he would walk up and down like a dog in heat. He could not sit and wait, and expect her to arrive. He had to do something to help her to arrive faster. His tension was the greater when he saw these four men – Whippetts, the minister, the overseer and the manager – sitting down and drinking as calm as cucumbers in the hot season, knowing what they had in their minds and knowing what they had to do, and still not saying one goddamn word.

Is this the way white people behave, he asked himself, over and over, as he poured their drinks, and smiled and laughed at their jokes, but remained tied up inside. Whippetts was not white. Nobody could even imagine that he was. Neither was Stella. He himself, he could only claim to be halfway white. This claim, and this loss of claim, worried him too. Why was Whippetts so close to the plantation people? He could understand Stella's position. She was nothing but a smart whore, a bitch. And himself? What was he? What was he?

The men were pounding the counter.

'Excuse me, gentlemens, excuse me,' and he left, shaking like a leaf, but smiling to conceal his nervousness.

'Biscombe, you still in business, or what? You still selling rum?' Rufus was angry, but not too angry.

'Busy, Rufus. I'se a busy man. But what can I do for you gentlemens?'

Rufus made a rough count of the men and told Biscombe to open three bottles of the Five Star Special. 'Let we see which way the wind blowing from.'

'Sure, Rufus, sure.'

A happy ripple of expectation moved through the men. Boysie was there. He was conspicuous in a clean suit of khaki material which his mother had ironed and which was as stiff as a suit of armour. He had a new, large, finely sharpened lead pencil behind his ear. In his hand was an exercise book, ruled in double lines, with the names and addresses of the seventy men present. Biscombe brought the bottles, opened them and dropped them on the counter. He brought a large glass jug of water which had no ice in it. Only the men in the special room got ice in their drinks. But the men did not care too much about not having this privilege since, to them, rum drunk straight burned a more joyous passage down their throats. They could not understand how the Anglican minister and the manager could drink rum mixed with ice and Coca Cola, and still have the presumption to say that it was rum. When Biscombe, out of kindness, offered to bring in some ice and more glasses, they shook their heads and begged him to keep 'those kiss-me-arse things' inside the special room.

The men were mostly young, strong and undedicated to any particular cause. Their only loyalty was to the money which they got from working on the plantation; and after work, to drink in the rum shop. They were poor, as poor as a cane-field worker is poor. For they worked only part of the year. That was during the reaping of the canes. For the rest of the year they repaired houses for their friends or neighbours, fixed old shoes, bicycles, and did other such around-the-house jobs. They had come tonight because Rufus had promised to buy them free drinks. They had come because he had made some rash promises about getting their jobs back for them. But they knew that the plantation was closing down half way in the crop season. They knew that Rufus and Boysie were the only two labourers to be kept on during the next two months before the canes were reaped. They knew the reason for keeping Rufus on the job. Everyone in the village,

54

except Rufus, saw through the motive of the overseer for retaining him, when the plantation could have hired a younger, stronger man to work with Boysie. But the men said nothing. Rufus was a leader of the people in the village. He was the leader because of the wisdom of his age, of his experience, because, apart from Mango, he was the oldest active labourer in the village. But perhaps, most of all, the men gathered in that rum shop had met to drench the thirst of their frustration and disillusionment, in the rum which he had promised to give them.

Biscombe finished putting the rum and water on the counter, and then returned to the other room. The rum was being passed round. The men took sips, large gulps, and cleared their throats as the fiery liquid hit the bottom of their stomachs.

'Christ!' somebody said, 'that is fire!'

'But why the hell we meeting at all?' Jo-Jo asked, looking at Rufus and then at Boysie. 'You ain't propose' the motive and motivations for this meeting, yet!'

'Shut up your blasted mouth, Jo-Jo. Wait till everybody have a taste o' this medicine! And then, you going to understand the wherefores o' this meeting.'

Rufus was about to chastise him. The muscles in his face tightened and he rested his hand on the ugly, knotted stick which was on the counter before him. But Boysie was still talking.

'I is the chairman o' this meeting.' He was speaking with a strange, clear tone of authority. Rufus glanced at him, and was proud and glad that he had chosen such a strong chairman. He knew the men could give trouble, might wish to back out of the business, and it was good to have a strong chairman to keep them in order. Rufus thought immediately of the House of Assembly where he had seen, once or twice when Jackson had taken him to Bridgetown, the workings of his party, of democracy. Perhaps, if something happened, he thought, perhaps I could make Boysie the Speaker of my party. His thoughts went back to the men present. He heard Boysie saying, '...and I will make the order when the time come', that Rufus is the speaker. He will have the floor. Now, since I is the chairman, Rufus, and Rufus alone, going to talk. Now, shut up your blasted trap and lis'en – or let me give you two-three lashes with this stick!'

'Bravo, Boysie!' Rufus said in his heart.

Boysie pulled his own stick from his belt like a sword. He placed it heavily on the counter. The men saw the cruel joints and notches in it. They saw Boysie's cruel eyes, too. They looked from Boysie to Rufus, and they remembered the destruction which Rufus had worked once on an enemy. But Rufus was smiling indulgently now, like a father.

Rufus began to explain the reason for meeting: the plantation was playing the arse, he said. Low wages, long hours, and if a man even sheltered from the rain, he was docked five shillings. He did not tell them that he and Boysie had killed a hole of young sugar plants. He felt there were larger causes for rebellion against the injustice of the plantation and the overseer. He said that the overseer was a criminal, a dictator; and the men, not knowing exactly what he was referring to, assumed that he was hinting at the unfaithfulness of Stella with the overseer.

'True, true, true!' they said. 'He isn't no damn man at all. He is a man-goose!'

Rufus explained that he did not wish any bloodshed, because, as they knew, once when some labourers tried to talk to the plantation owners, the whole business got out of hand and shots were fired and sticks were flashing about like arrows of lightning. He did not wish any of this to happen. All he wanted, he said, was to be able to sit down with the plantation owners and discuss these matters.

'Sit down with them!' Mango exclaimed. 'Be-Christ, if you ask me, we should jump down in their backsides! This is 1961!'

'But this is Barbados, though,' Jo-Jo reminded him. And that wiped the argument out of Mango's sails. The men grumbled.

'Now, I don't have to tell you that we works from sun-up till sun-down, twelve hours a fucking day, six days a blasted week, and for what? Twenty shillings! They is other places in this world, in this same West Indies, where a man could get three times, four times more wage than that – '

'I hear' from a cousin o' mine, they gets five shilling' in St Lucia, though,' someone interjected.

'Well, that is good! But that is St Lucia! We talking 'bout Barbados!' Rufus felt for the stick. His hand touched it and he waited for further counter-arguments and interruptions. But none were forthcoming. He continued. 'I don't know, 'bout you, but I know that I is a cod-fish-eating man, and all o' you must be too 'cause we gets the same wage. Now that ain't fair. The socialists say everybody should get the same wage, the same food in his guts when the evenings come, and be-Christ, the same piece o' change in his pockets, rackling 'bout, when the Sa'rdays come. Now, tell me if this is fair? The Jockey, that bastard what rides about on a horseback all the damn day, he get a twenty-shilling raise – '

'Oh, Jesus God!' somebody exclaimed.

' – it seem' strange, eh? Well, that happen' the same day when the same Jockey lay off you mens.' Emotion was springing up among the men. Rufus began to feel that the meeting was being successful. Now was the time to spring the bomb on them. He looked at Boysie and smiled. 'Now, lis'en. Lis'en good. 'Cause as you know, the plantation have spies. And spies might even be in this very shop right now. So, lis'en real good and Boysie will read you some o' the things that does happen in other places, in advance' places.' He went on to tell them about the letter from Jackson, giving it his own interpretation. The letter was addressed to all of them, he said, and it was their duty to listen to what it had to say. At the mention of Jackson's name, a great cheer went up. Rufus held his hands in the air, begging for silence, just as he had seen the Prime Minister do once at a political meeting in the Lower Green. He felt just like a Prime Minister. As he listened to the applause of his men, his people, his head began to swim and he imagined himself once again in the richly stained, panelled chamber of the House of Assembly.

When the excitement died down and sufficient fire and brimstone in the rum had worked itself into their passions and emotions, Boysie took the crackling letter from his pocket, cleared his throat five or six times, and began reading it aloud.

'*Dear Rufus*', he read, paraphrasing it to suit the temperament of the meeting. '*Life up here in Canada is the same thing as living in Goat-heaven and Kiddy-kingdom…*'

Cries of '*Hear, hear!*' went up from the men. The noise attracted Biscombe from the special room, where he had returned to join the plantation manager, the overseer and his other guests. He opened the door a crack and listened.

57

'They intends to riot?' the schoolmaster asked, when the noise filled the little room. He was so moved that he forgot his proper English. 'This is a damn riot in the offing! We have to do something!'

'We will,' the overseer said, gripping his revolver. Biscombe closed the door and walked back to the table. Stella was beginning to understand now. She looked appealingly at the overseer, but vengeance was in his eyes and he said nothing to her. Biscombe was suffering from his own conscience and he too could do nothing to comfort her. Her man was outside there. And here she was, sitting at this table with all these powerful men, drinking their drinks and listening to their plans to shoot Rufus. Oh, Christ! How the hell I get in this, she asked Biscombe with the silent appeal in her eyes.

'If these bastards think they is Castros, they lie! This ain't Cuba!'

'Patience, Turnbull,' the manager interjected abruptly. He had a plan. 'Now, listen. We have the evidence. Open the door a crack, Biscombe. Turnbull, take down what Boysie is reading. We are getting the evidence.' Biscombe opened the door and the noise of words and exclamations swept into the room.

Stella made to get up. But the overseer gripped her hand.

'Where the hell you going?' he asked. 'You is a communist, too? Siddown, woman!' He forced her into her seat. He looked at the manager for approval, but the manager had other greater things on his mind. The minister's face was impassive. Mr Whippetts was drinking and grumbling. Nobody seemed interested in Stella. 'You for? Or against?' Turnbull asked her. When she did not answer, he gave her a sharp slap across her mouth. Stella gasped. The schoolmaster opened his drunken eyes. The minister sighed and asked God for something while the manager just looked straight into her eyes. His were cruel, blue, icy. Biscombe slammed the door shut in disgust. He came back to the table and sat down.

'For? Or against, I ask you?'

'Shut up, Turnbull! Shut up! What the hell you asking the woman?' the schoolmaster snapped.

'Keep your arse in the schoolhouse, Whippetts! This is politics we talking! Not education!'

'May I inform you, you little *assinine* – '

'Gentlemen, gentlemen.' It was the minister, rising and unfolding his arms, as if he were in church. But being in a rum shop, and not in church, they paid little attention to him. But he insisted. 'Gentlemen!' He slammed his hand on the wooden table. An uneasy silence fell in the room. They were listening to him. 'Gentlemen. We will dispense with the present circumstances – circumstances under which I find myself with you. But as men, as grown-up men, and women, I think we're going about this the wrong way. The men are poor. Many of them have been laid off work. Now, just because one of them gets a letter from a friend and, and – that is no cause for alarm. And certainly no justification for guns! Everybody is getting excited. With the Federation coming, everybody wants to be a leader, and surely because the men meet tonight in the rum shop, it doesn't mean they are plotting to overthrow the plantation. This is not Cuba, as you say Turnbull – '

'You finish, parson? You finish, now?' Turnbull asked him.

'I think I will bid you goodbye – goodnight!' As he made to leave, the manager stepped between him and the door. 'Mister Manager?' he said, surprised. 'Are you blocking the passage of a free man?'

'You can't leave now.'

'You're a foreigner, parson. A foreigner. We been living in this island all our lives and we know how to handle things,' the overseer said.

Just then, as he took his attention off Stella, she made a dash for the door. But he was quick. He held her, and then pushed her across the room, where she fell against the table.

'Rufus! Rufus! Rufus!' she screamed. 'Rufus, they going kill you!'

The blow was quick and crisp. It fell across her mouth and silenced her hysterical screams. Turnbull looked at the others for approval.

'May God forgive you, Turnbull!' the minister wished.

'A tide – a tide in the affairs of men! A tide in the affairs of men,' the schoolmaster said.

Biscombe went over to comfort Stella. The manager stood by

the door, which was slightly ajar, and listened to the revolution being hatched outside.

Boysie's voice was rocky and loud with the rum.

'*... and if a man is a hustling kind of man, and if any of them fellars what working on the plantation is hustling kinds of men, they could bring home eighty, ninety, even a hundred dollars on payday. That is what Canada means. That is advanced, progressive living. And you men on the plantation should get up off your backsides and tell the plantation a thing or two –* '

'That is a damn lot o' money!' Mango said.

'A man could even buy up the whole plantation, the whole damn island with that kind o' money!' agreed Jo-Jo.

'*– and it is time you fellars down there on that plantation do something!*'

A loud cry went up. The men were ready. Rufus felt the meeting getting out of hand. All he had intended was a peaceful talk with the overseer or the manager. But now he saw that the tide of emotion was taking the whole business out of his hands. Something inside him told him this was not good. But he could not go against the tide of feeling after he himself had caused it to flow.

'Okay, okay, mens!' he shouted. 'We ready. But remember, no vi'lence. I is a peace-loving man. All we going do is go 'cross the plantation road and get the plantation people to see some sense 'cause as Jackson say this is a damn backwards place.'

'Biscombe, Biscombe!' they shouted. 'Rum, rum! Bring out a bottle, Biscombe!'

'You go, Biscombe! Take them some rum – four bottles, a dozen bottles. Even put it on my account,' the manager said. 'Take the rum and come back. We are waiting on you!'

Reluctantly, the shopkeeper left the room to attend to the men. He gave Stella a glance of allegiance. The overseer noticed it and warned Biscombe for his own good not to play any double-crossing tricks.

'Don't forget the police still 'vestigating a certain burglary, Biscombe! Don't you forget that!'

'Ready, Mr Whippetts?' the manager asked. The schoolmaster nodded. He was not sure where his loyalty belonged but, like

Biscombe, he was caught up in the tide. 'Mr Parson?' The minister nodded. 'Turnbull, you bring Stella. We are ready.'

'Biscombe, you is a goddamn good man!' Rufus said, thanking him for the rum and the service he had given the boys. 'You is one man we not going to forget if anything happen' to this strike business. Eh, boys?' The men cheered Biscombe. 'Biscombe is one o' we. We can't forget Biscombe!'

'Sure, sure!' Biscombe said. 'Biscombe backing you up! Biscombe on your side!'

'The men vote' unanimous to talk to the plantation, Bis boy. If we get that raise in wages, well, you know, as man, we spending most of it in this rum shop! Eh, fellars?' Again the men cheered Biscombe. 'And Biscombe, not one damn word 'bout this meeting to the plantation, eh? 'Cause all o' we in the same damn boat, one way or the other! But I know you ain' no bloody Judas. You is a gentleman! Eh, boys?'

Shouting and cheering, the men followed Rufus and Boysie out of the shop. They passed the six bottles of rum from hand to hand as they jumped down from the threshold of the door and into the pitch blackness of the night.

Crappo, returning from choir practice, wondered what was happening when he saw the five men and one woman walking through the tall weeds at the back of the house. He followed behind and saw them get into a large black motor car which was parked in the lane a few yards away. He returned home and going into the special room, where he sometimes slept, saw the remains of the drinks and the corned beef and biscuits.

He ate some of the corned beef and then stretched himself out on a bench, on which he had spread three washed-out flour bags. In a short while all he could hear was the distant barking of the plantation's dogs.

4

The large stone mansion of the plantation house loomed out of the darkness in front of them, like the resurrection of some mysterious ghost. Its great white pillars looked like terrible fangs, and the few lights still on, in upstairs rooms, seemed like the eyes of some monster which was the symbol of their livelihood and of their bondage to the plantation.

All the dark way across the dirt track and right up to where they were standing now, the men sang loudly, trying to hear their own voices, trying to drown the hard beat of the fear they had of attacking their bread and butter, trying to stir up some of the courage and determination which the demon rum had placed in their hearts, and which now this imposing incongruous pile of stones and mortar was sapping.

Rufus had chosen the song they sang. It was his favourite song: *Onward, Christian Soldiers*. They were singing it to the sound of their bare feet. For a time they had been shod with the steel of conviction, but now both feet and the conviction that they were about to do something which would release them from their bondage were as soft as the mud beneath them. The singing stopped, the marching stopped, as if someone had given the command to halt.

Rufus wished the effect of the rum and the inspiration of the letter had not worn off so quickly. But he too could feel the presence of the mansion that stared at him like some sacred authority. The mansion represented punishment to him, and to all who had dared to march against it with him.

'Attack, men, attack! We going pull down every blasted stone outta that house!'

But the men remained standing. They were measuring the distance between them and the house, between the house and their own safety.

'This our bread and butter that we attacking so?' Boysie asked. Rufus was ready to smash him to the ground. But he changed his mind, since no one else heard.

'That is traitor talk, Boysie,' Rufus said to him. 'Don't let the men know the leaders divided. That is a backwards way o' looking at things, man.'

They were about one hundred yards from the main entrance to the house. There was no wind, no moon, no breath; everything seemed dead, waiting for something to happen. And the men too, they were waiting for something to happen. Something. As long as it was not something they had to do.

'Yeah,' Rufus said, 'yeah. That blasted plantation house, we have to come back to that house on Friday forenoon to get pay – '

Crawling like black ants over black dirt, the men, with Rufus and Boysie trembling in front, shifted forward, forward, waiting, waiting for something to happen. Then the main body of men stopped dead in their tracks. The stragglers stopped too. And then, as if in two minds about running away or attacking, they moved on.

Near by, the large black car stood silent, like a tiger waiting to pounce on its enemy. The manager had his finger on the trigger of his revolver. Turnbull was ready too. They were crouching a few yards ahead of the car in a cluster of canes. The schoolmaster, Biscombe and Stella sat in the back seat of the car. The minister sat in front.

'Lord, I hope nothing don't happen – '

'They just going to scare them 'way, Stella,' the schoolmaster said, trying to make her calm. During the drive to their hiding-place, Stella had threatened to jump out of the car, and Biscombe and the schoolmaster had had to hold her down. She had cried, she had wept, she had threatened to tear out Turnbull's eyeballs. But they had kept her with them in the car. Now it was about to happen and her bad luck said she had to witness it.

'Lord, Lord, Lord!' she wept.

The minister was quiet. No one knew what was going on in his heart: whether he was praying for the souls of the men who should die, whether he was praying for the souls of the manager and the overseer who should cause the men to die.

'We not asking you to wash your hands in blood,' the overseer had said. 'We only asking you to keep quiet.'

But it was the manager who had made a more serious threat. He had promised to write letters, anonymous letters to the Bishop, informing him that a certain vicar found time to drink rum in a certain rum shop in a certain village. After this, the minister knew he was trapped. But he wasn't beaten yet. He had his own plans. Since it was the manager who had given the church money to improve its chancel and had bought new choristers' gowns for the choir, he knew it would be indiscreet to force himself out of the stranglehold which was now wrapped about him like a Boston crab.

Turnbull chuckled sadistically as the men walked past him and the manager, crouched like birds of prey in the dark canes. The plan was to trap the men between the guns and the dogs which were to be let loose at the signal of the first shot.

Fifty yards in front of them stood the proud bastion of the entire village. The men could see the whiteness of the house. Fifty yards –

Suddenly a shot rang out!

Brunnnng!

Two men fell to the ground. The mob was transfixed. Two seconds later the two men scrambled to their feet unhurt, untouched except by their own terror, and ran across the South Field, screaming and shrieking at the top of their voices that they were killed.

Then another shot! And another!

The second shot caught Rufus in his left calf. He held on to it and sank to the ground, shrieking.

'Oh, Christ, Boysie! Oh, Christ, they hit me!'

The men were scattering like ants when a stick is thrust into their nest. Mango disappeared through the canes. The three bloodthirsty Alsatians were pelting across the road to cut off the men.

'Run, Rufus, run!' Boysie shouted. 'Through the canes!'

'Come, Boysie! Back to Biscombe! Biscombe is one o' the boys, so he going to hide us out!'

'Heh-heh-heh!' chuckled the overseer. 'It was my shot that got heem! Heh-heh-heh-heh!' He and the manager walked back to the car. Stella sat like a dumb animal in the back seat between Biscombe and the schoolmaster. The minister, in the front seat, was muttering under his breath.

'We got heem!' Turnbull was saying as the car drove back to the house. 'We got heem with one!'

But nobody asked whom he meant. They knew who it was.

'Oh, my God!' Stella moaned.

'I'd be grateful if you dropped me off home as soon as possible,' the minister said.

'Going to say your prayers, parson?' Turnbull teased. 'Say something for me – for putting down this revolution in the village so pretty tonight!'

But the minister ignored his sauciness and asked God to have mercy on his soul. This he did in the secrecy of his heart.

'Well, Biscombe boy! You did your duty as a first-rate citizen tonight. Thanks for giving us the tip-off.' The manager was in a good mood. 'We'll have a snip of brandy at the house and then go back to your inn, old chap. But, thanks again, for giving us the tip – '

'Biscombe? You say Biscombe give you the tip 'bout tonight?' the schoolmaster asked. 'Biscombe, is you who did this informing?'

'But, Mister Whippetts, lemme explain – lemme tell you what I think was going – I really and truly did call up Turnbull here – but I thought nothing would 'ave happen' – '

An icy silence fell in the car, as it headed for the magnificent white house with its proud pillars waiting to embrace them.

Rufus and Boysie made slow progress through the dark cane field. Luckily the dogs were called off. Every now and then, Rufus had to stop to soothe his leg and secure the piece of shirt which he had tied round the wound to stop the rush of blood. Boysie was silent all this time. Only his maddened breathing could be heard. Rufus knew he had caused this terrible thing to happen to the men, had caused himself to be shot, and he knew above all that now was not the time to talk to Boysie. But he was glad in a way that he had borne the brunt of the preparations for the strike march, and also had suffered the most. Perhaps, he thought, in pain, he might use this as a means of impressing the men in the morning that they were fighting for their lives. He realized that his wound was the symbol of his having suffered for the good of all the men and women in the village. His few lessons in socialism and his talks with Jackson had taught him to exploit his misfortunes.

'This blasted thing hurting,' he groaned. 'But I glad it happen'. I glad, glad, you don't know Boysie – 'cause now I have something to show. Something to show.'

'From the beginning I didn' like this business. I could 'ave been killed. And, be-Christ, I think I too young to get kill' fighting for something that ordain' 'gainst me and my fortune. 'Cause, be-Jesus Christ, I live' too long in this village to pretend that I, or you, or all them mens what risk' their blasted lives just now, could change one iota o' what been happ'ning here since Adam was a little boy – '

'What you think went wrong?'

'What *you* think, Rufus?'

'A spy! A spy in the midst – '

'But you not thinking that I is – who you think that spy is, Rufus?'

He could feel Rufus's eyes watching him, although it was too black for him to see them. But fear curdled his voice and he remained quiet, waiting for the onslaught of Rufus's cruelty.

Rufus had to stop again to adjust the bandage, now wet as the mud through which they walked. Soon afterwards they reached the edge of the cane field opposite the rum shop. Boysie wanted to rush out and enter the shop, but Rufus held him back. At that moment a large black car screeched to a stop in front of the shop and the lights were turned off.

'Jesus!' Rufus swore, because he could not make out the occupants of the car, which he had recognized.

'The manager! How they find out, Rufus?' But he could not see the faces of the people who got out. 'One – two – three – four – five! Five o' them get out, Rufus. One must be Biscombe!'

'Biscombe? Biscombe, a spy?' Rufus said, noticing the implication in Boysie's voice. 'Oh, Jesus Christ, no, Boysie! You didn't see the way the man serve' up the drinks and treat the boys as if they is special customers? Biscombe? No, man!'

Still they waited. Each man silent, each man plotting. Boysie, to see what action he would have to take if Rufus accused him of being the traitor. And Rufus, wondering if indeed it could have been Biscombe, the only other man who knew of the scheme. Boysie had an idea.

'You didn't tell nobody, eh, Rufus? You didn't tell no outside person 'bout the plan?' he asked.

'Oh, Christ, no, man! What the hell you think me for? 'Course I didn't tell nobody 'bout the plan!'

'Well, you must 'ave talked in your sleep, then, 'cause you threaten to beat up anybody who tell the plan even to their wives or women. And I don't see how, since that is the case, the ins and outs o' this blasted scheme could 'ave got out!'

'Boysie, you accusing me? You accusing your own leader? Now, that is a thing that we don't put up with, not even in socialist situations. You have to try the man with judge and jury before you could accuse the man. Even so, I don't have to satisfy you with my whereabouts, 'cause I leading this mission. Now you get that straight!' He emphasized his point by grabbing his sinewy stick and shaking it threateningly in Boysie's face. For a much younger man, Boysie was very afraid of Rufus.

'I want a cigarette bad, bad!' Rufus said.

Boysie offered him one and they went farther into the cane field to smoke it without being seen. It began to drizzle very lightly and they opened their mouths and let the water drop inside. It was refreshing after such a hectic run through the canes. The prickles on the blades of the canes were giving them an itch and the rain helped to soothe it. Rufus was thinking of the letter. He asked Boysie if he thought they had followed the letter exactly as Jackson might have intended. But Boysie was still doubtful.

'Now if you don't think we follow the letter, why the hell you join in the march, then?'

'Because I can never tell.'

'How the hell you mean you could never tell, Boysie?'

'Well, look at it this way,' Boysie said, taking a deep pull on the cigarette. 'I don't believe in no damn socialist-thing like you, Rufus. And I still don't feel that if for thousands o' years we been living in this fucking shit, with the plantation breathing down our blasted necks, morning noon and night, I can't see how the hell we could change this by marching 'cross a road, sixty-odd starved-out men, and hope to turn this Clapham Hill village into heaven! That is what I mean. Second', I join' in the march because if anything good was to have happen' I wanted to be in on it. But I didn't think nothing was going to happen, though, 'cause – '

'You is the spy! Be-Christ, Boysie, you just admit' in a certain manner o' speaking that you is the blasted traitor to this cause! Gorblummuh, and to think that you is the first man I talk over the thing with!'

'No, no, no, Rufus!'

But Rufus was already on him. His stick fell once across the softness of Boysie's shoulders. The blow sank him to the wet ground.

'Oh God, oh God, Rufus, you have the wrong man!'

'Who is the right man, then, Boysie?'

'I don't know, Rufus, I don't know.'

'Well, how you know I have the wrong man, then?' And again the stick fell. This time it landed on Boysie's hand which he put out to ward off the blows.

'Gimme a match!'

'No, Rufus – Rufus, you – '

'Jesus Christ, I say give me a match!'

'The wrong man, Rufus, the wrong man, oh God! – '

But Rufus felled him with the third blow and he rolled on the ground in pain, writhing – and then he was silent like a fowl cock that had lost its head.

Rufus searched his pockets and grabbed the box of matches. He scrambled some cane trash and balled it into a heap.

'Should never 'ave brought this bastard in on the business – bastard as backwards as in the slave days – '

He lit the trash and blew on it to nurse the fire. The flames caught quickly. Soon he was sitting in a smoke screen. About thirty yards away, Boysie lay unconscious. Rufus watched the smoke change its colour and become almost orange. The canes were on fire!

' – heh-heh-heh! Long, long time I promise to burn down every blasted cane in this village!'

The rain was still drizzling lightly when he left the cane field on his way to Biscombe's Rum Shop.

Biscombe and the schoolmaster had a violent quarrel when they returned to the shop. How in the name of God, the schoolmaster wondered, could one man, meaning Biscombe, be so rotten. Biscombe stuttered and tried to explain. But every time he tried, he was cut short by Stella's accusing eyes. She had refused to go back in the car with the overseer and the manager, who had returned to the plantation house. And since those two had already used her for what she was worth, they did not insist.

'God help you, Biscombe, when Rufus find' out!' the schoolmaster said. Biscombe looked at Stella to see if her expression was registering the same thoughts. 'She not going to inform on you, Biscombe! She is a lady! So don't try to scare the woman. It is me who will tell Rufus.'

'But you take a part too! Whippetts, you had a drive in that black car too! We is all Judases,' he said. 'All Judases together. Me, you and this – this whore here, who says she lives with Rufus!'

'If I were a younger man, Biscombe, I would flatten your damn face with a blow!'

'Oh, my God! Oh, my God!' Stella moaned. She shook her head from side to side mournfully. 'The blame have to rest on me too. The blame have to rest on my shoulders too.'

The schoolmaster got up from the bench, put his white Panama straw hat on his head and made for the door. Biscombe wanted to ask him to remain. But he was ashamed to display his fear in front of Stella.

'You not going too, eh, Stella?'

But she only looked at him and did not move nor speak.

'Goodnight, Stella,' the schoolmaster said and left through the front door.

Biscombe did not wait, but went and closed and bolted all the doors and windows. He felt safer now. He went into the special room to tidy up and when he saw Crappo sleeping on a bench, he closed the door and came back into the front room where Stella was still sitting.

'Stella – Stella, lemme explain. 'Twasn't malice nor hard

feeling nor grievances in my heart for Rufus that I let out the secret – 'twasn't that – but you have to understand that as a proprietor – oh, Jesus Christ!' he exclaimed and kicked an empty bottle across the room.

He sat down on a bench facing Stella. She was looking in his direction. Perhaps she was looking at him, perhaps through him to see if anything was in store for her tomorrow, to see if she could see her future. Biscombe watched her. They could hear the rain drizzling outside and occasionally a dog would bark or a cock crow. The rain, the rain, the rain, always drizzling, always holding up the hour hand of time – the rain, the rain –

'Look, Stella – a couple o' dollars – a couple o' dollars, and let we forget all this, eh?'

It was so quiet now that the alarm clock ticking away in Biscombe's bedroom entered the room where they were sitting and joined their company. Biscombe ticked to himself along with the clock. It took his mind off things. Tick-tock-tick-tock –

'Biscombe! Biscombe!' someone whispered.

Biscombe sat upright like a bolt. Stella came alive.

'Biscombe?' the voice said, louder. They recognized it. 'Biscombe, open, man. I want a drink.'

Stella rushed up to go to the window, but Biscombe held her and pressed his hand over her mouth. He led her near the window and listened.

'Biscombe! Biscombe!'

'Yeah, Rufus?'

'Open, man, open. A drink!'

'Man, Rufus, I sorry, sorry – I in bed – '

'Well, lis'en! You lis'ning, Bis?'

'Yeah, Rufus, I hearing you.'

'The plantation find out! The bastards find out!'

'Oh Christ, Rufus, that is bad. That is bad!' When he said this, Stella stared hard and dirty at him.

'And you know what. They got me! Got me in the blasted leg. But don't tell nobody how I come by this cut. And, Biscombe?'

'I still here, Rufus.'

'You seen Stella?'

There was a pause, a short pause.

'Seen Stella?'

'Well look, Bis boy, if you see Stella tomorrow, or any time, don't let on that you know how I come by this cut on my calf, eh? I going home now – and thanks for the drinks. You is a real first-class pardner.'

'Good night, Rufus.'

'Till then, Bis boy – '

They listened until his feet disappeared in the noise of the rain hitting the tar road like pebbles.

The wound was so painful by this time that Rufus had to sit by the side of the road to rest. Every step brought a jab of pain as if a penknife were cutting into the wound. The piece of cloth he had tied round it was soaked again. He rubbed the cut with his hand to soothe it, but the more he rubbed the worse it hurt him. Jabbing, jabbing, jabbing was the pain, like a boxer trying to weaken his opponent.

If he could only reach the public standpipe, if he could walk that far, he would be able to wash the wound under the water. Perhaps he should try to bear the pain and get to the pipe.

He got to his feet again and limped his way down the black road, desolate as hell. Not a light was burning. Everything was sleeping. In great pain he reached the standpipe. He hopped up the two steps and turned on the cool water. The water stung the wound, but he did not mind. Although it was dark he could see that the water was red as it poured off his leg and rushed down the drain. When he had finished washing, he hopped on to the embankment beside the pipe and sat down. The pain again. The blood again. He could not go home in this state. His blood would trail all over the floorboards of the house and Stella would know. He would die if Stella knew he was out making trouble for the men and himself, talking politics.

If only he could stop the bleeding before morning. He did not like the idea of having to remain in the cold night, the raining night, with the wound bleeding –

He remembered once in a movie he had seen some soldiers wounded in the leg like him and the bleeding would not stop. Now, what did they do? What? Think hard, Rufus. Think hard,

hard, hard. They had scraped the wound. Taken out the bullet with a penknife. Yes, a penknife! Rufus looked hard at the wound again, and he put his finger in the cut, feeling for a bullet. But there was no bullet, only a nasty cut.

'Thank God!'

He ran his fingers through the blood which refused to clot, and he cleaned the wound. Then he remembered. Dirt! Yes, they had used dirt. He put some dirt, lots of it, over the wound. It burned at first. But soon the pain was less. He could stand on the leg, although he could not hit his foot too hard on the ground. He tried walking. Good! He could move more easily now.

He hopped about on the leg to try it out, and when he could walk more comfortably, he laughed and cursed himself for not using his head. He sat back on the embankment thinking of the march and the failure of the march. He could not decide within himself whether it was Boysie or Biscombe who had informed on him. He tried to reason out why either of them should want to hurt him. Boysie envied him, because of Stella. He always wanted to live with her, but the only reason he did not try anything behind Rufus's back was because he knew the power of Rufus's cruelty. Boysie would not do a thing like that. He knew the penalty involved.

What about Biscombe? Biscombe was his age. A man that old could not be a serious rival with a woman. Besides, Biscombe had more women than he could go to bed with, even if he had two women a night. Why put so much effort into getting Stella, whom he had slept with before? Rufus knew he could get Stella when he wanted her. Her poverty provided the motive. Biscombe owned a shop. To own a shop in the village was like owning half of the single women and a quarter of the loose married women. But Biscombe couldn't be so worthless! To give a man rum on credit and then turn round and inform on the man, all in the same night! Biscombe himself said he was on the boys' side. He said that with his own mouth. Tonight. 'Rufus, Biscombe on your side. Rufus, Biscombe backing you up!' That is his very word. It couldn't be Biscombe! No!

Rufus tried to piece together the events after the shots were fired. He remembered being hit. Then he and Boysie running. Then stopping near the rum shop. The black motor car parked in front of the shop. He was no longer sure of Biscombe's innocence. The car belonged to the plantation – people got out – five – Boysie counted five – they didn't see how many left – and then soon afterwards when he went to the shop and called for Biscombe, Biscombe said he was sleeping – sleeping – sleeping?

'Jesus Christ! Lord, let it not be Biscombe who let me down! Lord, no, not Biscombe!'

Rufus raised himself to his feet, his stick gripped firmly in his hand, and set out back along the road to the rum shop. He ignored the pain. He ignored the blood which he could feel trickling down his leg. He had to go back and see. Perhaps it was the pain making him think foolish things about Biscombe. Biscombe and he were friends since they were young men. He even got some money for the down payment on some lumber for building his house from Biscombe.

But why was the shop closed so early? Before the last bus from town came back from the country districts. No, the shop was closed too early! It was Biscombe. This conclusion put strength into his leg, and he hopped and ran until he was almost there. His head was clearing now. He remembered setting fire to the canes. But there was no fire. No smoke either. And Boysie!

'Oh Christ, Boysie! I left Boysie to burn in the canes!'

This took his mind off Biscombe for a while, as he scrambled through the thick darkened canes searching for his friend. He must have been really mad, really hurt from the shot to leave Boysie to die, to burn with the canes. He had actually set fire to the canes? The plantation canes!

'Rufus, you not using your head tonight! Rufus, you behaving like a thorough arse! Burn them canes, and spend the rest o' your life in Glendairy Prison? And after what happen' tonight?'

It was a long time before he found Boysie. When he did, Boysie was sleeping. Rufus shook him roughly. Boysie jumped up, stick in hand, ready to defend himself.

'Don't do that again, man!' he said.

'Boysie, I need advice! Boysie?' he said, shaking the dizziness out of his body. 'Boysie, lis'en!'

He explained his confusion to Boysie as they walked out of the canes. But Boysie could not say; he was not sure.

'I thought I was in Mammy' bed sleeping. What happen' Rufus, that I still in this blasted wet cane ground?'

'You must 'ave slipp' and fall down, man.'

When they passed by Biscombe's Rum Shop, a light was on. Rufus asked Boysie to explain that. Again Boysie wasn't sure. Perhaps, he said, Biscombe had got up during the night to pass water, or chase a thief, or do something.

'It don't mean that becausing a man have a light on that he is a traitor, Rufus.'

'All right, all right, you don't have to bring no blasted high-class logick to me, man!'

They walked on towards Boysie's house. The leg had stopped bleeding. Rufus had rubbed it again with dirt. The pain was going away. They said goodnight and agreed to go to work early the next morning.

5

Something about the clouds in the charcoal sky and the wind, which was not too energetic this morning, said it was going to rain all day. It looked like one of those days when the rain did not make up its mind to come down and drown you, and have it over with; one of those days when it just sat teasingly in the clouds. A steamy energy-sapping day, with a breeze seen only by the shaking of the leaves on the trees and the canes, but without the courage to come and revive you, or lessen the clammy feeling which accompanied a humid day in the island. It was on such a morning that the small gang of cheerless workers filed across the dirt track to the plantation.

There were very few men in the gang, most having been laid off from work. Women were in the majority carrying their agricultural tools like silent muskets over their shoulders, or dragging them in the dust. The men seemed tired, still asleep, as they scraped their feet, already weary before the long day's work began. They were talking under their breath about last night. Occasionally someone would laugh. But you could tell by the lack of music in the laugh that it was not really a laugh, but rather an observation of something that could have been laughed about, had the circumstances been happier.

At the rear of this battalion walked Boysie and Rufus. A different mould of leader from the boisterous, determined men of a few hours ago. They seemed quiet, licked-out, sagged and dry. Merely going to work because they had to, because there was no alternative. Though neither was talking, they both knew that the other was thinking of last night, and of what the manager and the overseer would say to them as soon as they checked in to get their agricultural forks. Surprisingly, not many people in the village knew about last night. Rufus was glad that the men found it necessary, and possible, to keep the matter so guarded. Some did know of it; but the failure of the mission, as Boysie called it, was a failure they identified with their efforts to improve their position. They had never found enough courage to rise up before. Now that someone had dared to face the plantation, even if fruitlessly, they were prepared to back him. Now there was one feeling in the village, and it was this feeling of a bond that the men and women in front were talking about.

When Rufus had got home, Stella was in bed sleeping. He did not really think she was asleep, but he did not wake her up, because he too had something to hide. He could not face her with the sad story of his failure. When she inquired about the ugly gash on his calf, he put the blame on the schoolmaster's dog. Stella knew the schoolmaster's dog was a monster. But he did not know what else she knew, and she did not tell him. Soon, however, it was morning, and he was awakened by her with a plate of fried bakes with two sticks of roasted cod-fish. He drank the hot green tea which made his belly warm and comfortable, threw on his work clothes and headed for the corner to wait for Boysie. From that time there was silence between them.

The same feeling of failure held his tongue quiet as he walked like a man to his gallows. Once or twice Boysie grunted something about the rain, but it was a general statement and so Rufus did not have to answer.

The large white plantation house was in full view now. It looked as if it had been washed during the night, painted with a whiter coat of paint. They could hear the hundreds of chickens and the dogs and the pigs and the cows in the stalls behind the house. Rufus felt something inside him tying knots. He was getting frightened. Suppose another trap was being laid, had been laid, and they were walking into it. Suppose there were police constables waiting inside the house. He looked about the large, clean-swept yard for a strange car, for a police van. But he saw nothing to cause him fear. Still, he was not comfortable.

They were too near the house to talk now. Respect and silence increased as the distance between them and the house diminished. It held such an awful power over them. It was this same power which last night had kept them tied to their feet. A heavy uneasiness fell over the crowd of labourers. Somebody in front looked back at Rufus and Boysie, but said nothing.

'The Jockey!' Boysie whispered.

'I seen the bastard,' Rufus replied.

The deathly silence tumbled down on them again. Now, not even the chickens were cackling. Everything was paying respects. Then the overseer came down from the front porch, his black book in his hand, his pencil in his mouth. He was dressed in a sparkling suit of khaki. His white cork hat fitted him smartly. There was a riding whip tucked in the top of his boots; all in all he looked like a hunter of handsome proportions, about to set out on an African afternoon safari. When he came forward, the men and women fell dead silent, their hands at their sides, lifeless, in complete submission, complete subjection, for this man, this overseer, held more power over them than the manager himself, whom they saw only when something vitally wrong had happened. The overseer hired and fired the labourers. He paid them at the end of the week; he slept with any of the women labourers he wanted, and to crown his relations with them, he would lend them money on occasion. If they were seeking employment in another part of the island, or if they were brave enough to leave working in the fields and seek apprenticeship at a trade, it was the overseer who buttered up the paper with a recommendation for their prospective boss or trade master. The overseer was the kingpin in the village. Although he could never be a school teacher, because he had little more education than Boysie or even Biscombe, he was approached whenever one of the village children was seeking admission at one of the few government high schools. Apart from the plantation itself, the overseer was the single most powerful enigma in the village.

On their left was a pile of agricultural forks, stacked like rifles. The men never took their forks home, unless they had extra work to do for Mr Whippetts who kept a large kitchen garden, or unless they were asked by the minister to work in his rose gardens. With the pile of forks were some hoes, used for weeding the grass from among the roots of the cane plants. The women's job was to weed. The men dug.

The overseer opened the book and began calling the roll. This ceremony usually took half an hour; and some of the labourers knowing this, and having got to know the time their names were called, had hit on the idea that they could come late, just in time to answer their names. But the overseer tricked them once by calling the names from the bottom of the list. Rufus was among those who were docked two shillings that morning. Since then he had always been early. He was early this morning.

The names were being called now.

'Millie?'

'Presunt, sir!' There was a strange daring in her tone as she walked towards him and marked her 'X' beside her name, at the place he indicated in the book. Millie was an old woman, ready to be bent in half like a hairpin, but she must work, because she was poor, and her children had all been married or left the island.

'Clementina?' the overseer shouted.

There was no answer.

'Clementina here?'

'She must 'ave stop' at the standpipe a minute to wash the mud off her foots, Mister Turnbull, a hell of a lot o' rain fall last night, yuh know!' It was Constance speaking up for her friend. 'But Clemmie soon come.'

'A shilling off!'

'But oh, Christ, Mister Turnbull! But –' Some of the men, not accustomed to this rudeness, gasp and wonder what is happening to Constance's intelligence. 'Clemmie swear' blind she coming to work this morning. She tol' me so to my very ears. And you don't have no damn right saying you docking her with a shilling, just for being late a minute, man, 'cause Christ knows we already too poor!'

You could hear pins falling in the silence. Then the overseer took control again. He was mad. Such rudeness had never happened before.

'Shut up, Constance!' he yelled at her.

'Don't tell me to shut up, you pissy-pissy red man, Turnbull! I talking for Clemmie's rights. I talking for the rights o' every man, woman and child present here this morning.'

'Jesus Christ, woman! You want to go back home right now?'

'Well, no, sir.'

'Well, shut up, then!' The overseer could feel the labourers siding against him. He could feel it in their looks, in their silence, in the way they were standing up facing him.

'Yessuh, Mister Turnbull, sir.'

So Constance held her peace, because she knew, after all, it was useless and dangerous to argue with him. The rest of the labourers breathed more freely. But still they remained docile.

'Constance?' he said, calling out her name.

'You hasn't heard my voice just now, Mister Turnbull?'

'Constance, you presunt or you apsent?'

'Oh, Lord, I present, I here, Mister Turnbull. I here, in the precious name o' Good Jesus Christ who is my shepherd,' she said. There was a wicked smile on her face. 'And I asking Him daily if He never intends taking me out o' the hands o' my tormentors.'

The men and women broke out laughing. Just as suddenly the laugh was smothered.

'Constance, you working today, or are you out spreading communism?'

Constance flung her hands in the air in mock appeal. 'Oh, Lord, Mister Turnbull, why you asking me such a stupid question? Sure, I working today! How the hell you think I going live, 'cepting I work, *every day*!'

'Answer then, woman!'

'Presunt, sir.'

The names were called and answered. When he came to Boysie and Rufus who were the last to be called, he gave them the impression that last night had never existed. This made them very uncomfortable, for they were sure that something worse was in store for them. But nothing happened. They took their forks and headed for the fields. Down the slight incline from the yard they walked, Boysie to the South Field, Rufus to the North Field. Boysie was so disgusted at having nothing said to him that he was jittery. He dragged the prongs of his fork over the rocks and the noise made Rufus angry. But Rufus did not say anything to him.

'And that bitch didn't even ask me if I had a cut, fall down, a dog bite me, nothing!' Rufus said. 'That bastard didn't even ask how I get this bandage round my leg!'

'That is white man' tacticks. They intend to make us stew.'

They fell silent again. They walked on with the breeze, which had sprung up, blowing in their faces. The sun held back a cloud and peeped out. It was a bright day after all. Just as they were about to part company, Rufus held Boysie by his shirt.

'What you think, Boys, if we hold another meeting tonight?'

The fork fell from Boysie's hand. He was speechless. Could this be a madman or idiot standing in front of him, he wondered.

'Don't get mad, Boys, don't get mad before you lis'en to what I have to say. Lis'en. I know how you feeling. I feeling worser, a thousand times worser. Have a cigarette,' he said, offering one.

'No, thanks, I stop' smoking since last night.'

'This is my reason for bringing up this topic,' Rufus went on, trying to choose his words carefully. 'Beginning with the letter. Now, maybe or maybe not, the letter from Jackson didn't have anyways and means o' solving the predicamunt on the plantation. I say, maybe. And I say maybe not, 'cause I not sure. But the letter show' me one thing, Boysie. It show' me how the world spins round in different countries. It show' me how a man, a' ordinary man like me or you, or any one o' them fellars what marched last night, according to Jackson's words, could make himself into a more better kind o' man. It show' me them things. Now, you don't have to be a socialist-minded kind o' man, or a communist, or even a Marxist, to know that what goes on in this island with a certain type o' fellar, me and you, ain't no bed o' roses. Now, you can't take no oppositions 'gainst that, Boysie, 'cause that is logick I talking now. The kind o' political man you happen to be, or not happen to be, don't interfere with that logick. That is basic and vital. And another thing, Boys – I soon finish', because I don't want to get you in more trouble – another thing, you remember me telling you only last Sunday 'bout the revolution in Russia? You remember that me and you was sitting down under Clementina' apple tree talking 'bout how in some countries they don't have no rich and no poor? Well, according to that same revolution, and according to the man who engineer' that revolution in question, the plantation make a big mistake by firing on we working mens. That is their mistake. 'Cause, if I remember the thing right, Jackson say – and is from him that I happen' to know all these important things 'bout socialism and the working class – if what he say is true, then the moment you see the plantation class get frighten' and start shooting off guns, they know the systum they have us living in is on the way out. It on the way out, Boysie. 'Cause, reason the thing for yourself. Why, in the name o' hell, you would shoot a man, when you know that you could beat the man with your bare hands? Why? The answer simple, simple. It is because you *think* you can beat that man, but you really can't beat him. You following what I saying?'

'Be-Christ, it going through one ear and coming out through the next. I don't comprend at all. But I say this. I warned you. I warned you 'bout the itchy hand the Jockey have. You ain't the first son-of-a-bitch he shoot.'

'I know, I know. I know my big mouth caused me to get shoot up. But that bullet have make me a new man. They make me a martyr. And now, I not only looking forward to tomorrow, or the next two days, or even payday, I looking to the futures. I dreaming, Boysie, 'bout that day, when I could look up in Turnbull' face and say "kiss my arse", when a piece o' this land I working on all these years belongst to me, when Stella could wear high shoes like the manager' wife, and let them make more noise, be-Christ, in the road when she walk', that you would think a rock-engine passing. I looking to the futures when them two starved-out childrens o' mine could go to Harrison College and Queen's College like the children o' the Rev, or the manager, or even like how Turnbull trying to get his two scatterbrain' children in at the Lodge School for Gentlemen's Sons. Them is the things I have in mind, Boysie. Now how you like what I said?'

'Lemme go and work for my salt-fish and rice. That is something I sure 'bout. Goodbye, and if you get any sweet-water drink from home this forenoon, don't forget me 'cause I thirsty as arse.' With this he left on his way over the boulders of earth.

Rufus watched him for a long while. Sadness filled his heart. Lord, Lord, why is it, he wondered, that when a poor man opens his mouth and talks about improving his lot, and the lot of his people, even his own people call him a communist? Why a man can't be a Christian-living, God-fearing, peaceable type of man, and still want to live a better life? Even the manager, who is supposed to be this educated man, educated at Oxford up in England, and the Rev, who studied all these hundreds of years learning how to read the Bible properly, even these two important gentlemen think a man is a bad man when he opens his mouth and begs for two shillings more on the little pittance he gets for working from daybreak to sunset. Why, why, why, why? He searched the cloudless skies, but he could not see the answer there.

Just before the plantation bell struck one o'clock, Rufus's son, Ezekiel, trundled over the warm earth with a three-gallon tin pail of cooling molasses water. He said his mother had got a piece of ice from Miss Gertrude this morning, and she had put it into the molasses. Rufus held the pail to his lips and kept it there until he had drunk half the liquid. He crunched some of the ice and spat the rest back into the pail.

'You not going back to school, boy?' he inquired, remembering that the bell had announced one o'clock, the beginning of his own lunch time and the end of his son's. 'Don't play no fool with me and say you playing truant, eh?'

'I going back now, Dad.'

'You better! I don't want you twirling no blasted fork in this ground! This land ain't mine.'

'And Dad, the schoolmaster call' me up on the platform this morning, and he say that he not giving me no more private lessons, 'cause they have certain fathers in the village, who don't know how to carry on theyselves. And he say that I can't enter for the scholarship exam no more, 'cause this island ain' the U.S.S.R.?'

'Whippetts say that? Whippetts say that to you?'

'The schoolmaster say that, Dad.'

'Never mind Whippetts,' Rufus said. And he made a mental note to deal with the schoolmaster this afternoon after work, or in the rum shop. 'Lemme see what you learn' today at school,' he added. Rufus always made a check on his children's progress in school. Although he often asked them questions which he himself could not answer, he knew instinctively, by the sureness and loudness of the children's answers, when they were correct. With the passage of time his instinct began serving him in the place of knowledge. He grew to depend on it, as he had learned to depend on and to listen to his own voice, a habit which his loneliness in the vast oceans of sugarcane fields had taught him.

'One and one?' he asked the little boy.

'Two!' Ezekiel shouted.

'Heh-heh-heh! You going good! Six and six?'

'Twelve!'

'Heh-heh! I going beat yuh with this one, though! Bet yuh! The capital o' Barbados?'

'Bridgetown!' Ezekiel sang out triumphantly.

'And Trinidad?'

'Port-o'-Spain!'

'How many days in a year?'

'Three hundred and sixty-six in a' ordinary year and three hundred and sixty-five and a quarter days in a leap year!'

'In a leap year, eh? Heh-heh-heh! You going good, son! Now run along and give Boysie a drink and ask him if he think over what we talk' 'bout earlier. Don't forget.'

Rufus watched his son with pride. He could see him right now as a Harrison College student, riding his brand-new green Raleigh three-speed bicycle, with the large book bag laden with big, important books: books about Latin, Greek, French, geography, books on the sciences, on English – books on everything under the sun, and Ezekiel mastering them all!

'Jesus Christ, I thank Thee! That boy more brighter than a damn new shilling! That is my boy!' he said and he smiled at the thick earth which he still had to plough after lunch. 'Christ, if I not careful, that boy will make me 'shame', 'shame' in front o' company, he have so much blasted learning inside that head o' his already! He is Einsteen the Second!'

The cool drink brought up some of the stale gas inside him. He patted his stomach, passed water on the prongs of the fork to clean them, and then he returned happily to his work. He was thinking of his son, and he was thinking of Stella who would soon come with the large bowl of food for his lunch.

'Heh-heh-heh! Three hundred and sixty-five and a quarter days in a blasted leap year! The longer a man lives the more he know'! Heh-heh-heh! I must see if Boysie know' how much days they have in a leap year.'

★

They were sitting in the shade of the pigeon-pea trees that ran round the border of the cane field. It was sunny, it was bright, it was like the Easter of life. The rain had changed its mind long ago and the breeze was strong and high. Rufus was squatting. Between his legs he held the large pottery bowl of split pea rice and boiled pig's tail. Stella had put many tomatoes in the sauce just as he liked it. The heavy solid rice and peas settled pleasantly and warm in his stomach. He was now running his index finger round the contours of the bowl to scrape up every semblance of sweetness that remained and the worn metal spoon could not reach. All the while he ate, Stella lay on her back, with the wind rippling over the waves of her legs and dress, watching him. She looked appetizing today. More enticing than the large bowl of food he had just eaten. The thinness of the cotton dress she was wearing exposed all the beauty of her body to him. To see her like this would send arrows of greed through his body. And when the arrows had burned their passage of desire in him, he would in turn become very tense and angry and bitter; bitter with himself, and bitter with her, although he could not explain why he was angry with her. He could understand being bitter with himself, for it was his fault that he could not satisfy the fire in her thighs. He knew this. He knew she knew this, although they had never discussed it. It would have killed his pride to have his woman of more than eleven years tell him that he was inadequate for her. Whenever he felt this way, he wanted to make love to her, to ram himself right into her, until he could hear her panting for breath and feel her fingernails cutting ditches of ecstasy into his body. He would live this pleasure in his mind and enjoy it. But when he lay on top of her, the dream would fade and he would think he was lying on the beach, on the warm sand, for the sand was passive and dead beneath him.

He wiped the bowl dry as a bone and handed it to her. She took it, put it back into the basket and handed him a large skillet of water. Rufus put the water to his lips and drank until his stomach was on the point of bursting. He had to feel this threat of intestinal collapse before he was satisfied. Then he washed the mud off his hands, sprinkled some more water on them and ran them across his face. Stella watched him like a cat watching a mouse, not saying a word. She had arrived about half an hour after Ezekiel had returned from Boysie on his way back to school. In all that time she had said nothing to him. Though not a talkative woman, she was not usually so silent. This strange behaviour worried Rufus. He thought of all the possibilities. Did she know about last night? Had the police come to the house after he had left for work? Did Mr Whippetts tell her about not entering the boy for the scholarship? All the ancient fears in his life and in hers sprang up again and confused him, and since he was not a very open man himself, these fears almost strangled him with curiosity.

They sat watching the wind sweep the dried pieces of cane blades across the field. His jacket which he had left on the shoulder of his fork was snapping in the breeze like the old weather-beaten Union Jack on the flagpole of the schoolhouse. It was such a lovely day! And he was so unhappy! If only she would talk to him, since she knew he was not a talking man. If only she would say what she was thinking, what she was waiting to hear. And if only he had the guts to talk to her as he could talk to Boysie or the other men in the rum shop. He watched her, when she wasn't looking, and he saw why the younger men in the village coveted her. Stella was desirable even if she was dressed in a crocus bag. He longed to be able to sit down with her, and run his fingers through the stubborn hair on her head, and play with the nipples of her breasts which had refused to sag despite her childbearing, and mash them in the palm of his hand, and giggle and laugh and talk about little silly things, as he had once heard the manager and his wife doing. He had tried once, but she repulsed him. His hands were too rough, she said. His mouth was too dirty, she said. His clothes smelt like mould, she said. When he had tried to contain his hurt and his humiliation, and had failed, he slapped her hard across her mouth, and went and got drunk as a dead man, with Boysie and Biscombe. Now, he wanted to try again. For this was his woman. Long ago, before she had begun to realize that he would never satisfy her, would never make her feel a complete woman, before she had become disillusioned with his inability to rouse her as the overseer could, or as Biscombe could when he was not too savage and excited, before she realized that she was married to a rough, stupid man, she used to tell him she loved him. But now their life was as riotous as a dumpling in a boiling pot. Rufus resorted to beating her with his stick. In this way he got rid of some of his frustration; and Stella, frustrated too, began looking to other men for the satisfaction and consideration which she did not, could not, expect from him. They had lived together all these years, but it seemed as if they lived together to tear each other apart.

Rufus was looking at her all the while, but she said nothing to him. She would watch him intently, as if about to say something, but then she would change her mind and turn her head aside.

'I see you done eating,' she said, putting the cloth over the basket. ' 'Zeke tol' you what Whippetts said? My child can't take the scholarship – and you and that Whippetts is drinking friends! You see now that you can't trust your own-own mother?'

'Ignore Whippetts, Stell! Me and him will talk over this thing, this evening in Biscombe Rum Shop!'

'Ignore Whippetts! Ignore Biscombe! Ignore the Jockey! When you going wake up, Rufus? When you going learn sense and know that them men ain't in your camp?'

'You telling me something, Stella.'

'I telling you what you should know. Biscombe, Whippetts and the Jockey on the white man side, and you thinking they on your side! But when you hear the alarm it will be too late, Rufus! Too late, too late, shall be the cry! Mark my words.'

'Everything going to be all right, Stell! just wait and see – just wait and see.'

'Like last night, Rufus?'

'You know 'bout last night? Tell me what you know 'bout last night.'

He was kneeling now, alert to catch every word that she was about to say, any word that might betray her. He repeated his question again and again, but she said nothing more. They continued to sit watching each other, baiting each other, while his desire rose and fell, and made him tremble like a leaf. Something about this woman made him itch, made him mad with lust. The greater the lust, the greater his failure to exploit it. But he held her close to him, and squeezed her soft body against the buttons and sweat of his coarse flannel shirt. Stella did not like him to force himself on her and she tried to free herself, but he was too strong for her. After some moments of struggle, she gave in and collapsed in his arms. Rufus lifted her like a baby and took her out of sight into the canes. He spread some cane blades to make a bed, pulled her dress over her head and threw himself flat on top of her. He had no time for the overtures of love making. Stella closed her eyes, trying to keep away the tears; and she asked God not to let her feel what was about to happen and to close her eyes against this rape. When Rufus touched her, she thought of Biscombe, and how he had cheapened her yesterday. Rufus sensed this stiffness, this frigidness, this refusal to grant him what he considered his due, one of the prime functions of their association – even if she did not enjoy what he was about to do, at least she ought to have the decency to pretend that she was enjoying it. It was her duty to enjoy it, or pretend to, he felt.

'You feel like a piece o' ice, you don't know,' he told her, when there was no co-operation from her. 'Just like a blasted piece o' wallaba wood underneat' me!'

'Love lacking, Rufus,' she said. Something about the simple, direct way she said it, made him feel guilty. He knew he was powerless to correct this and the feeling turned to hostility. 'Is love what lacking betwixt me and you,' she said.

'Open your blasted legs, woman! If the overseer could lay down on you, I can too! I is suppose' to be the man in the house; the overseer is only the outside man.'

But she said nothing to this, and he mistaking her silence for guilt, continued to perform the joyless operation. As quick as a dog, as rough as a bull, he did it, and then he was finished, exhausted, blowing like a cow. Stella stood up, looked him straight in the eye, and began putting on her clothes.

'You bitch!' His hand was swift and accurate. The thin cotton dress was ripped from neckline to hem. 'I have a mind to – ' The blow stung her in her face and she kept her eyes closed long after the sting had worn off. She broke out crying. The first time for a long time, as far as he could remember. He had forgotten she could cry. Now he liked it, to know she had emotions after all. He was glad he could make her cry. But he was sorry that, to do so, he had had to slap her. It would have been better, better for his dying pride, if he could make her cry when he was making love to her. Then the tears would be tears of joy, of ecstasy, of gladness, the same tears which the overseer used to brag about in front of the men, during a noisy evening of drinking in the rum shop. Rufus would agree with him and brag that he too knew these tears; and nobody knew he was telling a lie. 'You make me so goddamn vexed! Sometimes I look at you, and be-Christ, the first thing I want to do is kill you!'

'It ain't me you should kill, Rufus. Even if it is me, I not the only one.'

'Like who?'

'Like Biscombe! And the Jockey and the manager and the Rev and the schoolmaster! Them is your enemies. Not me. All I guilty of, Rufus, is finding pleasure and happiness when I can't find it in my own bed. And finding money when the man I lives with drink out all his blasted wages in the rum shop. Them is the crimes I guilty of, and God know', so He can't judge me too harsh!'

'You telling me something?'

'I not telling you nothing, because you and Biscombe is bosom friends. But I know Biscombe is a snake, a Judas.'

'You telling me something, Stella, but I don't know what it is. So before you make me give you a lash with this stick and make you talk, be-Christ, you hads better stop talking parables to me and talk English!'

His threat did not open her mouth and loosen her tongue. She was accustomed to threats and blows. They had no effect on her now. So, scorning his anger, she took the basket in one hand, hitched her torn dress with the other, and prepared to go home.

'Biscombe is not your friend,' she repeated.

'What the arse you telling me, woman?' Rufus shouted at her. 'How the hell you mean Biscombe and me isn't friends? We've been friends all my life. Is Biscombe who I tol' 'bout the strike. Is the same Biscombe who give the fellars free drinks. And the same Biscombe admit' that he on the side o' progress. And you telling me what! Looka, woman, get out o' my eyesight, before – ' He made a swing with his stick, but she was not there. 'Biscombe is the onliest man, saving Boysie, who know 'bout the strike business before we had the meeting!'

'Rufus, Rufus!' a voice was heard calling him. He looked round and saw Boysie running across the field to him. He was in a great hurry. Something had happened.

'Wait, Stella, Boysie coming. Let me ask him what he think. You wait and see!'

'Rufus! Oh, Jesus Christ! Something bad take place! Bad, bad!' He was out of breath from running, and they waited, Stella out of reach of the stick, and Rufus at his elbow, to hear what he was about to say. 'A police! A police fellar just done questioning me – asking me all kinds o' questions 'bout if I is a communist, if I ever get letters from Russia – '

'I going home, Rufus.'

'No, no, you wait here, Stella. You wait!'

' – the police know all 'bout last night. Appears he get it from Biscombe this morning – '

'From who?'

'He tol' me that Biscombe call' the police station early this morning and tol' them to be on the look out for two communists in the village – using my name and yours – '

'Well, Boysie? You still in two minds?'

'I don't know, I don't know, Rufus. I so far in the blasted sea, but I might as well go on swimming, 'cause either way, it look' as if the blasted waves going drown my arse, anyhow! That is how I stand.'

'You talking progress, Boysie!' Rufus said. He was glad that Boysie was implicated, was accused. Now he had him. He could not turn back. 'Well, I have a plan.'

Boysie and Stella listened to the plan. It would take place tonight, late. They were to tell all the men and make sure that Biscombe did not hear of it this time. But Boysie was still doubtful. Rufus convinced him by saying that everybody was against him, the plantation, the schoolmaster, even Biscombe. There was nothing to do but shake off the chains of bondage.

'You been talking and talking 'bout chains, but I don't hear none rackling on my body! As I say, I don't agree with this socialism shit, but I caught up in this tide o' circumstance and I have to swim with the tide.'

'That is advance' talk you talking now,' Rufus told him. 'That is all I want from you, Boys. I want sympathy in this cause from you. Now, don't forget the plan. Me and you going meet at the place mention' tonight.'

Stella was more disposed now to disclose some of what she knew. She told them about the manager and the overseer being with the schoolmaster, Biscombe and the parson in the back room while the men were discussing the meeting. Boysie and Rufus almost died with shock. The story was out. The letter was known. Their plans were open as the sun in the sky. It was time to plan. Time to correct all wrongs, and time to remind Biscombe to keep his mouth shut.

'What I couldn't understand though,' Stella went on to say, 'was how a man like the schoolmaster could lay his cards on the same table as the rest o' them white men! I can't understand why.'

'This ain't a matter o' white man 'gainst black man, Stell, darling. This is poor man 'gainst rich one.'

'Same blasted thing, Rufus. Stella talking sense. Poor man and black man is the same, same thing in this village, in this island. And rich man and white man is the same thing too. Look around and see.'

'Explain Whippetts, then. How Whippetts get to be a member o' that clique?'

'If you had heard Whippetts talking last night, and your eyes was shut, you would 'ave thought you was hearing a' Englishman talking 'gainst we poor black people.'

'See? See?' challenged Boysie. 'Whippetts only black, but he is a white man!'

Suddenly Rufus could see some light, but something was still puzzling him.

'But how you know all this inside story, Stella?' he asked her.

For a time she said nothing. Then, instead of betraying herself, she said, 'I get the story from Crappo. Crappo was there all the time, but they didn't know.'

'Oh Christ, Rufus, the Jockey!'

'Look, I going,' Stella said.

'Don't forget the plan,' Rufus warned her. 'Come, come, Boysie – back to the kiss-me-arse grind!'

PART TWO

CHANGING THE CIRCUMSTANCE

6

The night was black. It was silent. You could hardly hear the wind in the tall weeds behind Biscombe's paling. Rufus was crouched in the weeds, listening. He could barely make out men's voices inside the shop, though they reached him clearly in his hiding-place every time the back door opened to let in another customer. Since he had been there, the schoolmaster had entered; so had the minister, and the local constable, P.C. 454 Roberts, alias Barabbas. It was still quite early, for ten o'clock was striking on the school-master's old grandfather clock when Rufus was walking through the pasture from his house. Ten o'clock. Two hours before the time he had told Boysie he would be there. Stella was to be present behind the rum shop at that time too. But Rufus could not trust anyone. He had to be sure now that no one had the chance to betray him. That was why he had come earlier than the time he had told the other two to come.

Something in the Scripture lesson his daughter Conradina was learning that night struck him as being important to the mission he was embarking on. The words said something about the disciples selling everything they owned and possessed, and bringing the money and putting it into a common fund. It was a good idea; Rufus liked it. All the time he was waiting for the appointed hour, and all the time he was walking from the house to the weeds where he was now sitting and thinking, the idea of sharing, of having the villagers bring together all their possessions appealed to him as the only solution, the only defence against the plantation. He kept repeating the words to himself. '*And having land, sold it and brought it – and brought the money and lay it at the apostles' feet.*' Perhaps he could get the villagers to see reason tonight; perhaps he could get them to sell their land and their possessions – donkey carts, fowls, cows – and bring the money and put it at the disposal of the committee he was about to form. Perhaps –

But he remembered that the villagers had no land. If they did sell their possessions, who among them had the money to buy them? The plantation? He could not allow them to do that! The plan could not work. He must think of something else. But they were meeting tonight, at midnight, and he would have to think of something to tell them.

The back door of the shop was opening. He could see the schoolmaster tottering out, followed by the minister, and then the constable, Barabbas. Biscombe said goodnight, that he was closing up early, that he was tired, that he was going to bed. The customers said goodnight to him all over again, and faded into the thick blackness at the side of the house. Rufus balanced his stick in his hand and praised God for his good fortune. He had only to think of Crappo. He would wait a little longer before entering the rum shop. ' – *having land, sold it and brought the money and lay it at the apostles' feet* – ' The words of God, of the Bible. There can be no wrong in using the words of God for his own benefit. There would rather be a blessing. God would be on his side.

Someone was coming. He retreated back into the weeds and waited. A woman. She stopped just outside the gate of the paling and listened. Perhaps her heart was beating too loudly, perhaps she was listening to hear her conscience talking to her. Rufus waited. Then she opened the gate and entered the paling. He could not recognize the woman from where he was hiding. He would have to creep nearer. She was inside the paling now. He heard her knocking on the door, and then the light from the shop shone into her face. Stella! Rufus held his heart to see if it had stopped beating. Stella? A damn good thing he had come earlier. The door closed behind her and shut Rufus off from the conspiracy she was plotting with Biscombe. But Rufus wanted to hear, he wanted to know first hand. He crept inside the paling and listened. He could hear Stella mumbling, but the words were as dark and low as the night was black and scheming. Then he heard footsteps – coming round the paling and through the gate. He moved back in the darkness. A man! The man walked up to the back door, with Rufus just ten feet away from him, and knocked. Biscombe's feet stopped shuffling about inside. The night became tense. Rufus could hear whispering, scheming whispering inside the house. The man knocked again. Rufus waited. It was too risky to attack him. It could be the schoolmaster returning for a bottle of rum; it could be the minister – it could be anybody. The top of the back door opened and Biscombe's head appeared in the orange light. He gave the impression that he had been disturbed from sleep.

'Who the hell is that, this time o' night?' Biscombe growled, annoyed.

'Bis! Is me! Boysie, man! Open. I have a' information for you – real secret!'

'But Jesus Christ, Boysie, I in bed, man. You can't come back in the morning?'

'Bis, it real important! Rufus intend' to raid you tonight, man, so I thought that since – '

'Jesus Christ! You say raid? Rufus?'

'Open the door, lemme tell you, man.'

'Well, wait – no – look, I putting on a jacket and coming out. Hold on!'

The window was closed and the night sucked up Boysie's face again. Rufus wondered when to strike. Now? But he decided to wait. Wait, Rufus, wait.

'You catch me in bed, man,' Biscombe said, when he was outside. He closed the door behind him. 'Where you get this informations?'

'Look, Biscombe, promise. Promise. Promise you don't mention one word o' this. 'Cause you know what kind o' man Rufus is. And, be-Christ, I don't want to spend four months in horspital with a break-foot – But lis'en. Rufus know' 'bout you telling the plantation. He intend to hold a next meeting tonight in the North Field. All the men and some o' the women meeting him there. I going to be there, too, 'cause, as you know, he wring my hand and threaten' my life, if I don't turn up. But you know me, Bis. I not in this damn strike business. I is a young man who only want a piece o' pussy when the night come, and a rum to drink. Anyhow. He plan' coming here at twelve o'clock. Stella coming too. And I don't know how close you and she is, but she is a decoy. Beware Stella, Bis. You is my friend. She coming and she going take you outta the shop while Rufus carry out the raid, and then – '

'What the arse going on at all, Boysie? Stella just come in my shop telling me the same thing. She just now this minute tol' me that Rufus plan' to make the raid. Oh, Jesus Christ! Well, I never know I had so much o' enemy in this blasted village!'

'Stella there? You mean' Rufus's woman, Stella?'

'In the flesh! She just step' in the shop!'

'Heh-heh-heh! As man, Bis! What you waiting for, then? Put a good loading on her, and fix that!'

'But something I don't understand at all.'

'What is that, Bis boy?'

'You intend to join in on the raid too?'

'Well, as I just explain' to you, Bis, I had my hand twisted, so had to agree to be in leagues with him. But since the police start' 'vestigating me – '

'Police 'vestigate' you?'

'They come right in the blasted cane field! And that make me think. I think that even if I get involve', I can't stand up and see a damn good man like you suffer – not after all the free rum and drinks you give the fellars. Oh Christ, Biscombe, blood more thicker than water – as you understand.'

'Thanks, Boysie.'

'But Bis – Bis? I was thinking that inasmuch as I just put you on your guards – it stand' to reason that as man – you understand?'

'You asking for a drink?'

'I thirsty as arse, Biscombe!'

'Sure, sure, Boysie, sure! Wait here. I bringing you a whole full bottle o' Five Star. You is a man with plenty ettics.'

Boysie waited in the dark, humming to himself. Near by, Rufus was smiling at his good fortune. Boysie lit a cigarette and blew the smoke noisily through his mouth and nostrils. The door opened again. Biscombe came out with a bottle which he handed to Boysie.

'Thanks, Bis.'

'But you intends to walk out on Rufus, though?'

'Well, no. I coming back with him. But as you on your guards now, you will know how to organize things, eh? Organize yourself, Bis. And don't forget what to do with that bitch you have in there. She want' something. Put a good breeding on her. She is no blasted

96

good! Rufus is such a damn old man, he don't know how to load women. So you give him a lesson or two, eh, Bis, boy!'

'As man, Boysie. And thanks! I going back inside here, and if you hear screeling and rummaging all down the Front Road, well you will understand – heh-heh-heh!'

'It set for midnight. Don't forget!'

'No. And look, if you see that idiot o' mine, Crappo – he gone to a choir practice, but he don't know I know practice finish', 'cause the minister come and get his med'cine already – anyhow, tell him I say he could spend the night at his aunt, my sister. It won't be good to let the boy know what going on. Don't forget!'

'Sure, Bis – and twelve o'clock.'

Biscombe went back inside the shop and Boysie left, humming joyfully to himself. Rufus crept outside the paling and hid in the weeds waiting for Stella to come out. He had never felt so alone in his life. Not even when the judge sentenced him to two months three years ago for beating a man. Not even when Jackson left on the plane for Canada that rainy morning, and he had stood in the rain alone near the runway watching the plane fade into the grey mist. Not even a night ago when the bullet hit him. This was a new, cruel feeling he was experiencing. The fact that his instinct told him that he was going to be alone, that he was going to be betrayed that night – although he did not know by whom – made him very sad. He was sad because he felt he had the power to foresee his destiny. He sat in the weeds, with his head in his hands, and he cried and cried until his heart almost broke. He wished Jackson were here beside him, to help him; that he had never received the letter from him, the letter which put these foolish thoughts into his head – he wished that he too could run away, anywhere, even to Canada or the States, but he knew he could never run away, for even this form of escape cost money, and he had none. He was tied, hands and legs. Money, money, money – just what he was asking the plantation for. Just what he needed to run away from the plantation with, should the plantation refuse to grant him more money. But where, where – where would he get the money?

Rufus went back inside the paling. He was going to break the door down. He was going to beat both Biscombe and Stella.

Perhaps he would have to kill them. He wanted to do something cruel, something hostile, he felt so inadequate and frightened. But all he could do was stand there, outside in the darkness, while the creaking bed springs inside told him what was going on between his enemy and his woman. His heart was broken. He cried and cried, this time his tears were born of hate which he had no power to express.

Rufus watched Stella creep out through the back door of the rum shop and make her way home through the dark lane to tell him that everything was set for the raid at midnight. She did not know that Rufus had seen her. Tonight she was confident and brave. When she came out of the house, with Biscombe behind her, he could hear her laughing gaily and telling Biscombe not to worry about Rufus because he was an old man. Rufus only smiled. He had been waiting long for this information, and the long wait had paid off.

'Rufus will catch a damn fit if he know' you been here already Stell, darling love, and we been doing the thing, eh?'

'Serve him damn right!' she said. This was a new woman, not the Stella he knew. Not the submissive woman who remained dead as a piece of wood under him in bed at night. 'Serve him blasted well right, too! All these years I living with him, and he not thinking o' putting a ring on my finger, and make me into a lady like the other whores in this village. I right as hell to take a' extra man with him.'

'You could be playing with fire, though,' Biscombe cautioned her. 'You tol' Rufus 'bout the events o' last night? That you was in this rum shop whilst he and the fellars was out there in the shop arguing?'

'I tol' him certain things, but I didn' let on that I was a' eyewitness. And I will take this secret to my very grave. I wish' to Christ that the bullet did pierce his blasted heart!'

'You say that like you mean it, Stell?'

'I mean it, Biscombe. I mean it. I getting 'shame' o' that man. He come in the bed without washing his damn foots. Conradina soon going to Queen's College, and he hasn't got the decency to give that girl his name, and make her feel like she is wanted. The blasted man can't write his own name, and come saying he leading strike. Well, what the arse next, eh, Biscombe? You mean to tell me a man could lead a strike, and think 'bout becoming Prime Minister o' Barbados, and he can't even write a dirty word 'pon a piece o' paper? And all the time talking talking – 'bout when he is the Hon'r'ble Rufus This, and Hon'r'ble Rufus That – '

'No kidding, Stell, he does say these things?'

'That blasted man been talking 'bout strike, 'bout federation, 'bout socialisms and 'bout somebody call' Karl Marks – you don't know all, Biscombe. Rufus going mad as hell. And that is really and truly why I risk a beating from him tonight, and come and warn you. 'Cause if a man like him could ever think he could be Prime Minister o' this island, well, something vital and basic wrong, wrong, wrong with the workings o' his head. You don't think so?'

'No – I mean, yes! I didn' know. Anyhow, you run home and take care. I going prepare myself for the battle.'

'Biscombe, you think that some day – not tomorrow or even next year – but some day – a time will come when me and you – '

'Stella, you better run home now. We could talk this over tomorrow,' he said leading her to the gate in the paling. Unknown to him, he was walking within three yards of Rufus.

He closed the gate the moment Stella was outside and fastened the latches on it. The back door was closed, although not locked. Biscombe was trapped inside his own back yard, with the enemy inside the yard with him.

'Jesus Christ Almighty, you can't trust not one living soul these days! Not even your own blasted mother! Well, well, well, well!'

He was going to the back door, about to enter the house, when Rufus came from the darkness and touched him on the shoulder.

'Bis?' he whispered.

Biscombe sprung round, and when he faced Rufus, something was glistening in his hand.

'A knife, Bis?'

'I tear out your balls, if you try anything!'

'I am going to lash you, Biscombe, I am going to tar your backside with lashes – '

The first dropped between his shoulders. Biscombe did not

wince. He sprang aside from the second blow, and the third. He could feel the great pressure of wind fan him. He knew that if either of those blows had landed, he could have been a dead man. Fear was in his eyes and in his legs, and it helped him to parry and move about. Rufus was not moving much. He would wait until he could find his man, and then, whuff! he would throw the stick and hope for the best.

'I am going to kill you, Biscombe,' he kept on saying as he struggled for breath from the exertion of trying to catch up with Biscombe's surprisingly lithe body. Rufus fired a lash and it caught Biscombe on his hand. But he refused to drop the knife. Another lash, and Rufus saw the flashing blade before his eyes. He closed them and thought of the blind man who walked the village streets begging. When he opened them, Biscombe was standing over him, with the knife held to his throat.

'You going to kill me, Rufus? You stupid son-of-a-bitch! You going to kill a' important man like me, when you can't even read! That ain't fair, Rufus. *I* going kill you!'

Biscombe was standing over him; but he was not watching, he was not careful, he was not a fighter like Rufus.

'I just had your woman in there – I just had Stella, and I had her yesterday and the day before that, and the day before that. And I give her to the Jockey too. And the Jockey haves her at night and I haves her in the afternoon. And I telling you this so it would choke you! I want it to choke you – kill you! And you know why? Because you is a socialist. We don't have no uses for blasted communists. The manager say so, and the overseer, the Jockey himself, say so. Whippetts don't want no socialists neither. None o' we decent people in this village don't want no socialists. We going run you outta this village, Rufus, just like we run Jackson! You understand? You understand?'

Rufus lay very still, waiting for his chance. He knew what to do.

'What you say? You intends to leave this peaceable village? I'll tell you what, Rufus. I, Biscombe, will put up your passage money, if you decide to leave this island. But we want you out! Understand?' The thin blade was touching Rufus's veins. He thought he saw his blood trickling down his neck. 'Heh-heh-heh! I wish the manager could see me holding the great Rufus now!' When Biscombe laughed again, Rufus felt his chance had come. He took the risk and knocked the knife out of his hand in one desperate lunge. Biscombe stumbled, and in a flash Rufus was on him. He pinned him to the ground and rained the blows in his face until his hands were wet from the blood. He carried out his punishment in silence. Biscombe struggled once or twice like a chicken with its head cut off, but Rufus quieted him with a lash. When it was all finished, the night was still again, and dark, as if nothing had happened. Rufus left him unconscious in the yard and went inside the shop to find the money.

Rufus had to work fast. He wanted to find the money and hide it before either Stella or Boysie returned. The alarm clock on Biscombe's dressing-table, which he searched first, said he had twenty minutes before it was twelve o'clock. After he had found the money, he would have to make a telephone call. He was not very expert with a telephone, so it did not matter to him if the call had to be postponed, or made when Boysie came back. He would ask Boysie to help him make the call. No, better than that, he would make Boysie do the calling. He had to keep him from suspecting that anything odd had taken place.

The lights were on in the front of the shop, in the special room and in the bedroom. For a while Rufus sat in the special room, with his feet on the table. At last he was sitting in this privileged place. He closed his eyes and thought of himself sitting in the dark-brown panelled chamber of the House of Assembly – the members were applauding his speech on the dissolution of the plantations –

He jumped up and began searching for the cash box. He knew it was kept during the daytime on a shelf with the bottles of rum and falernum. But he also knew that Biscombe hid it when he retired at night. The lights in the shop were bothering him. He did not feel safe, he was uncomfortable with so much light shining round him. No thief, he reasoned, would stomach so much light. So he turned the lights off, and walked through the darkness feeling shelves and knocking down bottles and glasses. He was more comfortable. He was like a real burglar now, just like the expert thief, the diamond thief he saw in a movie in town two weekends ago.

He was in Biscombe's bedroom again. In the darkness it seemed all his senses were sharpened. He was thinking better and faster now. His hands walked over the old straw mattress, under the mattress, under the springs, and then they travelled under the bed itself.

'Christ!' he exclaimed, as he felt water on his hands. He put his feet under the bed and kicked the receptable on to the ground. He thought he heard coins rattling. 'Well, be-Jesus Christ! Biscombe worthless, but at least he have a sense o' knowing a joke from a joke!' He had upset the chamber pot which was guarding the cash box. Rufus thrust his hands under the bed and dragged the heavy cash box, with all Biscombe's savings, from its hiding-place and put it on the mattress. He ran his hands through the money, and the bills crackled and the coins sang. He liked the sound, new, deep and full. Money! Now he could think of escape, if the people rejected him.

Hurriedly he scrambled the money in his hand and stuffed it into his pocket. He did not bother to count it, since he knew he could not get past ten or twenty dollars. Besides, it was a waste of time to count money, when you had so much in your pocket. Rufus was chuckling when he put the cash box back under the bed. He poured some of the urine into the box and replaced the chamber pot on it. He moved out of the bedroom and as he reached the special room, he heard someone coming. He waited. It seemed he was spending all his life waiting, but last time his waiting had paid off. He would wait again. The footsteps came confidently round the paling and stopped. The newcomer was searching in the darkness for someone. Then the walking began again; it came through the gate, after unlatching the hook, into the yard. Rufus held his breath. Biscombe was still unconscious there. The footsteps approached the back door; he could hear them coming in. It was only ten minutes to twelve, ten minutes before the appointed time, so the footsteps must be those of someone who knew the plans for tonight. It had been arranged for Stella to call for Biscombe at a quarter to twelve; if possible, she was to take him for a long walk in the cane field. Meanwhile, Boysie and Rufus were to carry out the rest of the mission. Now, this intruder had come. He was searching in the dark room as if he knew what was hidden there. As if he knew about the plan. Rufus could hear him shaking the mattress in Biscombe's bedroom, and then he heard him knock something over – the chamber pot! There was a low cry of disgust. Rufus chuckled softly. 'Should 'ave drowned the bastard!' The footsteps left the bedroom and came into the special room where Rufus was. Give him a lash, he thought. No, that would scare him. He might escape before he was recognized. Give him a fright, then. If it was Boysie, he would really be frightened! No. The lights. He would expose him in the lights. That would tie him forever in a bond of silence and fear. Rufus's hand reached up for the light switch. He waited until he thought the intruder was close enough, very close to him, too close to escape. The uncertain footsteps shuffled for a while and then were still. Just then, the lights went on.

'Mister Whippetts! Jesus Christ! What – what – ?'

'Rufus? Rufus?'

'It won't look good for nobody to hear 'bout this, Whippetts. You better go home to your wife – go home.'

Rufus turned the lights off to save the schoolmaster from shame and embarrassment.

'Thanks for turning off the lights – and thanks again.'

'It don't look good to see a man in your position doing a thing like this – it don't look good.'

It took him a long time to get the telephone working. At last the distant voice of the operator somewhere in the black night was telling him to wait. Rufus checked the money in his pockets. It was there. He lit a match, looked about the room, judging the quickest escape in case Biscombe should regain consciousness and enter the shop. A bottle of rum, half empty, stood beside him; searching for a glass and some ice, he forgot the match in his hand.

'Jees!' he swore. 'Some ice – yes – some rum – yes – lemme drink and wait for this son-of-a-bitch – more ice – ' The voice was talking to him. Jackson was reached. Rufus was nervous. He had so many things to tell Jackson; he hoped he was not getting him up in the middle of the night – he had not remembered to ask the operator what time it was up in Canada – he must remember to ask Jackson. Here he is!

'Jackson? Jackson? Oh, Jesus Christ! It is really your voice, man! Jackson, I hearing you as if you was standing up beside o' me! Well, how things?'

'You wake me from sleeping, Rufus?' His voice was clear and cold. Perhaps he was standing outside in the road answering the phone. It was not a friendly voice.

'Jackson, look! Bloody hell happ'ning in Clapham Hill village, man. I have the fellars out on strike. We meeting tonight. And I have to thank you, Jackson, man, for sending that information 'bout Canada, and the wages, and the advance' kind o' living. You is a real first-class socialist-minded man!'

'What the hell you saying?'

'And Jackson? Jackson, you still there, are you?'

'Lis'ning!'

'The plantation know'. They lay off all the men saving Boysie and me, and – and – we had a march, but the plantation win the first round. Tonight is the second round. And so far, Jackson, we giving them licks! But I call' you up for some advice, Jackson.'

'Rufus, what the arse you telling me? I dreaming, or really hearing a voice talking?'

'Lis'en, Jackson. You paint' a real progressive picture o' Canada. I want to come up. Lis'en. I come into a piece o' money just now, and I coming up there – '

'Rufus, Rufus, Rufus!'

'I still here, man. You don't have to shout.'

'You wake me up from sleeping. I vexed as arse. I jus come home from washing off cars, and I tired as a dog. Rufus? Rufus? Lis'en to me! I say I tired as a horse. I write you a letter, but I had to write that kind o' letter – But, by the way, you not thinking o' making me pay for this blasted long-distance tellyphone call, eh? 'Cause I is a car-washer and the money is only eighty cents a' hour! Rufus? You still there? I sorry to paint a technicolour picture o' the place but, Jesus Christ, man! I couldn't let you know that up here in this country is the same slavery as what I run from back in the island – you understand, Rufus? Rufus?'

Jackson continued talking long after Rufus had dropped the receiver and was on his way out of the room. He heard Boysie coming in. He was so disillusioned that he did not try to hide from him. Boysie asked him about Stella and he did not answer. Rufus went back into the room, with Boysie behind him, and seized the bottle of rum. He could not find the glass and had to strike a match. Boysie saw the phone off the hook.

'You made the call?' he asked. But Rufus did not answer. He poured himself a drink instead. Boysie took up the receiver and began talking into it. 'Jackson?' he screamed when he heard the voice at the other end. 'Good Jesus Christ! Jackson this is your voice I hearing? When you coming back on a holidays? Well, look, then, send me a Roy Rogers shirt instead, then – yes, he still here, drinking. Yes, I lis'ning, Jackson. Tell him he get the wrong impression from the letter? I tol' him so already, but he didn't believe – and you going to write a new letter? Yes, well all right, and don't forget the Roy Rogers shirt – good!'

7

'I tell you, Rufus, I can't and never could understand how Stella' mind works,' Boysie was saying. He was drunk. Rufus walked on beside him without saying a word. 'You mean to say that though she know' the vitalness o' this mission, she turned round and won't turn up? And you say you didn't see Biscombe, neither? That is a funny thing, 'cause I swear I saw Biscombe tonight 'bout – '

'You say you seen Biscombe? You seen Biscombe?'

' – rightly and truly I did see Biscombe, but that was early, early in the evening. I seen him early, after work. But I still can't understand how Stella behaving – and Biscombe, too! Rufus? Rufus, you don't think somebody beat Biscombe, or that Biscombe over there at the plantation informing again?'

'Gimme a drink. I thirsty as arse, Boysie.'

'Where the hell I would get a drink from?'

'Five Star! Come, somebody give you a bottle.'

'Okay, okay, okay!'

They walked on in silence. Boysie was terrified of the darkness and of Rufus. They were coming to a deserted part of the road and Boysie held back a little, watching Rufus, and the hand that held the stick. He was almost certain that Rufus knew something. Otherwise how would he know about the bottle of Five Star? Boysie let him drink as much of the bottle as he wished, and did not even ask him to give it back. They were very near the deserted part of the road now. Boysie was being careful. He thought he noticed Rufus's hand move to the stick.

'Boysie, you believe that sometimes a man could know, could get to know what write down in the stars?'

'What you say, Rufus?'

'Nothing!' He stood still in the road. Boysie knew his time had come. He stopped a few feet behind, waiting for the first blow. But Rufus went on talking, talking to himself. This made Boysie even more scared. 'Boysie? I not going to that meeting. I going home.'

'But Rufus – '

'I have things that worrying me. Things that happen' tonight that I can't find a' interpretation for. Like Jackson. You hear' what Jackson say 'bout the letter?'

'I heard, Rufus.'

'And you believe what he say?'

'I believe what you say, Rufus.'

'Thanks, Boys. You is a real kiss-me-arse son-of-a-bitch, though!'

'What – what you mean, Rufus?'

'That you is a real first-class gentleman!'

'Oh Christ, Rufus, man, I know that, but, but – '

'You go to the people. Tell them I can't come tonight. I coming tomorrow night. Tell them the meeting postpone'.'

'They been waiting since eleven-thirty.'

They continued along the road. As they got near, Boysie whistled, giving the signal. Immediately a low whistle told him all was clear.

'Wait,' Rufus said, holding his hand. 'You wait, Boysie!' Boysie thought he heard a sharpness in his voice, which made him uneasy. 'Something happen' tonight. In the morning you going hear that somebody beat up Biscombe.'

'Jesus God!' Boysie gasped.

'Control yourself, man! Now the police going come' round 'vestigating. They going come to you. I want you to tell them that you beat up Biscombe, Boysie!'

For a long while Boysie struggled with himself, trying to make out whether he had actually heard what Rufus had said, or whether he was imagining it. But he was dragged from his bewilderment by the force of Rufus's hand on his shirt.

'You heard me? You admit you beat Biscombe!'

'But, Rufus – I was in the meeting with the people all that time!'

'Boysie! I not joking, man. Besides, somebody else seen you beating him!'

'Who? Who? Nobody wasn't there when I give Biscombe the tip – nobody wasn't there when I saw Biscombe this evening – '

'We understand one another, Boysie.'

'Jesus Christ!'

'Whippetts and me was there when you went in the house and beat Biscombe, and you come out with a bottle o' Five Star and money, and – '

'Money! Money? Good Christ Almighty! Man, search me! Look in my pockets – not one blasted penny!'

'I beat Biscombe. And I have the money. But you was seen beating Biscombe and stealing the money. Whippetts and me. And you is a traitor. So you have to bear the punishment. Don't forget I is the leader o' this mission. You is the second-in-command.'

The people began to number themselves so that Rufus might find out how many of them were present. It was too dark to recognize their faces. He waited until they had finished, then he began to tell them about his plans. Boysie was nominated the second-in-command, he said. Nobody was to return to work, not even the women. They wondered how they would live, how they would get money for groceries. Rufus tried to set their minds at ease by promising to share out a few shillings every Friday. He had come into some money he said, and it was to be put to the uses of the organization. The people did not believe him. There was an epidemic of suspicious coughing and clearing of throats. But Rufus could not detect who was causing the trouble, and he continued talking.

'They is a damn lot o' traitors in this village,' he told them. 'And the biggest one is Biscombe!'

'Biscombe?' somebody said.

'Yes, Biscombe!'

'And how we know you ain't one too, Rufus?' It was Jo-Jo. 'How we know you is a hundred per cent true as the Gospull behind this mission? Don't forget what happen' last night. I not letting no blasted Allasatian mongrel, or no damn bullet lick-loose in my backside! Not for you! Not for the Queen! Not for a fucking soul!'

There was silence among them. Boysie did not hasten to warn Jo-Jo that Rufus was privileged to speak. He was biding his time. He knew that his time was coming, and since he was not yet sure of how he would face it, he was disposed to remain quiet.

There was not a sound except for the crickets in the canes and, now and then, the canes themselves swishing their bodies like the tails of fly-infested horses before settling down again to sleep. The people were very quiet. In the distance, on their left, the last light in the plantation house went out. Immediately, it seemed that everyone was more relaxed and breathing more freely. They seemed to be rejoicing that the last silent eye watching over their actions was now closed. Only God above knew what was about to happen. Somebody sighed. It was a sigh that seemed as if it would bring down the entire world. Somebody else sighed. Then somebody was brave enough to cough. And soon everybody was easing his tension by coughing.

'First time I know these canes could make such a comfortable bed to lay down in,' a woman said. And immediately everybody giggled. To their right the last bus returning from the country district, like the last train to Glory, sped down the road, and then the night was again as dark as a cinema.

'Jackson in agreement with what I plan' to do,' Rufus was saying. 'Jackson say strike. And we intends to strike. Jackson say, as workers we have one weapon. That weapon is sweat and muscles. We have to keep these to ourselves, and make them lis'en – '

Somebody was coughing, clearing his throat sceptically. Rufus recognized Boysie.

'You have something on your mind, Boysie?' he asked angrily. But Boysie's courage faded into the limbo of the night. 'Beginning in the morning, I will divide the money in portions. And lemme tell you how I come on this idea – '

'How you could be in communications with Jackson, tell me, when Mister Jackson living up in Canada?' Jo-Jo asked. Boysie knew he had scored on Rufus, and again, as second-in-command, he refused to assert his authority. Jo-Jo went on asking questions: how could Rufus call Jackson? What had Jackson said? How could they believe that what Rufus said Jackson had said was really what Jackson did say? How could they know this was not going to be like last night? The people were becoming suspicious. Rufus was cornered. He fumbled in his pocket for the money. It was still there. He would count it, or get Stella to count it with him when he got home; then he would plan on leaving the island.

He would do that, because these people were too backward for him to spend all his old age worrying about their troubles, when all they wanted to do was to ask stupid questions.

Jo-Jo was still talking. He had a lot of things to say, he said. He had a lot of questions to be answered.

'How come that your own woman, Stella, was in the back room with the manager and the overseer and the schoolmaster on that particular night, and you didn't know? Or you playing you didn't know? And how come nothing ain't happened to you? Only a little cut by a bullet, which if you ask me, was intended for the rest o' the mens, and not for you! 'Cause we know, Rufus, we know you selling out the rest o' we by letting the overseer live with your woman! Is only why you is one o' the two mens still working on the plantation!' Jo-Jo was talking fast and loud. The effect on the people was electrifying. Rufus was becoming frightened. He knew they would rush on him, and beat him the same way he had beaten Biscombe. 'You answer some o' them questions and then, maybe, we could back you up in this venture. 'Cause, don't mind we is poor people, we is not blasted donkeys!'

'Shut up, Jo-Jo! Shut up! Boysie, as second-in-command, tell that bastard to shut up! I have the floor!' But Boysie was as silent as a dumb mouse. 'Shut up, shut up, shut up!'

'You didn't tell the fellars that the Jockey giving you twenty-five shillings for doing the same work as Boysie, and he only giving Boysie twenty shillings! And you make the fellars believe last night that everybody on this blasted plantation only getting twenty shillings a week!'

'Shut up, Jo-Jo! Or I coming for you!' Rufus made a dash through the blackness in front of him. 'You is a traitor! You is a damn traitor! All o' you is traitors! Biscombe! You! Jo-Jo! Boysie! The Jockey! The manager! All o' you is traitors 'gainst me!'

When Rufus's explosion was finished, they could hear Jo-Jo's whinnying laughter in the night, a short distance from them.

'Jo-Jo is a traitor!' Rufus said, hoping to stir up some sympathy among the people. But they remained as dead, as disinterested as the dew that was forming around their ankles. 'I telling you the truth,' he went on. 'A certain piece o' the Scriptures say that if you sell out everything you own, and bring the money and the possessions – '

When Stella returned from visiting Biscombe, she let herself in through the back door, turned down the kerosene lamps until they were almost out, and waited in the darkness for Rufus. She heard the last bus going past the corner of the street, and she knew it was about a quarter past eleven. She had just a little more time to wait. She got uneasy sitting in the dark room, and she opened the window that looked out towards Clementina's house a few feet away, and there she sat in an old rocking chair, humming to the music of the crickets. No light was coming from Clementina's house; she must be at church, Stella supposed. But she remembered that Clementina was attending the secret meeting in the South Field, and she felt even more alone and frightened. It was almost midnight now. Still, Rufus did not come back. In the distance she could see the headlights of the bus speeding down the road. It was time to go, even if he did not return. She would go back to the rum shop and wait in the darkness, perhaps wait at the entrance of the shop, until Rufus arrived. When he left home three or four hours ago, he said he was going to buy some cigarettes and that he would talk to the schoolmaster about the scholarship examination for Ezekiel. She was becoming worried now; she was getting scared. Had he found out that she had put Biscombe on his guard? But how could he? Biscombe would not talk to a soul about her visit. It was between her, Biscombe and God.

But I glad I do what I done, she told her quivering mind. I glad, glad, glad. He living with me all these damn donkey years, and not even have the decency to say that next year, or the year after next, he going put a ring 'pon my finger, praise God. Not even the decency to say so, even, as I would know, he don't mean one word of it! All that bastard doing is plotting strike, and 'struction and sufferation for the damn stupid people who ignorant enough to mind him, and follow him.

She could hear Conradina snoring. Perhaps she was thinking too hard, perhaps her thoughts were alive. She went into the room where the girl slept with her brother; pulled the crocus bag high over them and blew out the lamp in their room. She came into the living-room, put a piece of heavy cloth about her shoulders, and left. It was chilly outside. It was dark. She was glad for that. She would go back, and she would see what had happened.

That bastard who calls himself my man, probably in Whippetts drawing-room drinking rum, blind him! He have me in 'legiance with him. But if he think' I blind and stupid-foolish like the rest, he lie in hell! I know how to butter my bread, Rufus. If you thinking 'bout strikes, and getting shoot-up and thrown in Glendairy Prison, well you go on! But not me! I want to live! And live like if I is a white lady, darling!

It was dark through the back alleys, but she had travelled them often before and she knew them like the blisters on her palms. There was no light in the shop. Perhaps Biscombe was asleep. Or on guard. She laughed in her heart to see Rufus entering the shop and meeting Biscombe with a heavy iron crowbar over his head. She wished that Biscombe would kill him dead, dead, dead as hell, so that she and Biscombe might get married. Stella had had her eyes on the rum shop for the past two years, since Biscombe first began to take an interest in the joy between her legs. But he did not know her motives for the sacrifices she endured on his behalf. She waited. She listened. No sound. Not even the wind. She put her hand on the latch of the gate and it shouted at her. She stood still, waiting to hear. Suppose Rufus was hiding in the weeds, her conscience warned her. Suppose he was standing only a few feet from her, and was ready to kill her with a blow. Suppose – suppose –

She opened the gate, feeling her way carefully, closed it behind her, went past the bedroom and knocked gently and discreetly, giving the knock she knew he would recognize as hers. She waited. No reply.

'Something wrong!' Her instinct warned her. 'Something vital and basic wrong, wrong. Where Biscombe? Where Rufus? Where the Boysie who was to take part in this thing? Where everybody?'

Inside the shop there was no one. Before she turned off the lights, she went to the cash box drawer. The drawer was there. No cash box. She became terrified. Suppose someone were to come now and find her here. She looked under the bed. Biscombe had joked with her before that he hid the cash box under the bed, or under his pillow. There was no cash box. But she did not mind. She chastised herself for thinking of robbing him. Then she turned all the lights off, and –

'Where Crappo? Crappo not here!' She was frozen with fear. She went through all the rooms in the shop. There was no Crappo to be found. She turned the lights off. She shut the back door behind her. She must get back home. She must be home before Rufus returned. She jumped down into the yard, stumbled slightly and walked to the gate. She touched something. It was dark and she could not see. But she was frightened and she wanted to know what had frightened her. She stopped. She looked. Then she saw him.

'Biscombe! Oh God, Biscombe!'

When she shook him, and there was no answer, she rushed through the gate of the paling and out into the night. She must not be seen near here –

'If Rufus have a plan, I behind him a hundred per cent,' Clementina was shouting to the people. 'But that plan hads better have some foodstuffs and money inside it. You used a damn lot o' sweet words here tonight, Rufus, but them words didn't contain one piece o' foodstuffs. And although you did rightly and truly mention money, only God knows if you really have that money, and how much it is. And it must be a damn lot o' money that you hoping to come in possession of, and to feed all these black people with!' Groans and moans of agreement followed Clementina's speech. The people had had their fears expressed through her, and Rufus was not such a fool as not to acknowledge the influence she held over the people. Her position as an elder in the Church of the Nazarene gave her words the sanctity and the flavour of being blessed, a quality which Rufus's words could not hope to possess. He decided therefore to use Clementina to talk to the people. If she agreed to the plan, the people would think God was on their side. But perhaps he handed the meeting over to her for another stronger reason, namely that he was powerless to continue as their leader. He had been betrayed so many times that night. He was tired and hungry. He had been disappointed by Jackson. He could do nothing. But he was not willing to have all the power he now held in his hands slip from him. He would allow someone else to share this power with him. In that way he might avoid losing all his influence.

The people were waiting for him to say something. He wanted to choose Boysie. But Boysie was a traitor too. Would the people trust in a woman? Would they like Clementina as their leader?

'Rufus, the people waiting for you to say something more,' Clementina said.

Rufus was pulled from his thoughts. What spirit of weakness was this coming over him at the height of his power? In front of him all the able-bodied men and women in the village; in his pockets all the life savings of his biggest enemy; at his side a traitorous lieutenant whom he could keep in everlasting subjection; and a woman, faithless but living in the fear of him – and he thinking these thoughts? Surrendering power to someone else? And a woman, at that? He must be brave. He must be brave, for he must lead. These people were stupid, poor, backward, ignorant people, who had to be led. He could lead them. He could lead them. They would be pleased to be led. He could not lead them worse than the plantation had been leading them for generations past. It was his calling in life to lead his people from this prolonged slavery.

'Everybody stand up!' he shouted. 'Clementina going sing a song and lead us in prayer, whilst I want everybody, every man and every woman to come up to me, take a piece o' soil from this land what have our blood and sweat all these thousands o' years, and swallow it, and take a' oath to keep secret 'bout this meeting, and what we plan' to do. Everybody stand. Everybody sing. And file past me, one by one, and take the oath.'

The people got up. You could hear some of their bones dispelling the stiffness in them. Clementina cleared her throat and led the throng in a rousing prayer. But Rufus had to ask her to keep her voice down, since the plantation might hear.

'Hey, where the hell Jo-Jo gone?' he asked when they had all taken the oath of allegiance.

'Jo-Jo run and gone!' someone said.

'Blind him!'

Clementina was making the most of the prayers. Her voice was choked with emotion and the words came out as if she were gasping for life, as if someone were trying to thrust the words back down into her throat. The people shouted, 'Amen' and 'Hallelujah'.

' – in the toughest of tribulations I laughs, and I smiles, there is a smile on my face like the smile on the face o' Daniel in the lion's den, 'cause I know, yes, I know, Lord, that You on my side! You on the side of the poor and the 'umble – '

'Yesss, sister, tell it!'

' – and the piece o' Scriptures that Rufus mention' just now as having something to do with the arrangement he worked out for us poor peoples, well, let me tell you that that piece o' Scriptures is a damn funny piece o' God's words. It come from the Acks. Chapter four. Beginning at the twenty-second, twenty-third verse, or thereabouts. That piece o' Scriptures was base' on a serious bit of philosophy. 'Cause it mean' that Rufus intends to take bread from one Christian and put it into the mouth of another man who don't have his own, and who isn' no blood kin to that first man! That is a serious thing. That is asking for war. But childrens, God understand'. That is the meat o' human kindness, and that is what God talk' 'bout when He was walking this earth of ours. That is Christianity. Give unto others, not what you hoping you going get outta them, but praise God, amen, hallelujah! what you expects they in turn going to be *willing* and *joyfully* eager to give unto you!'

'Amen! Hear His word!' the people groaned.

' – call in that beggar man in his ragged suit offa the street, and let him sit down with you at that Sunday dinner table with the nice linen cloth what you only uses on a Sunday, and let him eat some o' that nice fried pork and black-eye peas and rice. You hear me? Do that! Open you pocket book, and turn it upside down, and downside up, open all the pockets and tear that dollar bill in half, and give the beggar man half. God watching. God watching – ' She was gasping for breath, as the tide of her emotions rose like the waves in the sea. The people were groaning. Clementina had them in her power, in the palms of her voice.

'Let we sing. *Abide With Me*. Come,' she said and she led them off into the mournful song.

Across the fields the plantation was sleeping. But the people could hear dogs grumbling. Rufus held out his hand and touched Boysie. Boysie replied by touching him. They understood. Rufus whispered and asked Boysie about Jo-Jo. Jo-Jo was a blasted backward man, Boysie whispered back. Rufus was frightened. Something was going to happen, he told his second-in-command.

'Take this,' Rufus said, handing Boysie all the bills he had in his pockets. 'The money. You be the treasurer. Get Mango, or one of the womens, or even Clemmie to help out, if anything happen.'

'How much?'

'I didn' have time to count it, Boys.'

'Suppose it is two hundered and you say it is ten hundered?'

The people were singing. Rufus and Boysie could whisper without suspicion. They could have walked off and left the poor souls singing out their hearts and their miseries to God.

'If anything happen' – and I not saying nor hoping that anything going to happen, but *if* – see that Stella get some o' that money. A third. Keep a third for me. And spend the rest on the people. But if nothing don't happen, meet me at Biscombe – no, meet me – '

'At my house. Mummy sleeping now, so the coast clear.'

'The coast clear.'

He and Boysie turned again to the people and joined in the singing. Their voices became one voice, one spirit, sad and heavy, reflecting the grief and the sorrows and the hope and the happiness that was within their hearts.

> 'A-bide with me-eee,
> La la la la-aaa,
> The darkness fall-alls,
> Lord, la la la-aaa;
> A-bide with me-eee – '

The satisfaction from the singing swelled their voices and they disregarded the secret nature of their meeting. Out of the darkness rang a shot, *brang!* tearing the hell out of the night. The singing stopped. Their breathing became hurried. It seemed that a lifetime had passed before someone said, 'Run, run, run!'

'Oh, Lord, in heaven have His mercy – '

Like animals saddled with fear and terror, the people scampered through the dark night, shouting, pushing, crying, and no one singing.

'Boysie? Boysie? The money!'

'Have it.'

'Run, Boysie, run with the money!'

But before Rufus could move, a light was shining in his face and a voice familiar to him said, in a tired, indifferent manner, 'That is the bastard who call' himself a Gandhi.'

The voice belonged to Jo-Jo, who was identifying Rufus to Barabbas, the manager and the overseer, and another white man whom he had never seen before.

The blows were quick and heavy and long. Rufus winced each time the truncheon fell on his body. Barabbas was smiling as he lifted the truncheon. The blows tore the shirt from Rufus's back; after a while he became numb, the blows were still landing on him, but they were having no effect. Barabbas went on smiling.

In a half daze Rufus felt that he was walking through a corridor in a strange house. Lights, lights, lights. Thick carpet on the floor – and the lights coming from shining sparkling things like diamonds – and then the door being shut, and the strange white man hovering over him with a thick, brown, shining leather belt across his body like the bruises left by the heavy, savage truncheon that Barabbas was wielding – and then the strange silence in the room, with the manager and the overseer looking on, and the strange white man mopping his brow, and Jo-Jo, like a disobedient boy, standing behind them by the door – and Barabbas holding on to a chair to regain his breath and his strength. And then, there was nothing –

8

When Boysie reached home, panting and frightened, he realized that his house was not safe. He set off again, running for a safer place to spend the rest of the night. He was scared without Rufus beside him. Although he had the money in his possession, and although he knew they had caught Rufus, and that they would probably charge him with some crime, yet he was not free of the overpowering shadow which this insane man had cast over his life. He was running faster now, going somewhere in this dark night that seemed darker than any he had experienced in the island. He would go to Mango's home, and see if Mango was hiding there, see what Mango was going to do. Without Rufus to steer him out of his confusion, he strayed and strayed until he came to Mango's small house. He knocked softly on the bedroom part of the house, and he waited, expecting to see Mango's face appear at the window and invite him inside. But a woman's face appeared instead.

'What the bloody hell you waking up my children for? You come to thief?'

'Is me. Boysie. Mango home?'

'Oh, is you, Boysie! No. He gone to some meeting some part o' the village. Say it is some secret lodge or some damn thing, but – '

'Thanks.' And before the woman had shut the window, Boysie was running through the darkness, searching it for Mango. All alone on a night like this. Nobody at home. Nobody knowing where anybody was – and he had to be alone with all this money in his pocket. He did not even have a chance to count it. Biscombe could have already told the police that he lost ten thousand dollars, or a million, and I won't be a damn sight better off, since I don't know how much I got from Rufus. Perhaps Rufus's woman would know what to do. So, he set off for Rufus's house. It was in darkness and everyone inside was dead asleep. Only the dog was alive, and he came sniffing and growling at Boysie.

'Down, Rover! Down, boy!' Boysie patted the dog on the head and tried to quiet it. He did not wish to wake the whole neighbourhood. Not on a night like this. Rover fussed about him and refused to be quieted. Then a window creaked open.

'Who' that? Rufus?' It was Stella.

Boysie dashed back into the shadows. The window remained opened slightly and he could feel the anxiety on Stella's face. She whispered again, asking the darkness if it was Rufus, or who it was.

'Rufus?'

'It's me, Boysie, Stella. Where Rufus? He come home yet?'

'Boysie? I not seen Rufus since nine o'clock. You seen him up at BiscombeRum Shop?'

'They got him, then. They got him.'

'Who is they? The police? Or the plantation?'

'Both.'

'He tol' you anything to tell me? Anything – like what to do 'bout the mission? Or anything?'

'No. I just come to tell you what happen'. You not seen Mango?'

'What the hell you think I does with my time, Boysie? Out looking for mens?'

'Sorry. I just thought – '

'Boysie? You heard anything 'bout Biscombe? You heard anything serious that happen' – '

'Like if somebody beat up Biscombe? You mean that? How you know?' Boysie challenged her. 'You know 'bout the robbery, too?'

The schoolmaster returned to the rum shop later that night because he could not sleep and because he wanted to tell Biscombe his side of the story in case Rufus began to spread it through the village that he, Whippetts, the imparter of knowledge in the village, was a common thief. He wanted to explain to Biscombe, before the rumours spread with the rising sun, that it was for some rum, for something to eat, for anything except the cash box and the little black book in which his outstanding debts were written, that his feet had misled him through Biscombe's back door like an ordinary criminal. Whatever happened, Mr Whippetts knew that his friend the minister must not hear of this. Neither must the manager know. Even if he had to give Biscombe some money to help him keep the secret, he had to have his assurance that he would not say a word about his small indiscretion to one living soul.

Mr Whippetts had tossed and turned in his sleepless, sexless bed, beside his wife who grumbled and cursed all the time, asking him not to jerk the springs. For a long time he had endured her recriminations and the heavy burden of conscience that kept him awake. He sat up in the bed, ignoring his wife, and then and there he decided to put a jacket over his pyjamas and take an early walk up to Biscombe's.

'You outta your mind, man? The sun still behind the hill, and you crawling out o' bed?'

'Mind your business, woman!'

With that he left her, grumbling and sucking on her teeth, worrying herself about his health and his safety. Mr Whippetts threw the heavy black oilskin mackintosh over his shoulders and went out. The early morning wind was chilling, and he walked briskly. The noisy mackintosh whiffed and whoofed as he sped along the street. He arrived at the shop, and he stopped in front, of it, wondering if he was doing the best thing. He could have chosen another means of ensuring that the story would not get around. He could have told Rufus that it would be all right for his son, Ezekiel, to take the scholarship examination. Rufus would have liked that. He was proud of his son, and proud of the prospect of him being a high-school student, like the manager's. But the schoolmaster realized that he had allowed that golden opportunity to slip through his hands. Now he had to take the more dangerous course in order to put a little matter right, which could have been dealt with so easily had he kept his thinking-cap on his head when discovered by Rufus.

He shrugged his shoulders, pulled the oilskin coat tight around his cold body and went to the back of the shop. The tall weeds shivered in the damp morning wind and they frightened him a little. He shrugged his shoulders again, getting more courage from doing so, and went through the gate. It was open. He walked slowly and carefully up to the back door, and there he stood listening for any sound inside the shop. It was late. It would soon be daybreak. But still he listened for some movement, something inside the shop, although he did not know why he expected this. As his eyes became accustomed to the darkness, so too did his ears grow accustomed to the strange silence around him. But it was not silence at all that he was hearing. He was hearing someone groaning. He listened. Yes, it was someone groaning. He pushed open the back door of the shop, and before him on the floor was Biscombe, writhing in the aftermath of pain from the beating.

'Good Jesus God, Biscombe! What happened? You was in the Boer War or something?'

Biscombe rolled his eyes, but said nothing. Mr Whippetts lifted himself through the door and helped Biscombe to a chair in the special room. Biscombe told him how it had happened, and who had done it. Mr Whippetts was smiling to himself as Biscombe related the savage beating which Rufus had given him. Now his problem was solved! It was so easy, he said to himself. So easy! And he had been worrying so much! He had almost listened to his wife and not come out. Now look what a wonderful solution! He must be firmer with that woman in future, he said to himself, making a mental note of his decision.

'You have witnesses, though?' he asked Biscombe, when he had settled him in his bed, and had wiped the cuts and helped him into his pyjamas.

'Witnesses? God is the onliest person who seen this thing. And I damn sure He not going to talk up in court, when it goes to court!'

'Heh-heh-heh!' the schoolmaster laughed, without telling Biscombe why he laughed. Only God, too, knew why he laughed. 'Life is a mysterious thing, Biscombe! Blasted mysterious!'

But Biscombe was in no mood for philosophical talk and he ranted on about having the police put Rufus in prison for life and throw away the key.

'It is only assault and battery, Biscombe, boy,' the schoolmaster explained. 'And that ain't the most serious infraction 'gainst the legal system!'

'And t'eft!' Biscombe snapped. He had discovered that the money had been stolen. 'All my blasted life savings!'

'But it doesn't follow – '

'Tell me what follow'?'

'Well, it is like this,' the schoolmaster said, sipping the rum which he had taken down from the shelf and was sharing with Biscombe. 'The legal set-up in the British system is like this. Don't mind that you know that Rufus did with intents maim you, and even though everybody in this village have reason to believe the same, it don't follow that the law o' the land will look at the matter that way.'

'If the law can't look at it that way, you tell me how the law o' the land intends to look at it, then?' Biscombe was in a rage. It was damaging to be beaten. Everybody in the village was against you when you were beaten, regardless of the reason. It was a shameful thing to walk around with bandages. Everybody talked and whispered about it. 'You is a' edicated man, Whippetts, so you tell me how the law o' this land intends to look at me?'

They argued for a long while about British justice. Mr Whippetts told Biscombe that under the law of the land every man was innocent until he could be proved guilty. And that was so, no matter how guilty the man seemed to be, or how guilty his enemies assumed him to be. Biscombe shook his head and began abusing the schoolmaster and the law and the British system. He was in pain, he said, and that ought to be proof that he was beaten. He was not a madman and he did not beat himself with a stick. Somebody had to beat him. And he knew who that somebody was. It was Rufus. What the hell then was the law waiting for? Mr Whippetts went on saying that the law could not come out in the open and say a man was guilty. It was not like that, he assured Biscombe, who was grimacing from the pain and the soreness of his limbs. The law could not do that. The law had to try a man by justice, the schoolmaster said. Justice!

'Justice could kiss my arse!' Biscombe said.

'Justice!' the schoolmaster said, mouthing the word with relish.' British justice!'

Biscombe grumbled and kept silent for a long while. Then he said, as if seeking Mr Whippetts's opinion, 'Why you think Rufus beat me up, Mister Whippetts? Why you think he pick' out me, instead o' picking out Turnbull the overseer, or even the manager, who is the people he should be fighting 'gainst?'

The schoolmaster watched Biscombe long and intently before he answered. It seemed as if he was arranging his thoughts; as if what he was about to say was to be a great shock to Biscombe.

'Because you are what you is!' he said. Biscombe was expecting some important explanation, something about his liaison with Rufus's woman, or even some mention of the fact that it was he who first informed the plantation about the first meeting, and he was a little disappointed.

'But why?' he persisted.

'You really want to know why, Biscombe?'

Biscombe did not answer. He was thinking. He was making sure to himself that he was strong enough to bear the hurt, the injury which he felt was in store for him in the answer the schoolmaster was about to give. When he felt he was sure enough, he asked him again.

'Why?'

'Because you are a son-of-a-bitch, Biscombe!'

Biscombe chuckled.

'You don't know where your blasted 'legiances lay! If you want to know the answer, the answer lay there, right there in them words o' mine.'

'You saying – although you didn't rightly say the words that I could hear – you saying though that it is because I on the white man side!'

'Pre-fucking-cisely – if you pardon the use o' the English language!'

'But you was on the white man' side that night, too! You was in the car, Whippetts! What is the difference?'

'The difference is simple, Biscombe. Number one, I is a black man like Rufus, and he would give me a second chance to prove myself. And number two, I is a' ordinary man. Not a blasted proprietor!'

'So they don't like me, eh?' Biscombe said, chuckling. 'Although I give them rum, although I give them credit, although I lend them money – '

'You late, Biscombe. Blood thicker than rum! You been shedding rum all this time and screwing everybody' woman. You been doing all them things what the white man does to the poor people.

Screwing them and fucking them up, and then asking them for mercy – ' Mr Whippetts stopped to listen. He cocked his ears, certain that he had heard something move. 'You hear something?'

'No,' he said, without trying to listen. 'Just the blasted prison cell locking 'pon that bastard!'

'No, lis'en. Somebody walking round this shop, man! Lis'en!'

The footsteps walked cautiously round the shop, stopping and walking in turn. Biscombe asked the schoolmaster to turn the light down. The schoolmaster was becoming nervous. Biscombe had shown himself to be uneasy.

'Who you think it is? Rufus?' he asked Mr Whippetts.

But Mr Whippetts did not answer. He had his own fear to defeat before he could think about what to do. Could it be Rufus, he wondered. Suppose it was Rufus, coming back.

' I don't feel good, Whippetts.'

'I know how you feel. As if something going to happen – '

'Mister Whippetts, I call you as my witness this night, or this foreday morning, I call you to witness that if anything happen to me, you and the manager and the overseer must lay the blame where it belong'. Lay it at Rufus's doorstep. If anything at all happen', we have to put the blame on Rufus.'

'But there wasn' witnesses, Biscombe. You asking me a damn funny request. That is false oath taking, you asking me to take.'

'I don't know who side you on, Whippetts. But whatever side you have 'legiances with, you can't shut your eyes to what happening in this village. A madman gone loose. I have to close up shop 'cause I is a sick man now. And the doctor sure to tell me take it easy. Whilst, however, the rum shop can't make money. So I get hit twice, in the magazine and in the hull! That is why I on the side o' power, on the side o' money – the white man side.'

'I on the side o' British justice, Biscombe,' the schoolmaster said, smiling. 'British justice!'

'A narrow escape! A narrow so-and-so escape, Boysie!' Mango was saying. He was breathing hard after the long run through the canes. When the shot was fired, he had dived under a heap of trash piled near by for manuring the young cane plants. He had witnessed the flight of all the people from the little watchtower which he had bored in the trash heap. He had seen Boysie flee; he had seen Rufus look round hopelessly for help, and he had seen the beating which the constable gave Rufus in the presence of the manager and the overseer, and the strange white man. At first he had mistaken the white man for the parson of the Anglican church, but when he heard the man giving orders to Barabbas, he realized that he was a police officer. And when the plantation's car came round, he could see the thick brown belt on his shoulder. When they had left for the plantation house, Mango crept out of the trash heap and ran for home. But like Boysie, he did not know how much Rufus was going to talk. It was the second time that something had backfired, and the second time that the victim, and the only victim, was Rufus. Perhaps he would feel he was having enough of the burden, while his followers reaped the rewards which he had hoped to get from his actions. This is the way Mango argued the situation with himself, as he ran across the black stretch of public road to his home. When he got near, he saw Boysie at the window. He listened, and decided that he should follow Boysie. He knew Boysie was closer to Rufus than he was; and this close relationship to the leader, for Boysie had become the leader now, caused him to suspect and envy Boysie. He would keep close to Boysie, and keep close to his freedom. He had followed Boysie to the schoolmaster's house, and when there was no answer from Mr Whippetts, he had followed Boysie to the rum shop. He waited in the darkness while Boysie shadowed the shop. Then when he saw that Boysie was lost and confused, he decided to join forces with him. He caught up with him as he was walking away from Biscombe's. He asked Boysie about the money. Did Rufus really have the money? Boysie told him he did have the money. But he said it was only two hundred dollars. In fact it was more than eight hundred dollars, but Boysie had hidden the rest in a cane hole opposite the entrance to the rum shop. He wondered if Mango had been following him when he hid it, but when he asked him a few questions, he was convinced that Mango was either a damn good liar, or he did not know where the six hundred dollars were hidden. Boysie had marked the spot, not by a stone, which would have been too elementary for him, but by sprinkling dirt over the spot and marking it in relation to the front door of the shop. A stone could be moved, he reasoned. The shop could not. It would take a storm to move Biscombe! Mango asked about the money again, and again Boysie lied.

'But you mean he was raising so much hell 'bout two hundred dollars? How the hell could two hundred people live offa that? And he have the rudeness to tell the people not to go back to work in the morning!'

'That is why I getting tired as arse with this whole strike business! Look at me. Look at you. We haven' done one blasted thing, and yet we have to live in the blasted cane field like common rats.'

'We have to make sacrifices for progressiveness sake though, Boysie.'

Boysie told him about the telephone call to Jackson. Mango was stunned. Boysie said it was true; and what was more stunning was that Jackson denied having anything to do with the strike, as Rufus wanted to say.

'Jesus Christ! That is false pretences!' Mango shouted. 'And to think that all them people could 'ave been shot – and for nothing! Because o' one stupid madman!'

'That's why I say, Mango, let we, let me and you cut out. Ignore the people. They stupid already. And nothing me or you could do going make them less stupid. If Rufus get hanged, another Rufus going come along tomorrow. Me and you, we in charge o' the organization now, Mango. I know how I could get my hand on a piece o' money. That piece o' money could do many things with. Passage. A trip to one of the other small islands, anything – '

'You talking like a blasted traitor, Boysie. And I 'shamed that I know you.'

'Jesus Christ, here goes another Gandhi the Second!'

'We have to think o' the people! That is what Rufus wants.'

'Well, let Rufus think o' the people, man! I thinking 'bout Boysie, because Boysie is people too!'

'But if – don't get me wrong! I saying if – if me and you go in partnerships, how would I know I could trust you? How would I know you and me going divide the money exactly in half, fifty-fifty?'

Boysie told him he could trust him, and Mango was convinced. They shook hands and sealed their agreement. They were to remain in the canes until they thought everything was safe.

They could not return to work, at least not Boysie. They had enough money to live well after they came out of hiding. Boysie decided he would try to go to one of the small islands and get married to a coolie woman. But Mango said he wanted to go where Jackson was, in spite of what Boysie told him Jackson had said the night Rufus called him on the phone. Mango was decided. Canada, he said, is a blasted big country, and in a big country a man like him could hide. The islands were too small. When these minor differences were settled, and they had agreed to spend about two weeks in hiding in the canes, all day, and only venture out at night, the further problem of getting foodstuffs, cigarettes and drinks came up. For a moment both of them were floored. Then Boysie thought he had the answer.

'Biscombe!' he exclaimed, ashamed with himself for not thinking of him before. 'Biscombe is the man!'

'Who side that bitch on now?'

'On our side, man!'

'Biscombe can't know which side he on, man, 'cause Biscombe is a two-tone man. He have to be on both sides. That is the way he was born!'

'Well, at least we could try.'

Mango said yes, but he really meant no.

'But what about the people, though?'

'Forget the people!' Boysie shouted.

'But the money we intends using on ourselves belongst to the people. Rufus say so.'

'Rufus thief the money and he give it to me. Well, I don't think the people count, 'cause as I said, the people like to be led like sheep. They like to suffer, so that they could sing and pray to God and get in the spirits and whatever the hell they like to do. It make' them happy as arse, Mango. You didn' see how them people behaved out there tonight when Sister Clemmie was pouring on the oil o' salvation 'pon them old, old wounds o' confusion and poorness? That is the people! And people don't change! I not wasting this good investment on these people, man.'

'We still have to think a little bit o' the people, though, Boysie, good Jesus Christ, man, have a heart!'

'My heart right here,' he snapped, patting his pocket, and rattling a few coins he had in it.

9

'We going make a' example out of you!' the white police officer was saying. Over and over again he said it, and each time he raised his hand to give Barabbas the signal to pour his fists into Rufus. 'We intends to make a' example out of you!' the officer snarled again. And again the heavy hand landed in Rufus's soft guts.

The three of them were alone in the manager's office. They had locked the door, turned on the lights, and had been questioning him for the past four hours. Rufus honestly could not understand why the questions were so serious, and so difficult to understand. He felt they were playing tricks on him. What did he know of a communist movement throughout the West Indies, which was preparing a revolution to overthrow the land-owning white people, and turn the land over to the poor black people? How could he ever know of these things, since he could neither read nor write, and the only letter he had received from abroad, in his whole life, described living conditions in a strange country, conditions which he had heard only a few hours ago, had not even been experienced by the man who wrote the letter? And the letter? They wanted to know more about the letter! Was it a document? What was a document? he asked them. But the constable gave him a blow in the stomach and bent him like a hairpin. When were they planning the big move? Which move? he asked. The constable hit him again.

There was blood running from his pores it seemed. He was stiff and tired, and sleepy. He wanted to be left alone, so he could collapse on the thick carpet on the floor, and go to sleep until next week, he was so dog-tired. But the questions were falling like rain, and he had no shelter from them, not even his ignorance was security now. The officer said he was pretending he could not read. He pushed the letter, the same letter which Jackson had written Rufus, in front of him, and commanded him to explain the meaning of it. Rufus looked at the mysterious characters on the soft, expensive paper, and blinked his eyes.

'I don't know what there, sir,' Rufus said.

'What the hell you mean?'

'Can't read nor write, sir.'

'Holy Jees!' the white officer exclaimed. 'Can't read nor write,' he added laughing, 'and saying he is a leader of these people! Who the arse you trying to fool, Rufus?' Again he held up his hand and again the constable was there with a blow. Rufus wondered why the white man would not hit him himself. Why was he making the constable do the beating? 'This is a lost case!'

The officer was becoming tired of the whole affair. He was sweating like a horse. The thick brown belt left a mark of perspiration across his shirt. He took a handkerchief from his pocket and mopped his face, resting one hand on the top of the desk. The constable was breathing hard and viciously. He too was sweating. He wiped the sweat away with the sleeve of his thick black night-uniform. They left Rufus for a while, as they wiped themselves, and stared at some imaginary piece of convicting evidence in front of them. Rufus held his head away from the brightness of the light, wondering if he was dreaming all that was going on before him. But the sting of the blows from the truncheon, and the weight of the constable's hands, even when he was not hitting Rufus, convinced him that this was not a dream. The officer spun round and stared Rufus in the face with his glassy steel-blue eyes.

'You are a blasted commie!'

'No, sir.'

'You lie! You lie! You are a communist! You are a communist because all black people are communists!'

Rufus glanced at the constable, who avoided his eyes. For some time the officer could think of nothing new to say, of no new angle, of no new development in the investigation. Rufus thought he saw a satisfied look on the constable's face, a look that suggested that he too was fed up with the uselessness of the investigation, that despite the role he was employed to play, he was inwardly glad that the officer could not bend Rufus suffi- ciently to get a signed confession from him. The officer mopped his brow again, and stuffed the dripping wet handkerchief into his breast pocket. He stamped about the room, trying to think of something to add, of some trap he could lay for Rufus.

'You belong to the Bridgetown Labour Movement?'

'Yes, sir. But my dues not paid.'

'Never mind, never mind. That is a communist party! And you is a damn commie, because you belong to that party! Right? Come on, say right!'

'But, sir, that party is the ruling party – what I mean to say, sir, is that – '

'They are all communists! You give a black man a little learning and, Christ, he turns round and tells you how to run the blasted show!'

There was a gentle knock on the door of the office. The manager appeared. He waited until the inspector went to him before he whispered some message into his ear. The inspector's face shone like a polished apple. He took his handkerchief out again and ran it round his face.

'And when you're finished, do come and have a spot o' brandy, Inspector.'

'Thank you, thank you!'

'And bring along the constable, too,' the manager added, before closing the door. But the inspector said nothing to this. He wheeled round and faced Rufus. 'What do you say 'bout murder?'

The shock left Rufus speechless. Had Biscombe died? Who could have found out? He wanted to know more, but the inspector said nothing more. He just stood there staring at Rufus as if he were a piece of rotten sugarcane.

'Stay with him, constable,' he said at last. 'I going to have a drink.'

The constable snapped to attention and clicked his heels. The officer replied with a salute that was as ragged and sloppy as a piece of wet chamois cloth. When he left the room, the constable kicked the legs of the desk to show his disgust.

'God blind you, man!' he said, forgetting himself in the presence of Rufus. But Rufus said nothing. He had the audacity to feel sorry for the constable. He wanted to talk to the man and beg him to come over to his side. But he knew it would be useless.

The constable was doing his duty. Even if part of that duty involved hating his superior white officer. 'You bastard!' said the constable. 'You poor, black, ignorunt bastard! Man, I would have wringed three-four-five confessions outta you by now!'

In a rage he loosened the belt with the ugly brown truncheon attached to it and swept it right under Rufus's nose.

'You idiot! You ass-head! How could you behave like such an arse in front o' the white man?' he snapped. Rufus watched him working himself into a rage. There was nothing he could do. The constable took a pair of handcuffs from his tunic pocket and snapped them on Rufus. He unbuttoned his tunic and sat at the edge of the desk, smoking and swinging his feet backwards and forwards in time with the explosive language he used to describe Rufus. A knock on the door startled him and brought him to his feet. He was fumbling with his belt when the door opened and the face of the overseer appeared.

'Leave that arsehole and come, man! The white man having brandy in the living-room. I going give you a drink o' strong rum.'

'Jesus Christ, Turnbull, you is a real friend!' the constable said, dressing. He glanced at Rufus as if to beg him, please, for God's sake, don't try to run away! 'Turnbull, you don't know, the white man come in here and invite me and invite that son-of-a-bitch for a drink, and he rufuse' to take me in! The man invite' both o' we for a drink!'

'Don't argue, man, with an officer,' the overseer begged him, 'don't argue with them! Rum tastes the same way and, if you ask me, officer, it gives a more stiffer hard on!'

'Heh-heh-heh-heh! Turnbull, you is a real son-of-a-bitch!' And the two of them went out of the room, their arms around each other.

Rufus sat with his hands handcuffed in front of him, and thought of his bed, how soft it would be now, and of the money he had stolen from Biscombe, and of the people needing him, and soon he was sleeping, sitting upright in the hard uncomfortable chair.

Rufus was emerging from sleep when he heard voices coming towards the door. He kept his eyes closed and listened.

'I really sorry for that bastard, though, officer,' a voice was saying. 'Real sorry. But, lis'en! He have a real nice woman. Nice, nice piece o' pussy, if you want some. Would screw 'pon a pin-point any time o' day, and cheap. One o' these days, man, officer, I going give you a' introducement, man!'

'Won't mind at all!' the constable said. 'Would take my mind offa that arse in there. But you said just now that all the fellars does let loose in this woman, and he don't know?'

'Don't know or don't want to know!' the overseer said. After this Rufus lost consciousness again –

'You got a madman in this van,' the constable was saying some time later, 'so don't let him get out, yuh! This man sell his woman for a job in the cane fields – take him down and lock him up in a nice cell, do.'

'Where the chief is?' another voice asked. 'Getting drunk again? And he didn' invite you in with him?'

'Chief? He couldn't even get a whore to confess that she ain't a virgin, if you ask me!' the constable said. 'Take him down. The Chief say call him here if anything more happen'. I have to go and see a man name' Biscombe at the rum shop.'

After that all Rufus knew was that he was being driven somewhere in the dawn that was breaking.

The tops of the cane fields in the east of the island were catching fire from the morning sun. Normally, every day at this time, the villagers would be opening their windows and spitting outside on the fresh dew, and yawning and stretching and calling out for their neighbours to get up and look out at the nice, lovely sun rising. This morning, all the windows in the village were closed, and even if the occupants of the houses were awake, they were not looking out. Stella had rushed over to visit Mango's woman after Boysie left, and she heard some story from her which made her try Clementina to see if it was correct. Rufus was shot again, the rumour went. They had him over at the plantation, dripping blood and on the point of death. Did Clementina know if this was true? Clementina rolled her eyes and looked up at the cobwebs in her smoky little house, and asked God for mercy and help. Never,

never, never, she repeated, in all her days on this terrible earth did she see such gnashing of teeth and shedding of blood. It was Sodom and Gomorrah, she testified. And she begged Stella to pray for Rufus, pray for the village, that destruction and desolation was coming. Stella made some exasperated sound and prepared to leave.

'Darling love,' Clementina said, resting her hand on Stella's shoulders affectionately. 'Darling love, you is the cause o' all this 'struction on Rufus's head. I know. I not as old and stupid as you think, Stella. You knock 'bout with the overseer – I know, I know he had Rufus working on the plantation while the rest o' the mens was laid off. We have to thank him for that. But he exact' a damn high price. And you should 'ave knowed that, darling, when you was in on the bargaining. It is a mother talking to you now. I going to beg you, please, go across that dirt track and talk to Turnbull. 'Cause Turnbull in a damn rage 'bout the people meeting tonight. I begging you, Stella, swallow a piece o' your pride and crawl back and ask Turnbull for mercy. He have the power to take back the labourers to work. And though Rufus make a real nice case that we shouldn' go back to them fields, and though the people might not go back tomorrow morning or the next day, they still have to go back, 'cause the pinch o' starvation and hungriness is a damn stiff pinch. So, please.'

'I don't have nothing to do with Mister Turnbull, Clemmie,' Stella said. 'I don't have no influence over Turnbull.'

'Oh Christ, Stella! You mean to tell me that what you gave him didn' sweeten him up sufficient that he wouldn't do a favour for you? You mean to tell me that that man suffer' a beating from Rufus, and you say he don't love you.'

'Turnbull married, Clemmie, you forgetting?'

'Married or no married, darling, outside woman taste a hundred times sweeter than a wife. I was young once like you.'

Stella was still not sure she could do anything to make the overseer change his mind. Clementina said that the people were behind Rufus; that they had taken an oath not to return to the fields. But that depended on the length of time Rufus was in prison. And this made Stella break down crying. Clementina was hard on her for crying. Those tears were false, she told her.

'Look, Miss Stella, the people in this village damn scared tonight! Everybody button down their windows and doors and they waiting to see what going happen. I know what going happen. But I asking you, as the onliest woman in this place, to go and beg Turnbull to lessen the punishment.'

'It serve' Rufus right!'

'You don't love Rufus?'

'Love Rufus? That nasty smelly bastard!'

'You have your sights on Biscombe, eh?' Clementina said. Stella looked at her but said nothing. 'I know. Poorness and sufferation is funny things. They does make a person think crooked. But you heard 'bout Biscombe? You heard somebody beat him to the point o' death?'

'No! Who?'

'You didn't hear? Where the hell you was when all this tragedies was going on, Stella, laying down under the overseer? Where you was? Sleeping?'

Stella walked out of the house without another word. Clementina stood at the door looking out at the dawn and shook her head from side to side, trying to work out the puzzle of Stella's life. When she could find no solution to satisfy her, she closed the door, and fell on her knees, and asked God to take her through this day that threatened to be such a terrible one. Outside in her small enclosed yard, the chickens were scratching the floors of their coops and the ducks were quacking for their breakfast. Clementina pulled the sheets higher over her head and waited for the knock on the door –

When Stella reached the rum shop, it was almost morning. A policeman was getting on his bicycle. He saw her coming and he waited until she was near to him. He examined her from head to foot, and when she passed him he turned round and watched the turbulence of her behind rolling carefree under the lightweight cotton dress. He made an observation which caused Stella to look back. The policeman laughed loudly and broadly, and rode off.

Inside the shop Biscombe was talking to the schoolmaster who had not left since he came back to find Biscombe beaten and unconscious in the yard.

'Where you was, honey?' Biscombe asked. 'Your man almost kill' me, be-Christ, and you couldn't be found no where! But praise God, they have him!'

'The police just left!' Mr Whippetts said. 'A plague going hit this blasted village. The plantation not taking back nobody to work. Not till the canes ready to be reaped. Rufus tol' the people to strike. The manager threaten' to bring in the volunteer force, he say they going to be a riot! Oh, Jesus Christ! He even threaten' to close down the school. My school! Well, it take me a damn long time to realize that one plantation and one plantation manager have so much power in this village! Now we got to do something. Something positive.'

'Where Rufus is, Biscombe?'

'In prison. You didn't go and kiss him goodbye?' Biscombe chuckled. 'I thought you would 'ave been in Broad Street at Fogarty and Cave Shepherd by now spending some o' the money the bitch stole from me! But I don't think he would give you none. He probably planning to leave for Canada tomorrow, though.'

'Where Boysie, Biscombe?' Biscombe shook his head. 'You know where Mango is, then?' Again Biscombe shook his head. He knew nothing, he said, and he did not give a goddamn about anything, except the profits he would be losing because of the ignorance of the ignorant black people in this village. 'We have to do something. And, Biscombe, I am 'shame', 'shame' that I ever – but that is past tense! From now, I know what side I on. If the manager want a fight and a riot, well, he getting one!'

'You better think o' your blasted job and leave those Africanated ass-holes alone! They is ass-holes! You didn't hear what Barabbas say? Rufus, Boysie and Mango should be shot – through the balls – 'cause they want to fight against the pricks.'

'You still on the white man side?'

'I on the side o' British justice!'

'That is the white man side!'

'Well, I on the white man side, then.'

'Biscombe, I never thought you was such a backward, two-tone son-of-a-gun!'

And with that, Mr Whippetts stormed out of the room.

Biscombe felt stronger when he had left. He looked at Stella and held out his hands to her.

'Come, Stella, I have you now.' He dug his head into her neck, and bit her, and ran his tongue round her soft flesh. 'Rufus not here now, darling love. You is mine for good. When he come out, if they ever let him out, you would be mine already.' He kissed her, and he kissed her. His hands exploring her body. In his ecstasy he did not know if she was returning some of the warmth and sincerity of his embraces. He was too happy to think. 'Who would 'ave thought that at long last you would be mine? Who would 'ave think that?'

'God works in a mysterious way, Biscombe,' she said, and buried her head in his shoulders. She was crying again. But Biscombe cared not for the tears. His mind was on sex. Though the stiffness of his joints and the numbness of his flesh worried him, he ignored all this for the greater pleasure of having Stella all to himself. It was worth the beating.

'Biscombe, I will have to move in with the children. All o' we have to live with you.'

'If you is my woman, you have to live in my house, and wash my shirt and cook my bittle. But be-Jesus Christ, you finish' holding up your dress and let the Jockey spy up under you, you hear?' And he gave her a slap across the face to emphasize the point. She closed her eyes and winced a little. When she opened them, she was smiling. Her lips were shivering. She had Biscombe in the palm of her hands. She pinned those lips on Biscombe, and wallowed her wet tongue inside his mouth, and rubbed her hands up and down his back, and tickled him and made him giggle like a little boy. Biscombe's eyes were like two pools of stale rain water. He had never expected such ecstasy.

'I moving in with the children in the morning, Biscombe,' she said, talking with her mouth sealing his.

'I love you, Stell, darling. Jesus God, how I love you!'

'It settle', then!' she said, and she got up, leaving him in the bed panting like a dog.

PART THREE

THE FAILURE

10

Something like a plague fell over the village. The villagers took heart after Rufus's conviction for assault with intent to maim, and refused to go back to work on the plantation. They endured their days of hunger with silence and gritted their teeth. The plantation almost panicked at first. The weeds were choking the young sugarcane plants. With the crop season only a month or two away, the plantation was without cane cutters. Unless men were found in time, it could mean a great loss to the plantation. But panic turned to hostility, and the manager threatened to put everybody in jail for not working, and for spreading communism in his village. In the first days of negotiation between the plantation and the labourers, Clementina, speaking for her people because Boysie and Mango were still in hiding in the canes, insisted that the plantation ask the judge to reduce Rufus's sentence. But Turnbull, representing the plantation, cursed and shouted. 'The judge has no blasted business in this,' he said. 'This is a plantation thing, and to hell with the judge anyways. We want you back in them cane fields by tomorrow morning, or if not – ' Clementina would not budge. All the time she talked with the overseer, she asked God to keep her mouth shut so she wouldn't say the wrong thing. The plantation got tired of arguing with the people and decided to do what it had not wanted to do, because of the increased cost it would involve. The plantation imported men from the country districts to cut the canes.

It was like federation day when the shy country labourers came down to work. Bottles, cutlasses and sticks were flying about. There were screams, police whistles and dogs snapping at people's feet. But when the hubbub was over, the plantation was still without cutters. The men from the country ran back home, frightened, saying it was not worth getting killed just for a few shillings. But the manager was not to be beaten. He had a few of the men who took part in the disturbance put in prison for three months. He made his influence felt by informing the education authorities that Mr Whippetts was a sympathizer. Mr Whippetts was placed on probation. The school authorities wrote him a nice letter in a large manila envelope one bright Monday morning as he was preparing for school, telling him that a gentleman from town was taking his place. That night in the rum shop, Mr Whippetts cried like a child. Biscombe laughed.

'Serve' you blasted right!' Biscombe told him. 'Now they have you by the balls. And I want to see how you going to wriggle out o' this necktie. It ain' me fighting 'gainst you, Whippetts. It ain' Rufus, neither. It is the power o' the land. The power o' the land, boy! And now you know, like Rufus find out, how the 'pliers feels when the powerhouse start pinching your balls!'

'I make a mistake, Biscombe. I make a mistake,' the school-master wept. 'I should 'ave known this island better than to sympathise wid the plantation. But I getting out. I getting out. I have enough save' up, and I taking the next plane for somewhere. I going somewhere – and find a job doing something.'

'What 'bout Mrs Whippetts?'

'Mrs Whippetts? She could always find a man! I running from this systum. First chance!'

Biscombe went on chuckling. He had no pity for Mr Whippetts, because he knew his own side had won, and he was not the sort of man to have soft feelings for an enemy. When he had that enemy down, he would step on his belly and kick him in the testicles. That way, he was sure to keep him down. It was this method he had used so successfully against Rufus. True, Rufus did beat him. But Rufus was now in Glendairy for giving him that beating. But look what Biscombe had gained. He was now living with Rufus's woman and was screwing her going and coming. He had her working in the rum shop from morning till night. It was the price she paid for his kindness in allowing her to move in with him, and bring her two children, Conradina and Ezekiel.

But Biscombe did not know what was in Stella's mind. She had set her mind on owning the rum shop outright. If Biscombe bragged to his customers about having a woman who treated him like a king, and who spent most of her waking hours lying down under him, Stella looked on it as the price of greater rewards, rewards she had planned for down to the last detail. When Rufus went to prison, even before the cell door had clanged behind him, Stella brought her children to live with her in Biscombe's house. She immediately put a tenant in her own house, paid the rent into the Government Savings Bank to gather moss, and told Biscombe that the tenant, whom she had carefully brought in from the country, was her cousin, and that she could not ask her for rent. The tenant kept her mouth shut because Stella reduced the rent by two dollars a month in exchange for her silence. Stella kept all this to herself, and watched with pride as the school bus stopped in front of Biscombe's rum shop every morning at eight-thirty to collect Conradina on her way to Queen's College, Ezekiel for Combermere School, and Crappo, Biscombe's own son, for some obscure private secondary school. Biscombe was paying the school fees for the three children. But Stella had looked ahead to the day when something, jealousy or just boredom, would make Biscombe look at her and suck on his teeth, and refuse to jump on her. So she clipped every cent she could from the sales in the rum shop, and she actually instituted a sliding scale of tips for herself from the richer customers. Biscombe saw this and praised her in front of his friends.

'That woman must be a Jew. Gorblummuh, I been slaving in this shop for donkey years and nobody never give me a tip. But look,' he would say, pointing to Stella putting the tips into a pocket under her dress, look, be-Jesus Christ, at that woman, and tell me iffing she ain' some kinda – some kinda –' Pride would not let the word come out, and he would smile and pat Stella on her behind and squeeze her when the customers were not looking. Biscombe himself began to accept tips, and as the extra money jingled in his pockets he thanked God for giving him the sense and the strength to stamp on his enemy, Rufus, and take his woman.

One day Clementina came screaming into Stella's ears about the slanderous way Biscombe was talking about her living common law with him. But Stella smiled and listened to Clementina's perplexity.

'That man talking 'bout you as if you is – is – nothing!'

'Man smart, but woman two times more smarter, Clemmie, darling love. You foolish?'

'But – but everybody know he living with you in the absence o' Rufus. And now that Rufus behind bars you should be journeying up and down Glendairy Hill taking some good strengthening home feed for the man! You loss your decencies, Stella?'

'No,' Stella said. But I gain sense. And you know, Clemmie darling, pussy is a funny thing. It is the onliest weapon a woman have. You give your man some whenever he want' some, and, be-Christ, it turn' his head right behind his back. Take Biscombe for example. He telling the Marrish and the Parrish that I nice, that I sweet. Sure! I know how to set his plate, and I know how he like' it. But I using my weapon. You don't see my two childrens going to High School? You don't see them sitting down besides o' the manager' children and Rev'runt McKinley' children on a mornings? How the hell you think they get there? By trotting up and down behind Rufus? A man who can't even give me two shilling to buy mens'ing pads when the month come'? No, child! It is this! This! This thing what God put up 'twix my crutch!' And she touched the apex of her legs, and patted it until Clementina could hear her hands hitting against her skin.

Clementina's eyes goggled as she marvelled at this woman. At last she slapped Stella on the back and went down the road laughing out loud, as if the minister of her church had just told one of his after-church dirty jokes.

In those days the men still had no money to spend in the rum shop. Stella saw this and frowned at it. She made Biscombe stop giving credit except to the richer men. She made Biscombe cut the tall weeds round the house with his own hands. She made him paint the outside and the inside of the shop. She made him paint a new sign on the front of the shop. It was to be no longer a shop, but a restaurant. 'Biscombe's Restaurant!' Although the villagers liked it and stood in the middle of the road and admired it, they went on calling it Biscombe's Rum Shop, and that it remained, although the sign was never taken down.

Then something happened. Two months after Rufus was locked up, something told the villagers they could not continue their resistance any longer. The money Rufus had talked of giving them every week was never distributed. They were getting worried. They had refused to complain before. But that was when they had food to eat and their small savings were still savings. But the bed springs, the little hiding-places in the old rocking chairs, the skillet covered tight as a drum and buried in the back yard under a tree, were now empty. Money. They needed money. Or they would have to go back to work. They would have to find Boysie and Mango. Or inform the plantation that they were willing to return to work – or tell them where to find Boysie and Mango.

While they were worrying about these things, sickness struck. It struck like a plague, like rain falling and drenching everybody. In the first week a woman died. The village gave her a nice funeral and Mr McKinley preached a long sermon. In the second week two children fell sick. Then there were five and as the days came and went so did the children. All died. It was time to do something. The people appealed to Mr. Whippetts, as the schoolmaster, for they had never recognized the man sent by the school authorities. But Mr Whippetts was powerless. The night they met in the rum shop, Mr Whippetts confessed he could do nothing.

'Even if I was still the schoolmaster, and a man with say and power in this village, I still can't do nothing.'

'And you know why?' shouted Biscombe who had just entered the room. 'You know why, Whippetts? Because you is the onliest man in this village what let his wife empty a pot o' pee on his head. Heh-heh-heh! The mistress empty the whole pot o' piss, and stale piss at that, right 'pon Whippetts head!'

Mr Whippetts made a dash for Biscombe but Biscombe was prepared. He raised the ripping-iron in a defensive grip, and when Mr Whippetts, who was the older man, saw the cruel, shining piece of iron, he changed his mind.

'Why all yuh don't go and talk to the plantation? Talk to Turnbull. The manager. The Rev.'

'You go,' Clementina suggested. 'You and him was buddy-buddy friends.'

'Not now, Clemmie darling love! Not now! Whippetts change' he colour. The white man let him down! So, not now!'

That was the way the meeting ended. With no one knowing

what to do. But they knew that something had to be done soon. Miss Gertrude at the food-store was giving no more credit. People had turned to making tea out of the leaves of the sour-sop, the Christmas bush tree, and the apple tree, and they had started eating the leaves of the beet plant along with the root. Potatoes were cooked in soup, as tea, in cakes, in a million ways. They needed money. Sometimes some of them on their way from the rum shop, where they got no credit, would stand and watch the sugarcanes dancing in the breeze, waiting to be reaped in two weeks' time. Then they would weaken and plan to go back to work, because they knew deep down in their hearts that it was useless. The plantation must win, because the plantation had money.

The rumours started to fly about the village: the manager was getting policemen in to guard the men he was planning to bring from another part of the country. Somebody said that if they had unions in the island, like the one Jackson talked about in the letter, the plantation couldn't behave this way. A man standing beside him hit him on the head with a bottle and told him to learn sense, that this was Barbados, and that this was a different story altogether.

Turnbull, the overseer, appeared one day, and announced that the plantation was willing to forgive and forget, and would take back the labourers. They had four days to make up their minds. By Monday morning, he said, and if not, 'all this blasted place going to be like fireworks!' When he said this, Mr Whippetts chuckled, and Turnbull snarled, 'Pot o' pee! Pot o' Pee!' and the schoolmaster kept quiet. The people did not even laugh, for they were on the schoolmaster's side and against the overseer.

'And if ever I put my hand' 'pon them two coots hiding out in the white man cane, well, so help me God, this village going to see federation!' the overseer threatened. But the people knew it was an empty threat. He would never get the chance to put his hands on them. He had to know where they were hiding first, and the people were pledged not to disclose their whereabouts. But a threat was a threat. They knew the plantation was winning, that the plantation had to win. That was the case all the time. The plantation signified final victory over them. Their outbursts, the march across the dirt track that night, and even their present resistance, were merely their death gasps, signifying that their last moments had come.

'Suppose we come back,' someone said. 'Suppose – '

The people waited to hear what the overseer would say. They were eager to know their fate.

'Suppose,' Turnbull repeated. But he said nothing. He left them standing in their confusion, and without a leader. He knew his victory was near. But no sooner had he disappeared round the corner on his way back to the plantation to report that the people were weakening than Clementina turned on the man and reproached him for showing signs of surrender.

'Why the hell you had to open your mouth and say things like suppose? Suppose your number-two had wings? What would happen? It would fly. But we know that can't happen, could never happen! Suppose I was the Queen o' England! Suppose I was the owner o' that damn plantation and I had you down trodden in degradation and sufferation! Suppose, suppose, suppose. This ain't time to suppose. This is the time now for all o' we to get up off our backsides and think 'bout something. We depend 'pon the plantation too much. We depend 'pon the minister o' that church too much. And you don't see that now hunger and sufferation step' in, the minister step' out? Brisk! brisk He not even coming over to the shop to drink his grog. He cocking up his arse upstairs o' Goddard's Restaurant in town. Man o' God? That is the Christian-minded minister we send for from all the way up in England to bring salvation to we? That is the shepherd o' we, the poor bleating lambs? Well, let me tell you, in case any o' you have yuh eyes in your behinds, that the pastor o' that church, the Nazarene, in his small way done more for this cause than the minister o' the church what have so much money.'

Somebody said, 'Hear, hear!' Clementina drew a deep breath and began again. She was in terrific preaching form. The words were tumbling out of her mouth as if they were greased with lard-oil. And they were coming out sweetly.

'I 'shame', 'shame', 'shame' to see the way my own people get on. You betray Rufus. You side with the plantation, well, now the said plantation spitting in your face. We have to do something. And I suggest we have a chat with Mango and the Boysie soon, before we talk to that coot, Turnbull, again. We have four days, and in them days we have to figure out a' answer to our whole lives.'

'I agree,' Mr Whippetts said. 'I vote we see Boysie and Mango, and tell them what cooking.'

'Well, seeing you is a man,' Clementina said, 'you better go and talk to them. I too old to say I venturing alone in them canes. A man might attack me.'

The people bawled. Even Mr Whippetts unlaced some of his propriety and smiled.

'What about Jo-Jo?' somebody asked.

'What about him?' Clementina wanted to know. 'What about him? The plantation convert' him. And he have a job cleaning out the cow-pens.'

'Oh, Jesus Christ!' exclaimed the man who had inquired about Jo-Jo. He clapped his hands hard and jumped about in glee. 'Jo-Jo is a cow-pen cleaner!'

'Well, if this is what socialisms does to a man, be-Jees, I voting strictly conservative in the next elections, then!' Boysie said, dropping the heavy galvanised bucket of water on the floor of the hut. 'Gorblummuh, two months now – maybe more, 'cause we don't have no almanack on the wall – two-three months now we been living in this cane field like two rats! And for what? Socialisms! Socialisms, my big fat arse I voting with the plantation when the next general elections come round, man!'

He left the bucket of water and sat down to get his breath. He had just returned from the public standpipe where he had to go every night when it was dark and when the villagers were in bed, so as not to be seen by the wrong person. Some nights he got the water without trouble. Other nights he had to hide behind a tree for hours while two children tried some version of love behind the wall at the standpipe. During their exile in the cane field they had lived mainly on sugarcanes which they ate at first to their hearts' content. But after a time, all the sugarcane did for them was to make them pass air with a vicious smell. This made Mango complain one day that something inside Boysie's belly was rotting. Boysie took offence and a big fight almost started. Apart from sugarcane, they ate potatoes stolen from the neighbouring potato fields belonging to Uplands Plantation on whose property they were staying. Sometimes a stray chicken would come within range and in a flash Mango would knock its head off with a stone, and in another flash the poor chicken would be held over a fire and roasted with its entrails still inside. Things were becoming hard. But Mango did not complain. Up till now Boysie had not told him where the money was hidden. He was waiting for this, and at night, while Boysie was sleeping, he would wander round their hut and scratch in the dirt, looking for the buried treasure.

'You been sitting down all the time since you come back, and you haven' said nothing,' Mango said, annoyed. 'You get any reports 'bout the people?' Boysie went on sulking, and occasionally uttering a foul word, with the evil expression and force of a human record player stuck on a record. Mango took the hint and kept quiet.

They sat in darkness in the hut, which was nothing more than a small clearing they had made. The sides consisted of canes and the floor was earth, stamped hard by their feet. There was no roof, since the canes could not bear the weight of one. Somehow, Boysie had managed to get possession of a large colour-print of Queen Elizabeth the Second, and this he had hanging from the top of a large, tall cane. There was another picture, that of Christ.

Mango was dressed in his only suit, a tattered, once-upon-a-time khaki-coloured piece of material, like a large bag with holes for his arms and legs. On his head was a very old felt hat. His clothes and person smelt like the earth after a long, heavy downpour of rain, when all the insects and dead fowls were still rotting. He carried himself like a man resigned to any fate, to any circumstance. He had carried himself this way all his life, and thus had earned the name Mango, suggesting that it was not he who was master of his actions but that, like the mango, he was a child of nature. He grew, he got ripe, he fell from the tree and he rotted. Mango was in this last stage of his existence.

Boysie on the other hand was a proud man. A proud man, but at the same time one who would sacrifice some of his pride for something he wanted badly. He was proud of his position in the organization, and he brought a military flavour to it, and to his dress. He adopted this attitude although he did not rightly know what the organization was fighting for, since he was against whatever Rufus believed in. But the organization was good to him. Rufus had named him second-in-command, and the title sounded good, like the generals and admirals in the war movies he had seen during the War.

Although his trousers and shirt were as tattered as Mango's, Boysie's bearing gave them an unexpected panache. Pride in his position told him to do this. He had turned his felt hat under at the sides to make it look like the hats admirals wore at the time of Sir Francis Drake. In fact he purposely made it look like the hat in Lord Nelson's statue in the middle of the town. Before he left home on the night he ran away from the policemen, he had torn the braiding from his mother's treasured cushion, which a friend in the United States had sent her. This he had pinned to his shirt to make epaulettes and wrapped round, his hat. During his trips to and from the standpipe, he had scrounged for further decorations, although he did not know what he would find. Luckily, some old coronation medals from the previous reign fell into his hands, and these he pinned to his stomach.

'Boysie, what happ'ning in the village?' Mango waited a long time and Boysie did not answer. All he would say was 'fuck you!' not to Mango in particular, but to everybody and to everything. 'Fuck you, fuck you!' he went on, like a gramophone record stuck in a groove. 'Any word from the commander? They say what the plantation say 'bout talking to the judge and letting off Rufus?' When Mango had had enough, he stood up and kicked over the bucket of water. Some of the water went on Boysie, who looked up and uttered his favourite word. 'You ready to talk now?'

'Whippetts coming to talk tonight. Clemmie tol' me so.'

'And?'

'And hell!' Boysie shouted. 'People deading like flies with tyfoy fever. People want to go back to work. Plantation threaten' to bring in more workers from the country, plus a' army o' police! And all you saying is *and*! You understand that mean' we have to move. And maybe keep on the move all the time them country bastards cutting the canes. Always on the move. That's me and you. Like rabbits in a cane fire!'

'I have a' idear, Boysie. Only a' idear, but take it for what it worth'.' He waited until he thought Boysie was paying attention. 'What about a letter to Jackson?'

'Why?'

'We have to tell somebody in the outside world what happ'ning in this island! We have to send out a' S.O.S. to somebody.'

'Why the hell you don't send a' S.O.S. to the plantation? Why you don't send a' S.O.S. to the Prime Minister o' the island? He is a socialist-thinking kind o' man.'

'Who is a socialist-thinking kind o' man? That man? If he is a socialist, be-Christ, the manager is a marksist then.' Mango thought for a while, turning over in his mind all the possibilities. 'The newspapers! That's it! The newspapers, 'cause the newspapers is the poor man' judge, and to-besides they getting a good story for nothing. All we ask is that they print big, big pictures o' me and you, and that they hand over a couple o' packs o' cigarettes. And be-Christ, before you could say Cockrobin, the whole West Indies know that slavery ain't abolish' yet in this island, and in a flash all the help coming in from the States, from England, from Russia, be-Christ, and we is kings overnight! And, and – '

'And I step' 'pon the wire and the wire won't bend, and that's the way my story end'! No, oh God, no, Mango! The letter is the best thing to do – '

'You really think so?'

'Yes. The letter is what start' all this hurricane, well, the letter would have to settle it! So get out pencil and paper and let we begin, Mango.'

'You get them out, Boysie.'

'Mango, you is the letter writer. Rufus say' so. I is the second-in-command, and as such – '

'Jesus Christ, Boysie! We don't have to quarrel 'bout a' insignificant thing like this. Rufus 'lected me as the minister o' propergander, and, gorblummuh, now you invading my territory. I say you write it.' Boysie started to curse, but when he stopped, Mango said, 'Write what I say to write. Now! You ready?'

'I been ready long, long time.'

' "From the organization of Cane and Abel – dated – dated in the year of our Lord, nineteen hundred and sixty-one, A.D." Get that?'

'What the hell you mean by this A.D. thing?'

'Heh-heh-heh ! You trying to tell me that you never receive' a court summons in your life, and you never seen that big A.D. thing write down 'pon it? Write the damn thing, man. A.D.! A.D.! You don't have to know what it mean' as long as it look' pretty on top o' the letter. Okay? Going on in the name o' God : "Rufus in jail. The plantation breathing down our arse – and – and we in the canes hiding. So, say something. Sign – " ' Mango waited until he thought Boysie had finished, then he took the paper from him and signed : Mango, Third-in-Command. He passed the paper to Boysie. Boysie took a long time writing his name. When Mango peeped over his shoulder, he exclaimed, 'Be-Jesus Christ!' Boysie had written: 'Boysie Cumberbatch, O.B.E., C.M.G., Second-in-Command of the Orgernization of Cane and Abell, Admirul of the Fleat.'

'You like a piece o' power, don't yuh?' Mango said eventually.

'Lack o' power is what have all o' we in this damn predicamunt,' Boysie retorted. Mango could find nothing to say to this. 'Well, if you satisfied, let we post it, then. A' envelope. You have one?'

'Where the arse I going to get a' envelope from? I is a book-keeper or a schoolmaster? Fold it up and write the address on the thing, man. That should do.'

'But we don't have the address, Mango!'

'That is true!' Mango scratched his head for a long time, trying to think of some solution. Then he looked at Boysie and said, 'Throw the damn thing 'way, man!' He changed his mind again and reached for the letter. He folded it in small folds and put it in his pocket. 'We could use this piece o' paper to go to the closet with. Save it.'

'What I wouldn' give for a piece o' woman now!' Boysie exclaimed. He was lying on his back on the warm trash heap that was his bed. A cigarette was dangling in his mouth and his eyes were closed. 'I wish I was a bird! Be-Christ, I would fly and fly and fly – all 'cross the Atlantic till I reach someplace different! Or a flea. Now, if I was a flea, I would get in that letter we was writing to Jackson, and when Jackson open' the letter I would jump out and bite his arse, and then turn in a man and – and – and – Mango! Mango!' he shouted, sitting up. 'Lis'en to this idear! Suppose we write a letter to the Queen on behalfs o' Rufus!'

'The who?'

'The Queen! Her Majisty.'

'You better turn in a blasted flea first!'

'If we write a letter to 'Er Majisty and ask she for a pardon for Rufus – you know, like how them big sons-of-bitches up in England does go to the Commons and make them big, long speeches and petition the Queen to have mercy and thing – like in the days o' Guy Fox and them fellars. 'Cause, be-Christ, the hist'ry books say she is we Queen too! So she have to bring 'cross a pardon or two for we, in the same way she going pardon the Englishmens, and – '

'You talking like them twelve fellars in the Bible, and I can't follow you at all, Boysie.'

'Lemme explain it, then. As I see it, the Queen is head over we. Don't matter she don't live 'mongst we, and that she living in that big, stone mansion, Buking'm Palliss, she still have her fingers on everything that happ'ning day in and day out in this island. In a certain kind o' way, you might say that the Queen is a kind o' God. And like God, the Queen have agents plant' all in this island who going to tell she which man in the island misbehaving, and which man not misbehaving. Now,' he felt in his pocket and brought out a coin, 'you see this? What this look' like?'

'A shilling.'

'Right! This is a shilling. But it is more than a piece o' change. You see this thing write down here? This image of this woman? Well, she is the Queen. Now this image is the passport she uses to get our loyalties. This is to remind we that every time our hand touch' a piece o' change, a shilling, a dollar bill, anything, she is responsible for putting that piece o' currency in our possession. And she working psychologies on we, 'cause she know' that a man, any man, is a happy son-of-a-bitch when he have a shilling or two rackling hell inside his pockets. So by putting that shilling, that image there, the Queen making sure that we don't forget she in the happy time, as well as in the bad times. Now, lemme turn this shilling round, and show you something real serious. You see this writing write down here? You know what language this is, old man?'

'Latin?'

'Latin! Be-Christ, you right, yuh! Latin in your arse! Now that is a serious language! That is the thing that make the Rev so lernid. Latin. And that is what make a man a' eddicated man, and what make a man not a' eddicated man. Conradina and Ezekiel and the plantation children all them learning this serious language. It is a language that they does use for all the important things that they don't want we poor ignorant sort o' people to know 'bout. Now, as you know, the Queen is the Queen o' England. And, be-Christ, she not writing this message in English, not even in broken English that we in the island could understand. No. She have a scheme. So she write it in Latin. Now, I going tell you what that piece o' Latin mean'. Is this. Keeper o' the Faith and Defender o' Justice.'

'But how in the name o' God you know all this things, Boysie, when I know you ain' went to no damn High School!'

'Is common sense, old man, common sense! The eddicated people don't like we to know what going on. That is why they have Rufus in jail, 'cause he yearning to find out things he shouldn't know 'bout. And when I say this, I don't mean that I agree eye to eye with all that Rufus stand' for. I don't. I is a conservative-thinking man, and because o' that – '

'Jesus Christ, somebody coming!' Mango whispered. Boysie jumped up and the coin fell out of his hand. He was confused and frightened. In the second that he heard the footsteps mashing the dead cane blades, he saw himself being thrown into a cell in Glendairy Prison for life.

'Lis'en – you hear something?'

'Yes,' Boysie said, backing towards the rear of the hut, into the thickness of the canes. Let we run outta here, Mango.'

'No, man. Hold yuh horses. We can't run, 'cause it ain' no place to run to.'

'Well what the ar –'

They could hear the heavy, searching, stamping feet coming at them from two directions. They stood, useless, and waited for their enemy.

11

It was Clementina and Mr Whippetts tramping through the noisy canes that Boysie and Mango heard. They had come a long way, and the cane blades were making them itch. More than once Mr Whippetts threatened to turn back, but Clementina entreated him to press on. Mr Whippetts grumbled, saying his place was in the school house, and not in the canes. But when Clementina reminded him that he was no longer a schoolmaster, he abused the manager, the overseer, Biscombe and the plantation, and pressed on. Just before Boysie and Mango heard the noise in the canes near their hut, Clementina had stopped to pass water. Mr Whippetts did not know what to do. He felt stupid turning his back on her while she held up her dress and pulled down her underclothes. But he did so nevertheless, taking an occasional peep at the dried sticks of her legs to see how she was coming. When he realized how undesirable she was, he cursed himself and said a prayer of forgiveness within his heart. But he could not take his eyes off her in time. Clementina caught him, and let fly at him. 'You worthless nigger-man!' she said, a laugh forming on her face. 'Why don't you take your eyes offa me? You don't see that I is a Christian-minded woman, and to-besides I old enough to be your damn grandmother?' She laughed out loud and Mr Whippetts became exceedingly embarrassed, not knowing if she would mention this piece of indiscretion to the villagers. He told her he was sorry and that they had better walk on and find the men. He was getting tired as hell, he commented. 'Just think, Whippetts,' Clementina continued. 'Just think. Supposing some-body appear' from somewhere in these canes and find me alone with you! Well, God have his mercy! Look how all my virtues what I lived with, and protected all these years, thrown way down the drain ! Look how I scandalized for life! And a decent-minded Bible-reading person like me!'

'Clementina, you crying wolf-wolf?' he asked. But she did not answer. Together they walked on and arrived at the open space in the cane field, just as Boysie was preparing to reach for his stick.

'Gorblummuh, don't do that again. Don't do that again, man!' Boysie advised them. 'If you coming to the headquarters o' the organization, be-Christ, you hads better announce yourselfs proper and good next time and say the password Cain and Abel out 'loud, 'cause I was ready with this stick. Every noise in these canes at night is a' enemy.'

'Cain and Abel,' the schoolmaster said, pointlessly.

'Peace, brothers, peace,' Clementina said, and straightaway she told them the purpose of their coming. The plantation gave them four days. The overseer was willing to take on everyone who was on strike. The people were worried. No work, no credit at the food store; and for the men, no credit at the rum shop.

'Biscombe change' he colour again!' Boysie wondered.

Clementina explained that Biscombe never had a different colour. She told him about Stella and how she was living with Biscombe, and had brought the children along too. Boysie whistled and hoped that Rufus wouldn't hear of this. Mango shook his head from side to side in disbelief, like a horse shaking the remains of a pail of mash off his face. When they had talked it all over and had discussed everything that had taken place in the village since Rufus's imprisonment, they still did not know what to do.

'We beaten bad, bad,' Clementina said. Beaten, coming and going, bad, bad, bad.'

They all kept quiet, pretending that they were thinking of some solution to their problems; and they went on fooling one another, until Boysie laughed out loud. But they ignored the outburst, putting it down to his nervousness.

'Why we don't ask the Labour Party to come up here and hold a protest meeting?' Whippetts asked. 'We fighting for the cause o' progress and the working man, so them should be backing we.'

'One o' the fellars asked the Prime Minister that already,' Clementina said.

'And what happen'?' Boysie inquired. 'What the bastard say 'bout coming up here and talking with the fellars?'

'He say he too busy in the House o' 'Sembly. He have

important gov'munt business to transsack, and he don't get paid for that!'

'Be-Jesus Christ! What I tell you 'bout this socialism-thing? Gorblummuh, at least the plantation give Jo-Jo, their party member, a job! Gorblummuh!'

'We lick'! Lick' bad, bad, bad! Lick' up from the day we born. They could 'ave keep all o' we back in Africa, at least we could be running 'bout in the blasted jungle and be happy!'

'What 'bout contacting this Jackson again?' Clementina suggested. She looked at Boysie for some comment on her suggestion. But Boysie avoided her eyes. Mango explained that they had just written a letter to Jackson.

'And what happen'?' Whippetts asked.

'Had was to tear it up. No funds. So we couldn' post it. But we could write another one, though. You think you could spare the organization a couple o' cents for postage, Whippetts?'

'Oh Christ, Mango, man, I damn sorry, I just had a piece o' change, but – you know – since the school job gone, man, things with me really bad in truth.'

'Is alright, Whippetts, we understand.'

'You really understand my predicamunt, Mango? You know, as a government employee, I can't get too mix' up in this thing, but – '

'I know! Call up Jackson!' It was Clementina again. And again Boysie avoided her eyes. He spoke without looking at her, or at Mango, or at Mr Whippetts.

'Lis'en. And lis'en good, 'cause this is the damn last time I saying this.' He coughed and spat against a cane plant. 'Leave out Jackson. Jackson deny he write them strike things in that letter to Rufus, yuh – '

'Good God!' the schoolmaster exclaimed. 'You mean we been treating Jackson like a member, and now he turn' traitor?'

'You mean Jackson ain't the Lenin o' this cause?' Mango asked.

'Jackson ain't no blasted Lenin and never was. He never write them things 'bout big job he have in Canada. He don't have no damn big job, neither. Jackson is only a blasted car-washer. The same thing he been doing in the off-season when he was living here.'

'Jesus God! You mean then that Rufus – '

'Yes, Clemmie, I mean that Rufus misled the whole village. But it ain't Rufus' fault. 'Cause even if Jackson was a half o' man, at least he could still say something, even if it is a lie, to cheer up the man. Lis'en. That night Rufus call', Jackson deny everything. He even tell Rufus he is a damn madman. And Rufus left the phone hanging 'pon the ground and walk out the place. And he steal five, six hundred dollars from Biscombe cash box, and he holding on 'pon every cent, 'cause he want to go up in Canada when he get outta prison.'

'Gorblummuh, I thought you say Rufus give you the money to keep?' Mango asked. Boysie ignored him.

'And all them people, all them honest, poor, decent people been suffering for nothing, in vain, on account o' one man' greed?' Clementina was rent in surprise. 'And I even bend down my knee' that night, asking God to bless the venture we been embarking 'pon, and nightly I praying and praying, and begging God for guidance!'

'Boysie, you sure you ain' have that money hide 'way some-where? ' Mango asked, with a threat in his voice. 'You sure, sure? You would kiss the Bible and say you telling the truth?'

'Cross my blasted heart, Mango, I don't know nothing 'bout the money!'

'Anybody have a Bible? Clemmie, you have one?'

Luckily, Clementina had one. She pulled it from the money bag she carried under her clothes when she was selling black pudding and souse at the street corner. Now that there was no money to buy pigs' heads and pigs guts for the black pudding and souse, she carried her next best friend, the Bible, in the money bag. Mango held it out in front of Boysie, who took it and kissed it four times, and said he was not lying.

'If I lying, may God strike me down dead, dead, dead right now in front o' all you.'

Mango frowned and gave the Bible back to Clementina. 'Okay. We been fooled by the man who is the leader.'

'That is socialisms, old man!' Boysie taunted. 'That is the way the ball does bounce, socialisms-wise!'

'Shut yuh kiss-me-arse mout'!' shouted Mango. 'Clementina,

Whippetts, I glad you come here tonight. We have to go back to work. Tomorrow!'

'That is a Friday, and half-day,' Clementina said.

'Well, tomorrow we going 'cross to the plantation and talk to the manager. All four o' we. Me, you, Boysie here, and Whippetts.'

'But, Mango, wait a sec, as I say just now, being a – '

'Why you and Boysie don't go, seeing you is the leaders after Rufus,' Clementina suggested. They agreed to that. Boysie and Mango were to walk out of the canes and go to the plantation the next day, Friday, and ask the plantation to take back the labourers. They were to pledge their loyalty to the plantation. Clementina made this point, stressing that now was the time for them to show the plantation, not that they were beaten, but rather that they were not vindictive. When they were ready to leave, Boysie said he did not agree.

'From now on, you shut your blasted mout' in big people's business, hear? Or I break it loose with my hand!' Mango shouted. 'Beg pardon, Clemmie, darling love. But this one-child idiot, acting like a thorough jackass!'

Boysie was silenced and after a while of idle chatting Mango announced that the meeting was adjourned.

'Meeting stand' a'journ',' he said. The Queen!'

The four of them stood at attention while Boysie sang every verse of the British national anthem. Tattered in poverty, but proud in spirit and loyalty, he stood rigid like a piece of iron. He sang loudly. Whippetts was ashamed of the display. But Clementina pushed him and got him to sing along with them. When the anthem was finished, Mango saluted Boysie, and the two of them made a series of pointless turns and about-turns, stamping their bare feet on the rebellious sugarcane trash, as if they were wearing boots.

'One o' these days,' Mango said, with a touch of pathos in his voice, 'one o' these good days, I have to see if I can't put my hand 'pon a nice second-hand grammaphone player. And get a record o' The Queen to play on these solemn occasions.'

'A blasted good idear, though,' Boysie said.

'Would liven up things a bit. Well, seal' and sign'!

'Sealed and signed,' the schoolmaster echoed.

'Maybe a Union Jack, too, eh, Mango?' Boysie said.

'Yeah. That is a damn good thought, Boysie! Maybe we could get a' old one from Whippetts, if Whippetts was still a headmaster. But perhaps next week, we could ask the manager to lend we a' old one offa the plantation.'

Going back together, Clementina and Mr Whippetts were silent, pondering the display they had witnessed in the hut, and the way the two men were behaving.

'What you think, Whippetts?'

'You will pardon me if I say, Clementina, that today I sorry, sorry as arse, to be a black man!'

'Trust in God, Whippetts!'

Biscombe was convalescing from a near victorious bout of fever. The fever had kept him weak and delirious for a whole week. Even now, his mind was only functioning half as well as it had done before, and that was not too well. It all started, his deterioration, just about the time when Stella moved in, lock, stock and children with him. Rumours started to fly about the village. Stella was moving in because Biscombe had more money buried in a gallon galvanized bucket in his back yard, and Stella was planning to get it. Another rumour said that she was planning to trick him into walking up the aisle with her in the Reverend McKinley's church, and that the parson was in on the plan. Still another rumour had it that the moment the ink on the will was dry, Stella planned to kill Biscombe with a nice dose of arsenic and call it a day. At first Biscombe ignored the rumours. Rumours were like the canes, frequent and flourishing. But when the fever tormented him, he had all kinds of dreams: Stella standing over him washing his neck in cold water which miraculously turned hot and scalding as it touched his skin, and all his pox-pitted skin falling off like the skin of a lizard in heat. Biscombe started screeling out in his sleep. Sleep began to run away from him. Suspicions crept in. He would pretend to be sleeping and watch her. The tipping business which she instituted in the rum shop put more money in her pockets than in the rum shop till. Somebody dropped a careless word one night in the shop, very late when Biscombe ought to have been snoring, that the overseer had pulled up in front of the shop one dark night, and that the woman who got out was Stella.

Biscombe stopped going to bed with her. He would test her. He stopped giving her clothes, and started beating her almost every night. The neighbours would open their malicious windows in the dead of night and listen to the blows raining on Stella's behind like a hammer on an anvil, and would pretend they hadn't heard. But Stella took her punishment and eased the pain with the prospect of seeing five hundred dollars to her credit at the Government Savings Bank.

But one day the storm broke. Turnbull rode up on his horse, tied it to a tree in front of the shop, and went round the back, unknown to Stella, and had a good heart-to-heart talk with Biscombe, lying half-dead and suspicious on the dirty straw bed. Biscombe kept quiet as a mouse in a barrel of cheese that night. Stella came in the room, rubbed him from foot to bald head in bay rum, put coconut oil leaves on his head, poured coconut oil on them, tied them in place, and left the fever to run through his body into the leaves. She brought him some chicken soup and Biscombe drank it. He listened to every single jingle of coin in the cash box, every snap of a bottle cap, every chink of bottle on glass. He was keeping a mental count of the sales that night from his sick room. The last customer left. Stella slammed the crossbars in place, blew out the kerosene lamps which she had instituted to save electricity, and went into the special room, which, because of the lack of money in the village, was now usually empty and which was used by her two children as their bedroom. The children were in bed. Sleeping like angels. She glanced at the dark corner of the shop where Crappo was cuddled up in a crocus bag on the floor. When she had satisfied herself that everything was in order, she retired to Biscombe's bedroom, her bedroom too.

Biscombe grunted and turned over. Stella took off all her clothes and cuddled up in an embryonic ball to escape the feverish heat radiating from his body. She had been nipping at the rum bottle during her long day in the shop and so she did not feel the cool iron crowbar which he had placed beside him. She settled herself in bed, said 'Lord, as usual!' and turned round so as not to have to put her hand round Biscombe's bulky body. He opened his eyes and came closer to her.

'Stell, darling love, you love me?'

'I love you bad, bad, Biscombe,' she said, without feeling, without putting her arms round him and without opening her eyes. 'I hoping you will see yourself able to put a ring 'pan my finger some day, some day, some good day, 'cause I not in any hurry.'

'Yeah,' he said and turned round.

You could hear his laboured breathing coming out in gusts of asthma. When he paused, you could hear the trees outside whispering to the wind and the wind whispering back, and the trees and the wind laughing at their jokes. Inside the house silence reigned. Biscombe interrupted it by coughing. Then he bounced round in the bed to let Stella know he was not sleeping, and to prevent her from being too comfortable herself.

'That half-white man went round here this forenoon,' he said, as if he were making a mental note of the event out loud. 'I say that half-white bastard Turnbull went round here this forenoon.'

But Stella remained silent. She could sense danger. She knew that if she was going to avert it, her strategy was to remain quiet, and hope that her lack of response would kill the argument and the fight which Biscombe seemed to be kindling.

'And he had a damn lot to say,' Biscombe went on. 'That man had a damn lot o' things to say 'bout you, Stella.' Stella was still holding her horses at peace. 'I say Turnbull had a damn lot o' things to say 'bout you. And, be-Christ, I thinking serious' 'bout asking you for a' 'count o' your stewardships. You heard me? Or you pretending you sleeping? You hearing what I talking to you?' And to test whether she had heard, or whether she was really sleeping, he turned over and put out his hand in the darkness to touch her. She stiffened and flounced away. Biscombe's anger was rising. He held out his hand again and touched her, and again she moved farther to the edge of the bed. 'You have to give me 'nough satisfaction, woman, you hear?'

'Niggerman, why you don't let me catch little shut-eye, nuh?' she shouted at him. Her words broke the thin thread which had held back his anger.

Biscombe wheeled round in the bed and grabbed the crowbar. He landed it right on her fat behind. Stella was so frightened and so shocked that for the first two or three seconds she could not find her voice. But when she did, the house shook.

'Gorblummuh, I had that for you a long time!' Biscombe said. 'Be-Christ, you think Biscombe is a fool? You think Biscombe is the village idiot! But, gorblummuh, Biscombe may look like the village idiot, but he ain't no damn idiot! I want you to get out. First thing in the morning, please God. And you take them childrens o' yours too!'

Stella, knowing that she had drifted out of her depth, remained quiet, writhing in pain and praying that there would be no more violence.

'You hear' I say move out? Well, I mean move out! And when I open my two eye' in the morning, I don't want to see you, or nothing that belongst to you in this blasted house, hear?'

'I will go. I will go, Biscombe. If you tired with me, I will go, 'cause if there ain't no love betwixt me and you to save any murderation in this place, I will go.'

'And, be-Christ, you right, right, right! 'Cause I treat you like a first-class lady, but you intends to remain like a whore.'

'You call me a whore, Biscombe? Is that the word you use? Well, let me tell you something! Your mother before me was a bigger whore. And iffing she wasn' a whore, how the hell the plantation manager o' Uplands wouldda lay down on her belly and get her stiff with child? Tell me, Mister Biscombe, how the arse you wouldda come in this world, iffing your mother wasn' a bigger whore than me? So you don't come putting on no blasted airs with me, hear? 'Cause I know how to tell you all the histories o' your forebears. And I know when to tell you when to get off. God blind you!'

'You call' my mother a whore, eh?' Biscombe said. 'You call' my mother a whore?'

'Yes! Yes! I call' your mother a whore, 'cause you call' me a whore. But lis'en. I whoring for a noble cause, Biscombe. I can't say the said thing 'bout your mother!'

'Gorblummuh, woman! Get out! Get out! Right now, you get out! You call' my mother, dead and buried all these years, a whore? Well, you get out, and take them no-father bastards o' yours with you, too! Right now!' And to impress her with the seriousness and immediacy of his words, he brought the heavy crowbar down on her behind again, and she bawled out murder. Then the children woke up and began weeping. Stella got into her clothes in a hurry, went into the special room, threw the children's clothes on them, and put them outside to wait for her. She went into the shop, pushed aside a half-empty barrel of biscuits and took the small bundle of money wrapped in a cloth, which she had banked there since her first day in the shop. She was glad she had prepared for this night. She was glad. But she was sorry that it had come so soon. She filled a large paper bag with biscuits and threw two tins of corned beef into it. When she turned to leave, Biscombe was standing in the doorway. She held the bag tightly in her hands and waited for him to say something. She was frightened. But, she would rather die than let him take the money from her. That was what frightened her: had he seen her putting the money under her dress?

'You really leaving?' he asked her, sorry now that he had told her to leave. 'You going leave me, in truth?'

'Blast you, Biscombe! I came here on your invitations. I slave' and slave' and put this place in shape, in shipshape, and, be-Christ, this is the onliest gratitude you could show! But, Biscombe – ' And without finishing she threw a jug of cold water over him, and when he ducked to get out of the way, she forced herself past him and rushed through the back door. The children were waiting outside.

'But Stell, darling, Stell, darling – '

'Take that, you son-of-a-whore!' she snarled, and then she slammed the door like a clap of thunder.

Biscombe ran after her, pleading. He stood in the cold, not thinking of his fever but only of making her remain with him. Stella pretended her mind was made up, but she wanted him to plead some more.

'But Christ, Stell,' he was saying, 'come back inside, man. I only get vex' as hell 'causing you refer to my dead mother as a whore. And it all start' out 'cause that malicious bitch Turnbull say' you renting out your house for money. But I have to say one thing in your favour, darling love. You have something in that head o' yours. And, be-Christ, if you could use it so damn pretty, well, you have to use it whilst you living with me. So, come back in the house, woman, and let we make up. You coming? Look, you two children shouldn' be out in the cold like this. Get back in there, before I tar your backside!' he shouted at Conradina and Ezekiel, who were cowering in the semi-darkness wondering what was going to happen next. You hear me? I is your father now. And I say get in there!'

The children appealed to their mother. What was she going to say about this? Stella put her hands around them and led them back into the house.

'Come, you go back in. This is your home,' she said to them. When the children were tucked in bed again, Stella went into the bedroom where Biscombe was standing. 'Now, you! Make this the last time you carry on like you pick' me offa the street, you hear?' she said. When he turned round and faced her, something worked itself in her heart and she ran to him and embraced him. 'Oh Christ, Biscombe! And you have such a bad cold with that fever! You ain't have the sense you born with! Walking 'bout in the cold with a two-hundred-degree fever! Christ, man, you really need a woman round this house!'

She spent the rest of the night rubbing him down in warm bay rum and putting a fresh supply of coconut-oil leaves on his head. When he was settled in bed, Stella got in and turned her back on him. But he was already snoring. She turned over and looked at him. She said her prayers a second time, the same prayer, and then she made a promise to herself. 'First thing Mondee morning, that money going in that bank account!' But she could not sleep easily with the money in her panties for three nights, and on the following day, bright and early, she sent Conradina into town, instructing her how to put the money into the night safe, away from temptation. Once that was done, Stella slept beside Biscombe like a child.

12

Mr Whippetts rushed into the shop at ten o'clock the following morning, Saturday, and interrupted Biscombe while shaving. Biscombe was mad, and he said so. He started to explode with the crudest language anybody had ever heard in the village. Stella heard him and came to the schoolmaster's rescue. It all happened so quickly that Mr Whippetts did not have a chance to explain why he was there so early. When he knew he had their attention, he opened the morning newspaper, still warm as toast and spread it on the counter. Biscombe dropped the old safety razor and his eyes popped out of his head. Stella was dumbfounded.

The headline read: STRIKING CANE-CUTTER ESCAPED FROM GLENDAIRY.

For some time nobody said anything. They looked at one another, as if trying to assess the danger each of them stood in if it was Rufus that had escaped. Though no one doubted it was Rufus, nor that the first visit he paid would be to the village, and that as soon as possible, yet they were not sure. And they did not want to mention it out loud.

'But how the arse! Biscombe exclaimed. 'But, but – how we know they mean Rufus?'

Stella looked at him sympathetically. Such a nitwit! Who else could they possibly mean? But she realized afterwards that Biscombe was hoping against hope. That he was fearing the loss of the things he had come to think of as his own: Stella and the children who had made him so happy. And Christ, this blow had to fall just now! Only this morning he had told Stella that perhaps, if everything went well, he was going to invite the Reverend McKinley over to the rumshop in the evening and make plans for their wedding. Stella, fortified by the prospect of security and given a new reason for living, had got out of bed very early and was working in the shop and around the house, cleaning, scrubbing, washing, like a mad woman. Now, that blasted ghost, Rufus was visiting them.

'What you think, Whippetts?' Biscombe asked.

'Be-Christ, Biscombe boy, this is one morning that I los' my thinking cap! I can't think nothing!' he said. But both Stella and Biscombe waited, and hoped that he would come up with some good idea, at least some way of preparing for the visit, if not a means of escape. 'We have to get in contact with Boysie and Mango!'

'Leave them two arses outta this!' Biscombe shouted. 'What you meddling up in this strike business for?'

'And what 'bout you? You not mix' up in it, too?' the school-master asked. 'Don't fear, Biscombe, if Rufus get out, rest assured he coming here first! I don't want to frighten you, Bis, but don't forget you living with the man' woman. And that is a thing that could make a man kill!'

'Jesus Christ!' Biscombe exclaimed. He could see it plainly now: Rufus coming through the window in the middle of the night with a long knife in his hand. 'Oh Jesus Christ, Whippetts, you is a' eddicated man, so say something, do something, some damn thing!'

'Well, as I see it, we have to notify Mango and Boysie. 'Cording to Mango, Rufus left money for the people, and Boysie still holding on 'pon it. Last thing I heard, Boysie making negotiations to clear outta the island, and run abroad with all the money. And second – '

'The plantation know'?'

'Biscombe, you not thinking 'bout notifying them again, eh?'

'Well, they ought to know!'

'Biscombe, when you going to learn sense?' It was Stella. This was the first time she had spoken. 'Leave the plantation outta this. This is a struggle that belongst to we, to we who don't have one damn thing to do with the plantation!'

'But I still think that 'cording to duty and as a citizen o' this village, the plantation – '

'Biscombe, wait! Wait!' the schoolmaster pleaded. He was becoming angry with Biscombe. 'Where the children? Stella get the children outta the house. Send them somewhere.' Stella told him that Conradina was in town on an errand for her; but he was not told what the errand was. Ezekiel was also in town on his way to the library. 'Good! Now, the radio ain't say nothing 'bout the break-out yet, and I hoping to Christ it don't broadcast nothing neither! And another thing! Don't let nobody else hear 'bout this. Clementina is the onliest other person what know 'bout it at the moment. And I have her confidences. If word get 'bout, well, the whole village gone wild. We have to wait and see. Clementina say she making black pudding and souse today, so when she appear' and anything new break, you going get inform'. I going back home, and see if that lizard make my tea yet!'

'Oh, Jesus Christ!' Biscombe moaned. He looked at Stella and his eyes told her that he was sentencing her for being the cause of all this trouble.

'Why you looking at me so?' she asked him, when Mr Whippetts left. 'You looking at me like I know something.'

'I should 'ave let you left my place when I tol' you to leave last night. I should 'ave done that! Now it too late! But I should 'ave kept my word.' Throughout the morning, Biscombe bemoaned the fact that he was so weak, that he was a coward, that he did not have the guts to keep his word. It worried him until he summoned enough strength to lift the receiver off the hook and call the plantation. Stella was in the rear of the shop and he had to talk softly. He could not bear losing her and he could not bear facing Rufus again. He did not see that either way he might be in the same predicament. The manager took a long time to come to the phone. He was talking to a police inspector, his wife said. If it was not important she would have him call when he was less busy.

'Important? You ask' me if it important? Look, woman, look, Mistress Manager, you tell your husband that if he don't want a riot in this blasted village today, he hads better call all the police in the Main Guard up here, 'cause I hear that Rufus get outta prison – ' Before he could finish, he heard a gasp at the other end of the line, and then the phone was dropped. In the background he could hear her hurrying. A minute later, the manager was at the phone. 'I just told your wife – ' Biscombe began. 'What? You know? And, be-Christ, you ain't done nothing yet? Who' side you on now, Mister Manager? You on them side? Oh! Well, now you talking! I agree with you. Bring up the whole police force, and if you could get the Volunteer Force too, bring them too. Yes, I see eye to eye with you. This village belongst to we, it don't belongst to no damn socialists. But one thing, though, don't let none o' the servants know what plan' – whatever you do, don't let that Bessie hear! You is a good man, Mister Manager. I know all the time I could depend on you.' When Biscombe hung up, he felt better. He even ate a large bowl of steamed cornmeal with fried pig's liver. He could only wait and see.

Towards afternoon the rum shop was filling up quickly. Men were sitting in the windows with their legs hanging outside. Though they did not have much money, neither Stella nor Biscombe objected. Stella even asked him to give them a little credit, and when Biscombe announced that for a special reason he was giving each man a dollar in credit, a cheer went up in the shop, and everybody started laughing. Some of the happiness seen in days of employment came back to the rum shop and to the village. But inwardly Biscombe was tense. Stella remained in the back, frightened that the next man to enter the shop would be Rufus. But as the afternoon wore on, she put this stupid thought out of her mind and waited for nightfall, when she felt Rufus would come out from wherever he was hiding. Conradina and Ezekiel arrived from town, and after Stella had satisfied herself that Conradina had put the money in the night safe and that all was well, she sent them out again to visit their grandmother who lived about five miles away. She told them they could spend the night there. Crappo, Biscombe's son, was out playing cricket with the boys in the village. The men drank and told nasty jokes, and were happy. One said this was better than when they were working and had money. But Stella and Biscombe served the drinks without smiling. The afternoon dragged along like a snail, purposely it seemed.

When the sun was high in the sky and the shadows clung close to the feet, so small were they, Clementina arrived with a heavy tray of black pudding and souse, and home-made bread with a smell so sweet and strong that you would think it could reach as far as the plantation. She sat down on a stool, like a queen on a throne, using an old newspaper to shoo away the flies, and an occasional man too, who came to 'talk over her nice black pudding and souse'. She had to beg, plead, almost kiss the butcher to let her have half a pig's head and entrails to make the local delicacy with. She sat in front of the rum shop, baiting the men with the provocative smell, like a queen claiming her kingdom.

She was wearing a dress with an all-over flower pattern. The neckline was high, she being a woman of God whose religion did not permit dresses which exposed even as much as the bones at the bottom of the neck. No rings, for she had never married. No bracelets. Her thin legs, like toothpicks painted black, were shining with grease and stretched out under the box on which the heavy tray stood. She was wearing canvas shoes, but had taken them off, because they were killing her bunions. A 'linen' cloth, made from a flour bag, washed under the public standpipe with washing soda, kerosene, marl and blue soap, and now whiter than the clouds in the sky, covered the tray. On her head was a piece of the same material as the tray cloth. Her dress, which she would have to wear to church on Sunday, was covered with a white apron pleated all round in a million pleats, and starched hard as dealboard. It had been ironed so often that it shone. Clementina was clean. She had to be. Otherwise, no one in the village would have entrusted their digestions to her black pudding and souse. She knew this. She also knew the penalty of being suspected of being dirty. Bessie, before she became the plantation cook, used to sell black pudding and souse, but one day somebody saw her putting her hand to her tongue and then with the same hand touching first the sore on her shin and later the black pudding and souse. From that day, if Bessie ever touched her sore, she never touched the black pudding with the same hand. Clementina was sanitary.

She kept an eagle eye about her. You couldn't trust children, you couldn't trust adults. So she sat on her throne, contemplating her sales and thinking about getting back home before it was too late to read over her text for Sunday's sermon. A fly approached. Her hand gripped the old newspaper. She was tense. Whap! The fly fell on the white ' linen' cloth covering the precious food. She looked round anxiously to see if anyone had seen her. Then she held the fly, now dead, disdainfully between her thumb and index finger, and flicked it into Purgatory.

'Haaii!' a voice called out to her.

Clemmie looked round anxiously. It was Biscombe. She cursed him all the way to hell and back again.

'You was in the last war, Clemmie, darling love? Man, you just kill' that fly like if you was a blasted machine-gunner!'

'Mind yuh malicious business! Your business in your rum shop!'

The men in the shop were listening. Biscombe climbed through a window and approached her.

'I hopes to Christ, Sister Clementina,' he said loudly, 'I hopes to Christ that you ain' kill' more o' them flies and they drop' down in that nice souse bowl, yuh!'

Clementina said something awful to him and turned her back. She got up off the stool and bent down very low, pretending to pick something up from the ground. The delicate, intricate, once-enticing embroidery of her longish panties was revealed. The men bawled as Biscombe appealed to them to look. Then a rousing cheer went up.

'You too old for that, woman! Too old, darling love. Goat your age ain't no damn kiddy, so sit back down quick, please. You can't give me giddy head with that!'

'Looka, Mister Biscombe,' she said, turning round, laughing, 'I have to ask you please to go to the devil in hell, and leave me peaceable to sell the little black pudding and souse, do. And if you intends to put some o' this niceness in that big mout' a' yours', well, you hads better hurry up and come quick, 'cause I have four pig's feet keeping for Rev'runt McKinley, half-dozen for the manager, two for Turnbull and two and a half for – '

'Woman, behave yourself! You playing you is so much o' man, look,' and he held on to her, and brought his mouth close to hers, threatening to kiss her in front of the men.

'Bet yuh I hold on 'pan you, and feel yuh up in front o' all these mens!'

Clementina turned her head in shame and embarrassment. The men laughed louder. Everybody was gay and happy, and half-drunk. Clementina went back to her thoughts.

Tomorrow is Sundee and I have to get up bright and early in the morning and run through the pasture and put ten shillings in that old t'iefing butcher man hand, he charging me so much o' money for this pig's head he think I born yesterday – nine o'clock is church and I have to preach the sermon, Lord, Lord, Lord, looka how I forgetting my spiritual duties and I not even sit down and read the Bible today, my mind so much on the few cents I going get from this black pudding and souse – I hope sales tonight going be good 'cause I have my eye 'pon a nice piece o' sharkskin the coolie man bring round last week and I thinking 'bout making it up in a nice high-neck frock – but why the hell these starving people don't come for the black pudding, they think I spending the whole damn night sitting down on my arse waiting for them to come and make a two-cent purchase and purchase twelve cent on credit, when I sit up all hours o' the morning making the seas'ning, grinding black pepper seeds, oh, Lord, till the pepper get in my eye and waiting the whole damn day for that wretch, the butcher man, to kill the damn pig and let me get the half a' pig's head to take home – Christ, and I thought the stuffing never was going to cook 'cause I must 'ave put in too much salt, but the pork ain't no damn good these days, it making the souse taste a certain way funny – anyhow, Lord, in thy precious name –

A little girl interrupted her. Clementina looked up savagely at the intruder, who told her that her mother wished to have some black pudding and souse on credit till Daddy came home. It was like showing a red cloth to Clementina. She was as mad as a bull.

'Look, look! Look here, you!' she said to the embarrassed girl. 'Trot right back and tell that mother o' yours sorry, that Clementina not made a sale yet, that as soon as Clemmie make' a cash sale, she could send you back.'

The girl went off in tears, for the men in the windows had heard. A short while later, Sonny, Mr Whippetts's part-time yard boy, came up to her tray. He was armed with a fancy basket made of coconut leaves. It had 'Jamaica' written all over it, so that the world could see that the owner or bearer of the basket had visited Jamaica. Sonny held this status symbol up to Clementina's face. The basket had a genuine linen cloth on it, and under the cloth was a large dish complete with matching cover, both genuine china.

'How?' Sonny greeted Clementina.

'Niggerman, you left your manners home? I old enough to be your grandmother, and how dare you talk to me like that and call me 'how'? You think you too big for me to hold on 'pon you and tar your backside, niggerman?'

'Whippetts say he want' big pig's feet this time, that last time you send small ones. And to make it six shillings in pig's feet, big ones, forty-eight cents in black pudding and send 'long two shilling breads, that he broke, and he going pay you in the turning – '

'Jesus Christ!' Clementina exclaimed, forgetting herself. 'Good Lord! You mean to say that a big schoolmaster like he can't know where to put his hand 'pan some cold cash and pay for his black pudding? I not made a cash sale yet! Tell Whippetts that! I say I not giving out credit, 'cause I ain't the Government Bank!' When Sonny turned to go, she called him back and dished him the order. 'Gimme the blasted gentleman' dish outta your hand, boy! Well! Some o' these high and mighty poor great bastards worser than the ordinary-class whores living in this village!'

'You would think a man in Whippetts position would be able – '

'What the hell you saying? Mind your manners, I tol' you, niggerman. This is me and Whippetts business!'

But Sonny wanted to talk and he went on about how Whippetts worked for so much money from the government and couldn't buy a simple thing like black pudding for cash, and that he didn't know how a man who had no children and no outside women could be always so broke. But Clementina ignored him as she made the first sale, on credit, for eight shillings. She knew she would get the money from Whippetts, but she hoped that no one in the shop had heard. Two more shillings, and the pig's head would be paid for. The rest would be profits. 'Lord, what a night this going to be!' she said to herself. The 'linen' cloth on the tray turned into a large piece of sharkskin material. She was happy now. She cut the greasy, sausage-like cylinders in one-inch pieces, basted them with a feather dipped in cooking oil and laid them neatly in the chinaware dish. She put the cover back on that section of the tray to prevent the flies from getting in. She opened the section with the large bowl containing the pickled souse. In this bowl were all kinds of herbs, seasoning, peppers, red peppers, black peppers, white peppers, nigger peppers, and cucumber, parsley, thyme, everything. She dipped the feet deeper into the pickled juice – 'Pig's feet is a sixpunce apiece, tell Whippetts that!' – and laid them beside the pudding in the dish. On top she spread pieces of fresh parsley in an attractive arrangement which made the bowl look like a model of the countryside, with mounds of rolling black earth (the black pudding), with white-grey stones (the souse), dotted with occasional trees (the parsley); and then she covered the dish and put it back into the basket marked 'Jamaica'.

'That for you,' and she gave Sonny a very small piece of souse, no bigger than a pebble. 'Hey! You hear' yet from that brother o' yours?'

'Who? That cane-rat, Boysie?'

'Look, niggerman, mind yuh manners! That brother o' yours is more man than you, yuh! He make' five times the man you is!'

Sonny burst out laughing. Then he told Clementina that Whippetts was having friends in. She riddled him with questions and at last he had to tell her. The manager was coming over to talk with Mr Whippetts, Sonny said. Big, big business they talking tonight!' Clementina made a note of it and told him to leave her tray. Soon after Sonny, the overseer stopped by on his horse, on his way back to the plantation. When he came to the tray, there were some small boys and girls gathered round, making small purchases. They saw the overseer and they moved back, but not briskly enough for Clementina's liking.

'Looka, you move one side, and let the gentleman see my tray, do!' she ordered them. 'Let the gentleman see my tray, please. He come to purchase. Not play 'round.' The overseer bought three shillings worth; and when Clementina held out her hand to receive the cold cash, the overseer handed her a cheque. Clementina smiled and bowed to him, but when he left it was something else. 'But what the hell these people think?' she cried. Just then Bessie was climbing the slight incline to the rum shop. The jealousy between the two women would not permit Clementina to give Bessie the idea that the overseer had worked a smart one on her. So Clementina memorized the amount of the purchase and tore up the cheque and gave it to the winds. The children scrambled after the confetti. 'Hey, Bessie!' Clementina called out, seeing the cook in a shining new dress. 'I never thought you was the same dress size as the manager' wife, darling!'

'Haul!' Bessie told her. 'I works for a good living, blind you!'

'It look' good, though.'

'Put the white man pudding and souse, and let me get back to my servants' quarters before dark, do. 'Cause I never seen so much o' police and gun in all my born days! Clemmie, you would think they expecting a riot or some damn thing. Turnbull have all he guns oiled and loaded. The manager, I left him sitting down at the window with a gun on his lap, and his wife upstairs pining 'way for man. Christ! I don't know how these white people does operate!'

'You say gun?' Clementina asked. 'You say gun?'

'More gun than what they have in a' army! And darling, that man, the manager, whole morning he walking up and down, through the kitchen what I just sprained my back scrubbing, all through the living-rooms and back again. And all the time he talking to himself like if he belongsts down in Jenkins Mad House and not 'pon a plantation what regulates the lives o' so much people! And then the radio in the kitchen say something 'bout a' excape' convict and Christ, Clemmie, it was like if somebody throw a white sheet all over him! He turned white, white, white, be-Christ, as a sheet o' white paper! So the same time the phone ring, and the Missy come storming in the kitchen, and I don't know what she whizzy-whizzied in his ear-hole, but, child, you would 'ave thought she told him his mother had just drop' down dead! That man ran out and pick' up the phone, and a minute after he telling everybody to lock up the doors and windows, that something going happen today. Now, Clemmie, me and you ain't no bosom friends, but I could 'part this little information to your ear, hoping that you understand it in confidences, since we is both Christian-minded womens together. Now, I ask you, Clemmie, I ask you, on the basis o' what I just tol' you, can you still turn round and say that them bitches is more mens and womens than we poor people? Answer that! And you know what the thing is? Lemme tell you, 'cause I know, since I been working round them for nearly ten years now. They lacking God! That's it, darling. God not in their hearts. I never seen that man take up the Good Book and try to understand the mysteries o' this world. I never seen that Missy tune in 'pon a church service in all the years I been cooking for them. He spends his time drinking brandy by the bottle and polishing that gun as if he expecting a war to break out in this peaceable island. And she? Suppose yuh could see her! Upstairs all day with a rum punch in one hand and a cigarette in the next, and flat on her back like the most ordinary person on the floor; and all the time she groaning like she in pain. Looka, Clementina soul, gimme the damn black pudding and let me get back, before that master mistake me for a damn black bird and shoot me, yes I licked my mouth with you enough. I have all them saucepans to wash up yet. Care yuhself!' And she left.

The moment she got out of sight round the corner of the cane field, Clementina pulled the cloth over the tray, told a child to watch it, and dashed into the rum shop, through the back door.

'Oh Lord, Biscombe! It is true? They expecting a riot!'

'Shhh Don't let the men in the shop hear!' He dropped the dish towel and came closer to her. 'Who tell you? The men didn't hear, eh?'

'Where Stella? Biscombe, you better get Stella outta this place before you don't have a murder on your hands. Take my advice, Biscombe. Get Stella outta your place, 'cause it sure now that Rufus in the land!' When Biscombe did not look as if he understood the seriousness of the situation, she pushed past him and entered the bedroom. Stella was changing the bed. 'You! You have trouble on your hands. You lis'en to me, 'cause I old enough to be your mother – '

13

The night Clementina and Mr Whippetts visited the hut in the bowels of the cane field, neither Boysie nor Mango slept. Mango was thinking of tricking Boysie into showing him where the money was hidden. And Boysie was laying schemes for getting the money without Mango knowing. All through the night, each laid his plans like a fisherman laying a net for fish. Each was jealously watching the other, and since both were convinced that the other was watching him, neither could afford to shut his eyes for fear of missing the one opportunity of success. Whenever Mango left the hut to pass water, Boysie was close behind. If Boysie held a cigarette in his hand, Mango was at his elbow with a match. But because of this mutual distrust, their plans came to nothing. Boysie was about to disclose where he had hidden the money and offer Mango a share, when an idea hit him. It was so simple, he laughed aloud to himself, and this made Mango unhappy, because he did not know the reason for Boysie's sudden joy.

'Gorblummuh!' he exclaimed, his temper as foul as an addled egg. Gorblummuh! I spending all my time in these musty canes, and you could laugh, and make a joke at it! Gorblummuh!' But Boysie refused to be tricked. He lay on his back, with his hands propping up his head, and dangled the cigarette in his mouth, moving it from corner to corner. 'How you think this thing going end, Boys?' Mango asked, becoming friendly again. 'You think this going come to a conclusion like the riot that fellar Castro had in Cuba? You think we is the same brand o' hero men like them Cuban fellars?'

'Heroes? We is arse-holes, if yuh ask me! 'Cause, if it is one thing I know, it is this. However this thing end up, the plantation bound to win in the long run! And I say this, Mango, boy. I say this. If I wasn' present, if I wasn' laying down in these canes with you all these days, and suffering through this thing, I wouldn't know, or think it could still happen in a blasted civilized place like this island. A man coming from another place and seeing how we live, and get on, won't think he living in the twentieff cent'ry at all! He would have to think that this is some kiss-me-arse part o' Africa where the English forget to build closets and went 'way without leaving the natives food and things.'

'That is what have me unhappy in a certain fashion, too. Boysie, I been thinking that only we who gone through this kind o' thing really know what it is to be black people. And not only black, but black and blasted poor, at that! I can't rightly believe if I still living or dead. This is like some topsy-turvy dream, or something. Or like a picture you been seeing during the war days when a group o' fellars get lost from the rest o' the army, and they fighting the whole blasted war by themselves, and don't know why they fighting, or if anybody care if they fighting. And, be-Christ, everybody, every single one o' them soldier fellars want to drop them guns and run home, but – '

'They can't run ! They can't run, 'cause by running they going to get a bullet in their arse, bram!'

'You know, in a certain way o' thinking, I wish Rufus was here with the fellars. He ain't no eddicated man, can't make out a A from a B, but he have something we don't have. And that is guts. Pride. Will-power. I don't know if it take' somebody damn foolish like Rufus to try to have things righted in this island, but I know that they have lots o' eddicated sons-o'-bitches down in that House o' 'Sembly and they so damn important that they ain't farting on their own people. That is the funny thing 'bout socialisms that I can't understand.' Mango went on talking about socialism and how the Party did not even send a man to see if Rufus was dead or living. Boysie watched him closely, waiting for the moment when he thought Mango was so carried away with his thoughts that he could take a chance on making a sudden dash through the thick canes, circling round him and then losing him in the vastness of the cane fields. Mango was comparing Rufus with Toussaint L'Ouverture of Haiti, and his eyes were travelling far away with his thoughts, when Boysie sprung up like a jaguar and made the break. Instantly, Mango stopped thinking about Haiti and put all his energy into catching Boysie.

'Oh no, yuh don't!' he said, when he had caught up with him. 'Them is schoolboy tricks!'

'Oh Christ, Mango, man! Man, I was only trying to frighten you, man. Jesus, Jesus, man! I won't do a thing like that, man!' He walked back with Mango to the hut and spread himself flat on his back, with his felt hat over his face, pretending to be going to sleep. Mango's voice rambled on like a day of rain, monotonous and depressing, and Boysie waited and waited, until suddenly they both heard a crackling near by. Boysie was awake in a flash. Mango was sitting up. It took them only a moment to listen and sniff before they knew what it was.

'Cane fire!' Mango screamed. He seized his hat and bolted through the canes.

Boysie ran after him. He turned back and started to search for the spot where the money was hidden, but the smoke was getting near and thick. He ran into the hut and ripped the picture of the Queen from the wall and set out after Mango.

'Mango Mango! Wait, man, we have to get out o' this together! Mango, wait, man!'

The faster he ran through the thick canes, the faster the flames followed him.

'Cane fire!' somebody had shouted, and in an instant all the men jumped through the windows of the rum shop and ran up the road towards the burning canes. Biscombe came to the front of the shop panting and swearing. Clementina, who had not yet made a cash sale of any significance, watched the people running away, and then looked down at her tray laden with delicious unsold pudding and souse, and wept. Biscombe came out and stood beside her, watching the black birds of burnt cane blades floating in the afternoon wind.

'Praise God, it is Uplands Plantation, and not *our* plantation,' he said.

'You own a plantation? How you mean – '

'If it was our plantation, Clementina, I would be sorry for them two bastards, Mango and Boysie! But what I really mean is that I glad it ain't the manager' plantation, 'cause in that case, it would mean no more work for the fellars in this village. And more than that. It would mean no more business for this rum shop. Drunk or sober, mind yuh business, Clemmie, darling. I is a business man, and I have to thrive on the poor people,' he said, winking at her. I in the same boat as you. You is a capitalist too.'

'Blast you, niggerman! I is a Christian-minded woman,' she said, annoyed. 'Looka, don't let Satan ride me this peaceable afternoon!'

'Watch the rum shop!' he told her and bounded back inside for a pair of canvas shoes. In a minute he was outside again. 'Watch the rum shop for me, Clemmie. I running over by the plantation. Mango and Boysie is threats to this place!'

So Clementina was left alone with all her pudding and souse, watching the men and women of the village run past her to the fire. She spread the cloth properly over the tray, put the stool under the box which held it, and went behind Biscombe's paling to pass water. Her mind travelled back to the night before, when she had worked so hard to get the pudding and souse made, her first effort for such a long time. Now all that time and trouble were in vain. The cane fire would take a whole day to be put out, and the way it was burning told her that perhaps the other plantation, the manager's plantation, was in great danger of being burnt to the ground. Clementina wished an evil thought. She asked God to let the manager's plantation burn flat, flat as a bake.

Lord, Lord, all my time wasted in vain and I now in the same position as when I started, Lord, the money I borrow' to buy the seas'nings with, the flour with, the potato with, and now I owe the butcher man money that I didn't even spend or use to a good purpose, and, Christ in heaven, look how I can't get that piece o' sharkskin material for that dress I wanted to wear to the Church outing – Lord, Lord, You forsaking me in my old age.

The manager met Biscombe panting down the road. He stopped the car and Biscombe jumped in. In the car was Turnbull. The first thing the manager asked was if Biscombe knew anything about this fire.

'Biscombe, you know who started this fire?'

'I just been coming to give you word 'bout them two outlaws, Mango and Boysie. They been living in the canes all this time. So it's obvious. The finger pointing at them.'

'You seen Stella?' the overseer asked.

'Stella gone home – ' Biscombe began, but changed his mind and said, 'Stella gone in town.' He did not know how much the plantation knew about Rufus, and he did not know how much they knew about his living with Stella. The overseer said nothing, so he assumed the question was answered.

'You know, of course, Biscombe,' the manager was saying, as the car reached the edge of the burning cane fields belonging to the Uplands Plantation, 'you know, of course, that we fear that Rufus is in the vicinity. He escaped, the bastard. But, so help me, Biscombe, if I see him within a mile of my plantation – ' He did not finish what he was saying, but instead he caressed the trigger of the rifle he carried on his lap. Biscombe saw it and moved closer to the door of the car. When Turnbull stopped the car, the manager jumped out and ran up to the rest of the plantation officials and senior employees who were surveying the damage and running about like champion hundred yards sprinters.

'And, be-Christ, to think we had the whole police force on the plantation this morning!' Turnbull regretted. 'If you see Stella, tell her for me, she better hide that man she lives with real good, 'cause I have a special bullet for him! And whenever we find him, he paying for this! Even though he didn' set the fire! But he paying for this! You tell Stella that!' He moved away from Biscombe and went to join the circle of dejected plantation officials.

The wind changed direction and drove the fire towards the onlookers. Some of the men who had been sitting the whole afternoon in the rum shop windows were now beating out the fire with the tops of canes. They were stripped to the waist. The bosses of the plantation were standing by, looking sad and useless. One of them said it was a shame that there was no fire brigade. But another reminded him that a fire brigade could never put out a cane fire. Only men could put it out. And they had to get scorched and burnt to do it. But the men did not care. They were hungry and they were wild, and they would have money after the fire was put out, and they would stand in the rum shop and joke and laugh about how near they went to the blasted burning canes and how a whole handful of red hot canes fell on their backs and they didn't feel one damn sting, not even as much as a flea bite. The plantation owners knew this. They raised the reward for putting out the fire from five shillings a man to ten shillings, and suddenly the canes were filled with so many men and boys that you would have thought, it was the people on fire, and not the canes. The women stood dangerously near, holding their men's shirts and shoes in their hands, and directing them to danger points. A strange happiness fell over them. There would be drinking and money in the village tonight. The bosses were smiling now, for the fire was leaving their plantation and going with the wind towards the other plantation. The manager, seeing this, said goodbye, and hustled Turnbull back to the car, but before it started off, he got out, and the people wondered why. They watched him go over to Biscombe who was talking with Mr Whippetts. Then they saw him turn away annoyed and go back to the car. Turnbull mowed a passage through the onlookers and the car sped down the road.

'The manager want all you womens to go back and help out on the plantation! You hear? The manager want you to go back. This is Uplands. You belongst to Clapham plantation. So, come!' Biscombe was shouting above the roar of the crackling stalagmites of red hot canes. A few women moved away. Then all of them turned, and soon there was a throng of black women, running, dashing down the road to their plantation.

'Jesus Christ!' Whippetts said in disgust.

'What you grumbling 'bout?' Biscombe wanted to know. 'It is their plantation too! That is their bread and butter and salt fish!'

'Well, be-Jesus God, you can't do nothing bad enough with a black man!' the schoolmaster said. 'You coming too?' he asked after a while, and together he and Biscombe jucked-jucked down to their plantation in his antique Ford Prefect. On the way they waved to Clementina, sitting like a lighthouse in front of the deserted rum shop.

'Don't t'ief my money, eh?' Biscombe shouted at her. But the ancient little motorcar was making too much noise. However, Clementina waved back, and all the way down they could see her teeth and her hand like the weather-worn Union Jack over the school house.

Dusk was closing in on the men and women fighting the fire. For hours and hours the men, those whom the overseer could persuade to save the cane fields on their plantation, beat the canes to put out any traces of fire. When the traces became flames, and the flames a sea of burning orange, they ran out of the canes hollering. But then they ran back again to the fringes of the fire, keeping up their unrhythmic drumming on the sugarcanes. The women formed chains from the three nearby water-wells in the yard. When they had reached the plantation almost five hours ago, they had seen poor old Bessie, the cook, throwing a bucket of water on the east wall of the house. The factory which was a hundred yards from the main plantation buildings had seemed in no danger of being burnt, since it was built almost entirely of stone and had very few wooden windows. But when the manager saw the fire clutch it and squeeze it like a noose, he uttered a cry and hung his head. All the work in preparation for the opening of the factory, all the greasing, the shining, the polishing, the new tools, was in vain. The fire was claiming all that now. Some men laughed when they saw this, but they laughed only because they could think of nothing else to do, of no other way to express the tense emotion inside themselves. The women were throwing bucket after bucket of water on the walls of the house. Whatever happened, the manager had ordered, never let the house catch fire. Bessie, due to her position as an inside worker, was in charge of this operation. More than once she had to upbraid a woman rudely for throwing water through a broken window pane.

'Looka, you!' Bessie snapped. 'Throw that water proper'. You want to wet up all the master' things?'

The woman made a disgusted noise with her lips and threw the next bucket of water on the walls without opening her eyes.

The wind shifted again. The fire came towards the men beating the ground and scattered them in the yard. Uplands was burnt to the ground. The fire was now concentrating on Clapham. The air was filled with pieces of black trash the size of crows, and the wind was carrying fragments of fire with it. Behind them, on the west, the fire was raging unmolested. But when the manager saw the danger to the house, he ordered all hands to grab buckets and save at least that one relic of the plantation. The woman to whom Bessie had spoken laughed out loud and threw the next bucket of water right through the broken window.

'Watch me, Bessie! Watch me!' she teased her. 'I going drown ever' blasted piece o' shift and clothing that belongst to that master o' yourn! Watch this bucket o' water! Splah-dammm!' The water struck the window and shattered it. All the women in the bucket brigade laughed, and for a moment or so the fire burned carefree.

'You worthless wretches! You ought to be lock' up!' Bessie stormed. But the water fell into the house, nevertheless.

Just about this time, the fire fighters heard a noise like men marching and singing. They stopped to listen, and soon, in the brightness thrown by the fire, a ragged battalion of men appeared with Boysie and Mango at their head.

> 'John Brown's bo-dy lies a-mold'ing in the grave,
> John Brown's body lies a-mold'ing in the grave – '

The voices were rich, the voices were loud, and the men were full of spirits. Boysie, with his medals shining like the testicles of a dog in the moonlight, could be seen a long way off. He brought the men to a crisp halt, and after some pointless saluting, he left them and marched forward, his feet pounding the gravel in the yard as if he were wearing boots, and stood stiff as a telephone pole in front of the manager.

'Reporting for duty, sir!' Boysie shouted. 'Comp'ny o' forty-odd mens, ready and willing to assist, sir! With Admirul Boysie, Commander-in-Chief, and of the Fleat, sir!' His hand went up to his hat like a flash of lightning. The manager, himself an ex-Army man, replied with as sharp a salute. When this was done, the men scattered, took the buckets out of the hands of the women, and set to work on the fire.

'Jesus God!' Mr Whippetts said.

Biscombe, standing beside him, said nothing. Instead he spat on the ground, and mashed the spit with his feet.

When Stella reached the plantation yard, the fire had almost been put out. Some people were already in the kitchen where Bessie was fussing about, serving hot cocoa and hard biscuits, and asking them please, not to make so much noise in her kitchen. Stella joined them. Mr Whippetts and Biscombe were called into another room with the manager and Turnbull. They were drinking brandy. The manager's wife was not there, as she had been sent off earlier, when the fire threatened the house, to a cousin in town. But she was told of their success later.

The overseer took time off to go to the kitchen with a large bag of money. The people had not seen this bag for some time now. They waited patiently until he came to them, then they stretched out their hands and took their hats off, and thanked him and blessed him. The women bowed, and prayed for him, and asked God to bless the manager. All the while, Bessie was fussing and asking them not to trample down the whole kitchen, but to behave as if they had manners. When the overseer came to Stella, all the people in the room watched closely for some sign, some indication of favouritism. But the overseer could sense the eyes on him and he did nothing to give cause for gossip.

'Let me show you why the manager nearly went mad when the fire start threatening the house,' Bessie said to Stella, taking her by the hand and leading her through a passage into a sitting-room. Stella looked around her and marvelled at the riches and wealth, the luxury in that room. Rugs, thick as the grass outside, and chairs shining like gold. Above her head, something glistening like the stars in the heavens.

'What the hell is that?' she asked Bessie.

Bessie winked at her and assumed a superior manner knowing that Stella had never seen one before in her life.

'Child,' she said, pretending it was common knowledge in her circle, 'child, that is what makes a woman a lady! That thing above your head like the stars in the heaven is a chandylair! Yes! Chandylair!'

'Man, Bessie, it damn pretty, too!'

'Many's the night when the master and the missy gone out to cocktail parties, and I here alone, darling, I draws up a chair, and I sits right under this thing. It keeps me company. 'Cause, I argues, that anything so damn pretty must be good. And if it good, I want to be near it all the time.'

'Bessie, don't laugh when I tell you this,' Stella said. 'Don't laugh, Bessie. But if it is the last thing before I dead, I have to have one o' them hanging up in my house. I is a woman, too! If that so-and-so in there – I mean your missy – could have one o' them, well, Stella could have one too!'

'When you put in 'lectricity, Stella?' Bessie said, laughing. 'When? Them things don't operate 'pon kerosene oil, yuh!'

Together they went out, hands round shoulders, laughing, to join the rest of the people.

14

'Gorblummuh, Clemmie, when I tell you we drink rum over there at the plantation this evening, well, I mean rum! R-u-m!' The man held out his hand and Clementina put a piece of pig's ear into it and poured a ladleful of pickled juice on top of the pig's ear. Then the man sucked ear and juice into his mouth noisily, and said, 'Emmm!' as if something was tickling him at the back of his throat. 'Gorblummuh, Clemmie, you will pardon me for using such emotional language to your face, you being a religious kind o' woman, but, be-Christ, the rum flow' like water. Everybody get blind drunk! Even the manager! And he come outta the front room, red, red as a cherry, and say he hiring all the mens bright and early Mondee morning. And he ask' the Jockey, God blind him – pardon my words, Clemmie, but I have in my rums tonight – he ask' the Jockey if he pay all the fellars and womens. Man, Clemmie, be-Jees, I wish somebody would light another fire right now! 'Cause that like it is the onliest time when a poor man could get a few shillings to rackle 'bout inside his pocket-lining! And when I tell yuh we drink! Man, we drink that white man rum like if it was ice-water.' Clementina was smiling now. The men were coming back from the plantation in groups, half-drunk and rattling the money in their pockets, and laughing as if they owned the entire island. Clementina saw the piece of sharkskin material for her dress clearly before her eyes. Nothing could take it from her now.

'Come, come! Spend some o' that easy money in my tra!' she shouted at the men filing into the rum shop. 'Come! You ain't see poor Clemmie here struggling? Spend some o' the manager money on this pudding and souse!'

The men would stop and taunt her, and touch her breasts, or rather the place where her breasts used to be, and say nice things to her, and then spend some money with her. Clementina would laugh for them to see, but inside she held a bitter contempt for them, because they did not spend enough, and because they spent more in the rum shop than with her. But the night was progressing fine, bearing in mind how unpromising the afternoon had been. Stella came back and told her about the chandelier. Clementina sympathized with her, but when her back was turned, she told the women who came out with dishes and plates for their Saturday night rations that Stella was an idiot, 'a' arse to think that chandylair does burn 'pan kerosene' The women laughed at Stella, and the next minute forgot her, for they too were happy because their men were happy. The snuffbottle, filled with kerosene and with a piece of cloth serving as a wick, burned brightly in the middle of the tray. Clementina's face was bathed in a soft orange light, and when a breeze blew, the flame sent its shadows walking across her face and her own shadow sprawling across the public road. Little children playing near by jumped on Clementina's shadow in the road, and called it a 'brute beast' a 'monster' and a 'man-a-kete', but Clementina didn't care a damn, her pudding-and-souse tray was being emptied faster than she had expected. Before the news came on the radio at ten o'clock, she had about one hundred shillings, eighty sixpences, and innumerable penny and one-cent pieces, rattling hell in the jew-bag she carried under her dress and apron, protected from the eyes of man.

Somebody in the shop raised his glass and proposed a toast to Rufus, who, he said, had made all this possible.

'To Rufus!' he said. The men echoed him. When they had drunk three such toasts to Rufus, the man said, 'Today is a funny day. I bet not one a' you sons-o'-bitches know what particular day today is?' He waited a respectable time for the men to guess. But none of them knew. And triumphantly he said in a superior manner. 'Today is the Eyes o' March! Yes The Eyes o' March!'

'And what so blasted fancy 'bout that?' someone wondered.

'Well, the professor going to tell yuh now!' He took a big drink from his glass while the men waited anxiously to be enlightened. 'Now, the Eyes o' March, meaning the first day the Eyes o' March fall on that particular day what now we know as the Eyes o' March – '

'But what day is the Eyes o' March, though?'

'Man, let we lis'en to the news, do! a third man said disgustedly. 'Turn up the damn news, Biscombe, boy. Eyes o' March, my arse! I want to hear the score in the test match!'

'Not in my rum shop! Not in this rum shop!' insisted Biscombe, coming into the shop just in time to hear the announcer saying something about a prisoner still at large. When Biscombe turned the switch off, the prisoner's name was almost blurted out for the men to hear. That would have been the end of sales that night! That would have been a riot, right there in the rum shop, for the men had grumbled all the time they were helping to put the fire out, saying that if Rufus was there, they were sure he wouldn't want them to work for the plantation in any kind of way. Biscombe had heard this and mentioned it to Mr Whippetts, who agreed with the men. 'They know their rights, boy!' Mr Whippetts had said. 'They waiting for their leader. And it is only luck that the fire burning while Rufus still in prison.' Biscombe quickly reminded him that Rufus was not in prison, but at large. At which Mr Whippetts stammered and said, 'But, but – but, oh Christ, Biscombe! Suppose Rufus round here this very minute killing himself with laugh – right round this very place looking on and laughing! You remember he tol' you he going burn down the canes?' Biscombe swore it was Rufus who had burned down the canes. But he was not sure, though this had not prevented him from telling the manager when they were drinking brandy in the house. All these things Biscombe recollected as he turned the radio off, leaving the men grumbling. Since it was the nearest radio and since they were indebted to Biscombe for having given them free drinks earlier, they did not bother to smash the place to pieces. But they grumbled and drank.

Then Mango and Boysie appeared, completely drunk, and dressed in some second-hand clothes which the manager had given them for their help in putting out the fire. Boysie was wearing a polo shirt, discarded army boots and green army trousers. Boysie stood like a general in the middle of the door, and laughed like a jackass.

'Mens!' he shouted, as if they were over at the plantation and not standing there in front of him. 'Mens! Say what you like, the manager is damn decent man. He on the side o' labour! And you know that tonight. He take all o' you inside his kitchen, feed yuh, put a piece o' change inside yuh pockets, and send you on yuh way rejoicing.'

The men went on grumbling. They were waiting for Rufus. But then Mango stepped in, dressed like Boysie. He too extolled the virtues of the plantation. He took two green, three-gill bottles from his hip pockets and placed them noisily on the counter. The men's eyes bulged.

'The strike over! The strike over, 'cause now the rum flowing like water!' He put a bottle to his lips and drank, but the men turned their faces away. The man went back to his story about the Ides of March, and his drinking companions listened attentively, what he said being more interesting than tales from the plantation. Finding themselves ignored, Mango and Boysie went through the shop and sat in the special room with Biscombe.

'You hear'?' Biscombe asked them.

'Hear what?' Mango inquired.

'Rufus!'

Boysie sprung up from his seat. His eyes were wild, the glass in his hand was trembling.

'Breaked jail,' Biscombe went on. 'It in the papers this morning, but me and Clemmie and Whippetts hide the paper, hoping the fellars won't see the picture in the paper.'

'Be-Jees!' Mango said, watching Boysie. 'I glad! I glad, glad, glad, 'cause now I going find out something.'

'Shut yuh arse, you hear?' Boysie warned him. 'Shut yuh arse, Mango!'

'I going hear some funny things when I see Rufus,' he said. He took a victory drink from his bottle. Then he said, 'You know where he hiding?'

'Nobody ain't seen him.'

'Is Rufus who set that fire!' Boysie said, bringing his hand slapping down on the table. 'Is him! I know!'

'But did you see! You damn Judas!' It was Mr Whippetts's voice. He had entered the shop without being noticed, Boysie looked round nervously.

'You don't have to see a thing like that to know a man like Rufus would do it.'

'You wearing plantation clothes now, Boys. So you is a plantation manager too! Admiral Boysie!' and he, laughed at him. 'Give me some o' that poison you selling for rum, Biscombe.'

'We all interested in this. We all in this, 'cause all o' we went over there, and drink the man' rum and eat the man' biscuits and corn' beef. We is all traitors.'

'But some o' we is bigger traitors!' Mango argued. 'Some is Judas traitors.'

Boysie made a dash at him, and only the bulk of Biscombe's body managed to keep them apart. The schoolmaster sat giggling. Just then, Conradina came to the door of the room and asked for her mother.

'Outside talking with Clemmie,' Biscombe told her. Conradina left.

Boysie and Mango started a big argument. Boysie was a thief, Mango said. Boysie had all the money Rufus stole from Biscombe, he told Mr Whippetts when Biscombe left to fix the drinks. But Mr Whippetts only laughed.

'Biscombe, Biscombe!' Stella called out. 'Where Biscombe?' she asked Mango as she burst into the special room. Then she ran into the shop and, overcome with emotion, blurted out so that all the men could hear, 'Biscombe, oh Christ, Rufus in the village! Connie just seen him!'

Biscombe dropped the bottle; the men came to life. Somebody laughed like a hyena, and immediately they filed out of the shop and left Stella, Biscombe and Conradina standing looking at one another. Stella told the child to go away, and with Biscombe she went back to the special room. She took a piece of paper from her pocket and handed it to Biscombe.

'Connie say he give you this,' she said.

Biscombe took the paper, trembling and scarcely brave enough to read it. He then threw it on the ground. Boysie picked it up and read it aloud: 'Biscum I going kill you tonite.'

'Somebody must 'ave write this for him,' Boysie said chuckling, ' 'cause we know Rufus can't read nor write!' He looked round and laughed, and expected them to join in with him. But everybody else was serious and tense and frightened.

And Connie say he went round by the house looking. And when he didn' find me or she, or 'Zeke, he kill' the dog. He kill' Rover,' she said, breaking down in tears. 'Rufus kill' the dog – oh God!'

'You getting on like you wanted him to kill me instead!' Biscombe snapped. But she continued weeping.

'Well, Biscombe,' Mango said, leaving by the door, 'night-night!' and in a flash he disappeared.

Mr Whippetts stood up next. He poured the rest of the rum from the bottle into his glass, swallowed it at once, and put his straw hat on his head, knocking it in place. 'Biscombe, God help you tonight. I better go and see if the wife have anything left back for supper!' He slipped into the darkness outside. Only Boysie and Stella were left. Boysie looked around him, wondering what he should do. He wondered if Mango was really going to search for Rufus and tell him. He wondered if he won't be safer here, in greater numbers, than at home, with only his old mother for protection. Biscombe was looking at Stella with the same fear in mind. He looked at Boysie too to see if he could expect any help from him.

'You is who put me on my guard the first time, Admirul Boysie,' he said. 'I hope you stand back now and protect me.'

'Biscombe? Biscombe?' Stella said, harnessed with her share of fear for what was about to happen. 'I hope you don't judge me too harsh', Biscombe. I don't want you to think that – ' Without finishing, she took a firm grip on Conradina's hand and led her out of the room. On the way out she collected Ezekiel and the three of them hastened out of the house. Biscombe was dumb-founded throughout all this. But he was vexed too.

'What you going to do, Boysie?' he asked.

'Biscombe boy,' Boysie said, with a smirk on his face, be-Christ, I think I just get sleepy, sleepy as hell. So I think I going home.' At the back door he turned and said, 'Take care, man.'

'God blind all o' you! God blind all o' you!' Biscombe screamed. 'All o' you is freeloading bastards, that's what!' When his anger left him, his loneliness and terror closed in like the dusk at evening-tide.

Clementina was watching the procession passing by. It was getting late. The last bus, which had passed her at eleven-thirty, was almost due to come back down. But she did not think it was so late that all the men would have gone home at the same time on a Saturday night. Just as she was about to enter the shop and find out the reason for this stampede, Mr Whippetts passed and whispered in her ears, 'Clemmie, you better close up shop! Something bad going happen here soon. Goodnight, and God bless!' He walked away from her. She gathered up the scraps of black pudding and souse which she usually gave the village children, and started counting her change. The snuff-bottle was dying. But her spirits were high. The night had been kind to her. God had saved her. The butcher man would get his money; the coolie man would get his instalment for the clothes she had bought from him and had almost worn out, and the piece of sharkskin material would be on her back in a few days. God was a good God. That was how Clementina summed up her trying day. Now it was time to go home.

Suddenly the lights in the rum shop went off and she was left in a sea of blackness except for the feeble, flickering light from her bottle. Something must be wrong, she mused. Biscombe had just put out the lights, and he didn't do that normally. Then she heard the bolts and latches. She knocked gently on the front door, and for a long while Biscombe did not answer.

'Biscombe?'

'Christ, Clemmie, darling love! You still out there? You ain't heard what set up?'

'I saying goodnight now, Biscombe, and God bless.'

'God bless, darling love. You better be careful. Last bus just gone down, and the night dark as hell. Nobody out there to carry you home?'

'I all right, man. I not able with these slick young mens in this village. One o' them just ask' me a question.' She laughed sensuously. But Biscombe did not join in. He was still inside and up till then had not opened a window to see if it was Clementina or her ghost talking to him.

'How you make out, Clemmie?'

'First class! Sol' everything! Well, God bless now!'

'Hold on tight 'pon that money bag, then!'

'I have God as my guardian,' and with that she left the door and went back to her tray.

Rufus was in the canes opposite, near the edge, watching and hearing everything from the moment Stella announced his arrival. But he was content to wait. He liked waiting. He remembered that all his life in the village was one long wait. In prison it was the same thing. But he had managed to do something about it there and had broken out in a guard's uniform. Now that part of the waiting was over. He had come back for the money. His plan was to hide it, go back to prison, come out again whenever they decided to let him, and then set sail for Canada and join Jackson. Now the waiting was almost over.

He saw Clementina snuff out the light, throw the bottle into the bushes, check her money bag and put the empty tray on her head. Instantly, she faded into the dark night. Rufus gauged her progress down the road, trying to make up his mind whether to go after her or not. But he decided to attend to Biscombe first. This time he was sure there were no witnesses. Nobody had seen him, except Conradina. He had wanted her to see him and had had the note written to Biscombe. He crept out of the canes, looked left and right, and then dashed across the road like a mongoose. He stopped running when he had reached the shadows under Biscombe's bedroom window. He listened carefully. He could hear only a man's movements inside. Crappo was probably out. He climbed up and put his mouth to the jalousies, and then called out softly, 'Biscombe?''

He knew Biscombe recognized his voice, for he heard him jump. Then he heard something fall, something heavy like a piece of iron. He knew Biscombe slept with the ripping-iron and the cash box as bed companions.

'Biscombe? I come back for you!'

Again he felt the shudder of Biscombe's terror inside the house. He jumped down just in time to hide from someone coming up to the front of the shop. The man went to the door, and rapped heavily on it with a stick.

'Biscombe! Biscombe! This is Barabbas, man! Open up this blasted door!' The policeman continued rapping heavily on the door, as if it were a piece of limestone he was trying to chisel. But

Biscombe refused to move. Rufus dashed through the bushes and disappeared.

'Biscombe!'

At last Biscombe, certain that it was the policeman, came to a window and opened it only a peep.

'Oh Christ, Barabbas! I glad you arrive'! Rufus just been here!'

'Where? Here? Man, why you didn' say so? Is he we looking for – ' and the constable's voice faded away, leaving Biscombe alone once more in a world of enemies. He shut the window and bolted it. But Rufus was too far away by this time to know.

Clementina walked out of the pitch blackness of the road which wound interminably between two cane fields and into the weak light from the electric street lamp. You could hear the winds talking to the canes. Her tired bandy legs seemed hardly to cross one another so slowly did she walk, as though she were feeling brave, or going to a funeral, instead of home. Clip-clop! the old canvas shoes beat on the echoing road, quiet and still now as a graveyard. She hummed to keep herself company, and told herself she was not afraid of the dark.

> 'Rock of Ages, cleft for me –
> Let me hide myself in Thee – '

Her voice was tired and distant, her strength was ebbing. She was almost under the street lamp and she looked just like the 'brute beast' which the children had said her shadow looked like. The tray was balanced on her head. Her left hand was in her pocket keeping the money from rattling. Her right hand clutched a large stone ready to stun an assailant, just in case. She had always carried a large stone in her right hand when walking the lonely roads at night, even when returning from church. Clip-clop! clip-clop! Precarious progress. Only a little way along this stretch of road, and then turn left, up the incline and – Lord, You is so good – down the little hill and into the nutshell of her house. But even that short distance was as dark as hell, darker than any part of the road she had already travelled. She should have asked Biscombe to accompany her home. Or she should have taken the last bus, if she hadn't been hoping to sell the scraps of pudding and souse. Man is too damn greedy, she said to herself, and then she sighed. Ahh, Lord! The sugarcanes on either side of her now seemed to be sleeping. Even the few blades that hung over the roadside and into her face were in bed too. It was quiet. Quiet, quiet. Wait, Clemmie, darling love! Stop a minute! And lis'en, lis'en good, good, and hear if you ain't hear like they is somebody walking 'long behind you all this time! You hear somebody? Or you hearing your own two tired old foots dragging 'bout in the white man road this ungodly hour o' the night? Lis'en! Oh Christ, no, Clemmie! Ain't nobody, not a living soul behind you, and there ain't a living soul betwixt you and your home, save God! So, hold up your head and walk on brave in the knowledge that God –

What' that? Somebody in them canes? Somebody make a noise? Ain't no noise, darling love! Is only Satan trying to tempt you and cross you up, love, and make you turn your eye offa God who guiding you like a lighthouse light through this black, blasted, black night – clip-clop-clip – clip-clop – clip –

'Rock of Ages – '

Somebody behind me? Somebody could be tracking behind me all this time, and I don't know? Lord, I 'trust my care in Your hands!

'Let me hide myself in – '

Child, why you don't try to put the Devil outta your mind and concentrate 'pon – clip-clop! clip-clop! She increased her speed in the darkness; the canes closed in on her like a triumphal arch, and the road grew smaller and smaller until she thought she was walking through the middle of a cane field. She imagined the end of the world where all was darkness, and legions of sounds trailing her, and her shoes refusing to break their silence and tell her she was still walking, moving, and not standing still in this lake of blackness, and –

Bram!

A man jumped down from the canes and stood like Satan in front of her. God! The tray fell to the ground.

'Money or yuh blasted life!'

The large stone crumbled into marl. The man tore the money-bag from her dress and the money tumbled out in the road. Clementina screeled all the way back up the road to Biscombe's Rum Shop, crying, 'Murder, murder, murder, murder, murder, mur – '

194

15

Breathless, and in terror, Clementina reached the rum shop. She banged on the door and shook it, screaming for Biscombe to open. But Biscombe remained as quiet as a mouse.

'Open, Biscombe! Good God, Biscombe, open the door!' She shook and she shook, and still Biscombe refused to answer. 'Biscombe, is me! Clemmie! Good loss! Open the door, man! Somebody just rob' me! The man in the canes hold on 'pon me, and steal all me black pudding money! Biscombe? You sleeping? Open, nuh!'

But the more she shook the door, the quieter Biscombe remained. She could hear footsteps behind her. She could see knives sharp as razors held over her throat; she could see demons descending upon her, and still Biscombe refused to answer. She tried again and again, banging and screaming, and bawling out murder. But nobody heard her. All the houses around remained shut, black cubicles in a deaf, black night.

'Good God, please, Biscombe! Open the door and let me in – '

The money bag felt good in his hand. Running through the jungle of night, he held it tight in his right hand, as he brushed the cane blades aside with his left. 'Heh-heh-heh-heh' he chuckled, over and over, as he ran through the canes. He had money now. Not as much as he had taken from Biscombe, but still money. All he needed now was the passport, and then he would jump on a ship, or an aeroplane, and get clean away. But now he was just running, running fast but going nowhere. He laughed at Clementina and chuckled to himself, and he laughed at the people in the village, and at the plantation and at Turnbull, the overseer.

'Now I have money and I could make a man outta myself, and leave all this slavery behind me. Maybe I could even store 'way on one o' them ships what come up 'long the wharfside and carry the horses to the other island in. I could store 'way in one o' them big boxes, and maybe land in Trinidad, Aruba, Curaçoa, even in a small island. But the where and how ain't important, as long as I land somewhere. Lord, Lord, Lord! Look how easy I come through! Maybe after a year or two, I could even write back some nice airmail letters and tell Stella how I getting on. Put a couple o' nice money orders in and make her stand at attention, and harken. Heh-heh-heh-heh! And when I get over there, I could even learn how to read and write, and send back some big, pretty letters written in Quink ink like what Turnbull use' in that black book he have. Look how the fellars in the rum shop reading the letters, and saying all the time, 'Man we was wrong as arse 'bout Rufus! We take a six for a nine, as far as Rufus concern', 'cause look how the man progress' so damn far, and we still here twirling the blasted fork in the white man cane field!' Maybe, after a couple o' years, I end up in Canada with Jackson. Up in that rich, progressive, advance' country, and wearing nice, nice clothes, and a Hamburg hat just like the manager' own, patient-leather shoes, collar and tie – Oh, Jesus Christ, it is such a' easy thing when you have a couple dollars in your pocket and you know where the next meal coming from! Maybe even send back for the family, Connie and 'Zeke and Stella. And then after a long time in that country, and when I have more money than a' idiot, more money than Lord Bowring, I coming back and buying up the kiss-me-arse village, and renting out house and land, and driving 'bout morning, noon and night in a big, big black Humber car like the plantation car. Jesus Christ! Walking 'bout the road with raincoat under my arm just like the Rev, gold teet' in my mout', and I talking big, big just like that man Jackson talk' 'bout up in Canada. Lord, Lord, Lord! It taking me a week to drive 'round my estate and I bowing down low, low and respectful, at the people renting from me. Bowing at Clemmie, bowing at Miss Gertrude as she bring in the rent for renting the food store, bowing down at Biscombe when he bring round the money for renting the land the rum shop standing 'pon. Christ, Christ, Christ! And I giving him a hee-hee-laugh, and Biscombe saying, 'But Mister Rufus, sir, please lower the rent. Things rough with me this mont'!'

The smell of burnt canes dragged him from his reverie, and he realized for the first time how tired and haggard he was. But he must lumber on through the compassless canes to find a spot to sit down and count his money. The ruts of the seared canes made a familiar noise in his ears and they punched his feet like in the old days. He was home. He was nostalgic. But he knows he must leave all this, the scene and domain of his endless labours, because it is no longer safe. For so many years, his world has been the cane field, and now that he is fleeing from his world, he finds himself back in the cane field. And the cane fields lead him one way only, right back to the plantation.

The darkness was becoming less dark. Perhaps morning was coming. He was walking slowly now through a thick field, and when he came to the edge of it, he stopped and wondered. 'Blasted funny! Funny, funny, funny! I walk' and walk' and walk' a whole night through canes, and the canes end up in front o' the blasted plantation house!' Indeed it was strange that Rufus, who knew the cane fields like the palms of his hands, should wander about, and when his wandering was over, should have appeared in front of the house, the last enemy he should have wanted to face.

The house rose out of the dawn like a monster. Rufus stood and looked at it a long time. He wanted to know it by heart, every window, every door he wanted to remember, for though this was his enemy, it was also the biggest house in his life. He would be leaving soon. He saw the pillars still standing like strangers to the rest of the house. They were unscorched. The trees were standing too, untouched by the fire. He cursed himself for having started a fire which could not consume the house and the trees, as it had consumed most of the sugar canes. But he became frightened. Perhaps, no fire can ever burn down this kind of a house. Perhaps this kind of a house is invincible. Cannot be destroyed. For it had survived since the time of his grandfather, who had worked as a yard boy on the plantation. Everybody, well, practically everybody, born in the village, worked for this house, or in this house, some part of his life.

The old horse-drawn carts, without horses in them, and looking like relics of a Punic War, were resting near the house. The factory, proud as a whore, stood in the yard, and it too was scarcely blemished by the fire. Its tall chimney reached to the skies, and Rufus had to raise his head high to follow the magnificent brickwork whirling and whirling, smaller and smaller, until it seemed scarcely bigger than the mouth of a bottle. But the factory was dead. No smoke came tumbling out of it now. No sweet, sickening smell of boiling cane juice. There was nothing here but Rufus, the stillness and God, and the manager inside that fort of a house, sleeping in a room, a passage away from his wife.

The power of that house drew him closer to it. He was so near that he could put his hand out and touch the pile of agricultural forks and hoes which the women used. Everything was as idle as unemployment. But he walked quietly up to them and rubbed his hand over the handle of a fork. He looked at it closely and saw that it was his fork. His fork! This was the weapon with which he had eked out his living in the broiling sun and cane fields!

Now it was in his hand. The feel was so familiar! More than forty years he had been lifting this fork in the air, and throwing it into the blasted earth. Rufus inhaled deeply. He balanced the fork in the air, and he kept it there a second or two, and then, wham! he flung it into the ground. But this ground was gravel. The fork cried out. And Rufus cried. 'Yahh! yuh bitch!' The prongs made a ringing noise, and in an instant a light went on upstairs in the house. Then another. 'Heh-heh-heh! I leaving you behind, fork! Yahh!' and he flung it into the hard gravel for the last time.

Dogs were barking. More lights went on. Running feet of dogs came at him. Rufus dropped the fork and beat it into the guts of the canes. The money bag in his hand, he scrambled over the ruts, stumbling and out of breath; but he went on regardless. Death was behind him. He must not let it catch up with him now. The dogs faded out, and he panted his way through canes, through gullies, across a road, Uplands Road, until he found himself in Uplands Plantation. He was walking now, dog-tired. The bag seemed lighter than when he grabbed it from Clementina. But he must not stop now to check it. On he walked, thinking of Jackson and of Canada, and of leaving the island. The letter came back to his thoughts and he regretted not having replied to Jackson. He came to a clearing in the canes which the fire had circled round.

This was the only break in the long monotony of canes, and he walked to meet it. He saw a piece of cloth, like a jacket, and he thought he had seen it before. But his mind was as tired as his body and he could not waste strength to think about it. Something glittered on the ground. He picked it up, held it close to his eyes, and chuckled when he realized it was a shilling. Almost new. Instinctively, he held the money bag up, but when he peered into it, it was empty. The money had fallen out. He put the shilling into the bag, and put the bag into his pocket. A sign painted on a piece of cardboard lay on the ground. Rufus looked at it, wondering how it got there. But the mysterious words only swam before his eyes, and he did not know what the sign wanted him to know. He folded the piece of cloth and laid it on the cardboard, and put his head on it. The sign read, 'Cane and Abel'.

He took the money bag out of his pocket and held it tightly in his hand. Soon afterwards, fatigue and indifference crumpled his body and mind, and he dropped off to sleep, unknown to himself, in the headquarters of the organization which he himself had formed.

16

The whole village was talking about it. Although it was Sunday, the rum shop had never been so crowded, except on that day when Adams had returned from Europe where he had represented the whole Commonwealth at a conference in Paris. On that day everybody in the island and in the village had been glad to be black. On this morning everybody was sorry to be black. Because it was a black man who had been run in by the police. It was not a morning for merrymaking, but the men drank rum after rum, and talked about the night's happenings, although they had not been eyewitnesses. Clementina postponed church and her sermon to be there. She regaled the crowd in the rum shop with her story of the hold-up and robbery. Biscombe had given her a free drink to celebrate Rufus's capture by Barabbas. She held the glass in her hand, rolled her eyes, gesticulated, and spoke her lines like Miss Rhinehart disclaiming Shakespeare.

'Well, darlings, let me tell you how it start' out. Look me, walking down that lonely, dark road, almost at midnight, and I singing the songs o' the Lord, and walking brave in the spirit, and then bram! this man jump out o' the canes, and come telling me that he want my money. My hard-earned cash! Well, be-Christ, if he thought he had me tricked, he lie! Bram! I fling the money bag in his face! Pop! the string break. The money all over the road, and brisk-brisk he put it through the canes! Darlings, I had God walking beside o' me that night!'

The people laughed and called Clementina a saint, and clapped their hands, and thanked heaven that at least one woman in the village was not a coward. Clementina stole a glance at Biscombe and winked. Biscombe winked back.

'And then I took a cool walk up here, and wake up Biscombe. And like a gentleman, Biscombe put on his clothes the minute I knock' at his bedroom window, and come out and help' me look for that crook! That worthless crook who say' he robbing helpless womens!'

'If I had o' had a gun!' Biscombe said, 'be-Christ, I would 'ave put one right in his arse!'

The men cheered again, and leant over the counter and patted Biscombe on his shoulders, and called him the hero of the village. Boysie was present. He was drinking like a fish, and before noon came, he was losing his words in a mumble of drunkenness. He told his story of going home, and sitting up all night at the window, waiting for Rufus to appear.

'As I tol' Biscombe last night,' he went on, addressing the men and women, 'as I had to say to Biscombe last night, I was damn sorry a piece o' sleep take hold o' me and caused me to go home. But old man, if it wasn' for that, me and Biscombe and Clementina would 'ave been tracking down that bastard the whole night all 'bout them canes. And this morning, I would 'ave been – '

'You worthless two-timing liar!' Stella shouted. She had just entered the shop. 'You worthless, Judas-lying so-and-so! What the hell you telling these people? You been doing what? You would 'ave been doing what?' She turned to the people and laughed out loud in ridicule. 'Don't lis'en to this lackney bitch, hear me? I pass' round by his mother' place seeking shelter, and this bastard stand in that house and won't open the door. Me and my two children had was to go and beg the people I have living in the house to give me a night lodging! And this Biscombe! Well, Biscombe, you is the worst – '

She turned to Mango to bear her out. Mango lowered his head, content to drink the free drinks and forget all about it, now that it was over.

'Mango ain't going to talk, 'cause all you niggers is the same thing. But I talking. And I talking plain, plain, plain. And I don't give a damn if I hurt anybody feelings. Rufus is my man. You all know that. And you all know that I been living with this bitch, this red-skin' bastard all the time, whilst I should been running down to the jailhouse with little good bittle for the man who fathered my two children. And when I look round and see all you Judases in here drinking free drinks from a Judas, a more bigger Judas, well – ' And she broke down in tears, and walked out of the shop. The people left their glasses on the counter for a while, trying to make up their minds whether to continue drinking or not. But their minds were made up for them when Biscombe appeared with a large tray of biscuits and corned beef. The men forgot their loyalties to Rufus and to Stella, and they scrambled for the food like ants.

'Jesus Christ, I can't wait to get back to work!' one man shouted, his mouth full of biscuits. Be-Christ, I going to swing that cutlass like lightning!' He pushed his hand in the bowl of the corned beef and stuffed some into his mouth. Eating and talking at the same time, he continued, 'And you hear' what the white man say' when we had that big freeness Sa'rday night after the cane fire? You didn't hear the man say "Well, fellars, bright and early Mondee morning!" And you know what that mean?'

'Rice and salt fish!' shouted Jo-Jo. 'Rice and salt fish! We is working mens. Not politicians! I know from now on you ain't going hear one bastard in this village talking 'bout striking, or no damn foolishness 'bout socialism, or even mention the name o' Jackson.'

Biscombe left them at the front of the shop and retired to the special room where Mr Whippetts, the overseer and the minister of the Anglican church were sitting. Clementina got away from the crowd and joined them.

'Forgive and forget!' Mr Whippetts was saying when she appeared at the door. He saw her and blushed. But she winked at him, and he gathered courage and went on. 'I say, give every man his due, and things going run smooth as if they greased with cart-grease. So, Turnbull, I know I cussed your arse coming and going, but now I stand up and bow down to you for the way you save' the village from a big riot! Forgive and forget!'

The overseer gave a cunning smirk, and lifted his glass and joined the schoolmaster. Then all of them drank the toast.

'It seem' like a year pass' since I seen you in this room drinking rum, Mister Rev. I been wondering if you lost yuh appetite for little good med'cine.'

'Why you don't leave the man o' God, you demon?' Clementina chastised him. 'This is the man o' God, and he have to answer to one Man! And that Man is God! Right, Rev'rund?' She gave him a push in his ribs and made him smile.

'Heh-heh-heh-heh!' the overseer started laughing. 'Heh-heh-heh! It was licks like water this morning! Licks like fire went in poor Rufus backside. Man, I never seen a bull-pistle whip lick a man so! Like if Barabbas went mad, or like some kind o' machine was in his hand, and he giving Rufus whop, whop, whop, whop, one, two, three, four, fast, fast, like 'lectricity! Jesus Christ! Well, he burn' down the blasted canes. But we still going reap them. Bright and early Mondee morning! And I know them fellars out there have itching hands to start swinging them bloody cutlass! I only hope to Christ I don't get in the way o' one. 'Cause, ping! and off goes my blasted hand!'

'Won't be a bad thing, neither!'

'Who say so?' he asked, looking round. 'Who say so? Oh! Is you, Clementina! I forgive you, 'cause you is a woman. I thought I heard Boysie' voice.' He went over and patted Clementina on the head. She wiped his hand away, as she would have wiped her bottom. 'Friends, Clemmie, darling love. You forgetting I give you a tip for that damn sour pudding and souse you sells? Friends, Clemmie, darling love.' But Clementina's face remained vexed. 'But guess what?' he asked them. 'Guess who I see this morning, bright and early in the cane field?'

'Rufus?' wondered Biscombe.

'No! We had Rufus licked and handcuff' long, long before morning come. We find him laying down sleeping, and snoring like a dead man, with a piece o' paper mark' "Cane and Abel!" – oh, Jesus Christ! you hear that? – "Cane and Abel!" We find him laying down like a dead man, holding the money bag with one kiss-me-tail shilling inside it! But I talking 'bout somebody else. Boysie!'

Biscombe became attentive again.

'Who, who?' he asked. 'Boysie? The Boysie we know?'

'Boysie! And he was looking 'bout in the burnt cane and trash for something. So I creeps up behind him, and then he hold down and pick up this thing like a skillet and, be-Christ, bram! he put it through the cane ground like a blasted mongoose!'

'Wait! Wait! You say a thing like a skillet? A tin tot? He pick' it up and run?'

'Don't tell me you lost a skillet! Full o' you know what? 'Cause I sure that is what it had in!'

Biscombe rushed out of the room, and climbed up on the counter and grabbed Boysie by his shirt collar. The men were astonished. They had never seen Biscombe exert so much effort.

'God blind you!' he said, holding on to Boysie and tugging him. 'God blind you!'

'But, but – but!'

'No buts! Gorblummuh, I going squeeze you till you fart up every penny o' that money! You make a innocent man get jail for money you t'ief, God blind you!'

Turnbull and the others rushed out of the special room to see this spectacle. But Biscombe held his hand to Boysie's neck and squeezed.

'Talk! Talk! Tell all these people, everybody here what know and what you know. Talk! Or, be-Christ, I kill you dead, dead, dead as a blasted nit!'

When Boysie talked, and the people had heard the scandal, they all left the shop feeling guilty and ashamed. When Biscombe eventually let him go, Boysie slipped out of sight and was not seen for the rest of the day.

'Gorblummuh! Gorblummuh!' Biscombe said over and over again, as if he had run out of words. 'Gorblummuh!'

'You mean that – ?' Clementina began.

'Pre-zactly!' the schoolmaster said. '*That* is the mistake we made. We nearly kill' the wrong man.'

'But Rufus still have a piece o' blame to take for all the sufferation he put this village through, though!'

'But just the same, not all!' the schoolmaster insisted.

'Christ!' Biscombe said, 'look now, I have to go and face Stella, and tell she sorry, beg pardon and forgiveness.' Displaying no immediate inclination to do so, he added, 'More rum, gentlemens?'

'And so you is the schoolmaster o' this village again!' the overseer sneered at Mr Whippetts. 'Bright and early Mondee morning you'll be the goddamn schoolmaster again! And the best rum drinker this side o' hell!'

'More rum, gentlemens?' Biscombe inquired again. He was breathing more easily now. With Rufus back in chains, a great anxiety was taken off his mind. 'More rum?' This time the minister smiled.

'But, Miss Clementina, why you don't decide to come over and join my congregation?' the minister asked her. The Church of England is a solid foundation. And, and – think of the benefits! Perhaps you could be a – a lay preacher, or even help take up collection on Sunday mornings – '

'Not on your bottom dollar! Not on your bottom dollar!' Clementina cried. 'Your church may have a damn solid foundation, but the manager o' the plantation goes there. And I swear blind, before God, that any place where that brute goes, God ain't there! And to-besides, Rev'rund, sir, you not going to let me get up and shout out loud, loud for my Lord, and testify, and shout to the house tops that I have God in my heart. Are yuh? So, thanks, but not on your bottom dollar!'

Biscombe and Mr Whippetts roared with laughter.

'But think o' that collection bag, Clemmie!'

'Biscombe, whenever I bring myself so low as to t'ief, I t'iefing so much money that I would be in a position to buy out you, the manager, the plantation and the whole bunch o' you hypocrites.' And so saying, she got up and stamped out of the room.

The men wondered what had been said that annoyed her so.

'More rum, gentlemens?' Biscombe pleaded.

If you were to stand for more than a minute under the berry trees in the Court Yard in Coleridge Street, when they were in bloom, you would hear the berries dropping from them as they shaded you from the savage sun. If you were waiting for a friend or for a trial to end, as were Boysie, Clementina, Biscombe and Stella, you would be hit by thousands of them. You would mash them with your feet to kill time, and laugh inwardly at their whispered pleas for pity. The trees were now in bloom. The berries were falling. And while the four of them were waiting, they trod them under foot, and listened to them crying out, while they pretended that their thoughts were far from the trial they had come to witness.

Rufus had been brought to court to be tried for arson. The court yard was full. People from all over the island, attracted by the escape from Glendairy – a million to one chance – and by the sensational cane fire, large pictures of which had appeared in the newspapers, were gathered in the yard. All but four of these people had come to see him punished, but those four had come for the opposite reason. They wanted him back in the village with them, and so they stood outside the court while the jury was reaching its verdict.

A detachment of police marched by, stiff as corpses, dressed in their stifling starched tunics and thick, black trousers made from a kind of horse-blanket material. On their trousers was a murderous two-inch red stripe. It was hot and windless, but despite their black-hole-of-Calcutta uniform, the policemen could afford a smile.

A woman came screaming out of a magistrate's court, with a man fumbling slowly behind her. He did not want the people waiting in the Yard to know that there was any connection between them. But the woman wanted them to know.

'Be-Christ, if you is man now, *take* that thirty shilling fine outta your backside! *Take* it out! The Lord is my judge! And the magistrate is my protector! Take that fine outta your arse, you hooligun, you!' The man tried to lose himself in the crowd, but they had seen him already. 'I going to live and see you in hell. You full up my guts with three children, and you say you not supporting not even one o' them bastards o' yourn?' Eyes followed the woman, cursing her. Eyes followed the man, pitying him. Then a policeman, who knew the woman as a regular customer of the courts, approached her and asked, 'Wait, Pearlene. You lives in the courthouse? What the hell you in for this time?' 'Const'ble Francis,' she screamed, 'I see my ship come in! I see it come in! That no-teet' bastard there, look, that one there, yes, he with the patch'-up hat on he head – '

But the attention of the crowd was drawn to two policemen coming down the steps, bringing a man with them. He was handcuffed. They led him into the court where the jury was filing back to deliver their verdict.

'My fingers cross'. My fingers cross',' Stella said. She drew closer to Clementina with whom she hoped to bear the sorrow of the decision. Clementina put her hand round her and drew her closer still. Clemmie, what you think? My fingers cross'.'

'Trust in God, darling,' she told Stella. Even if they send him up for twenty, thirty years, God give him that time for a purpose. And the day he come' out, you wait and see, Rufus going to be a better man. Ten times a more better man.'

But Stella was not listening. She followed with her eyes some of the people who were rushing back into the court. They waited, Boysie and Biscombe with her, and they hoped against hope. Mr Whippetts went up the steps of the court. But no sooner had he got inside than the people came pouring, shouting out.

'They throw the book at him! They throw the book at him!' a woman shrieked. 'The judge throw the book and the pen at him!'

Stella started to cry. She held Clementina closer and shook her head. 'My fingers still cross', Clemmie. My fingers still cross'.'

'Keep them cross', darling love, 'cause God watching,' Clementina told her. But Mr Whippetts came out, downcast, his eyes fixed on the berries that had fallen.

'Twenty years!'

'Twenty years, he say?' Stella asked, not really asking, but as though talking in a dream. 'Twenty years. God! My fingers cross', Clemmie.'

Biscombe moved from beside Boysie and took Stella by the hand, and led her away to the car they had hired for the trial.

'Come, Stell darling. Let we go home to the children. They must be waiting for their food.'

'God give him that time for a purpose,' Clementina said, shaking her head in grief. For a purpose – a good purpose – '

ABOUT THE AUTHOR

Born in Barbados in 1934, Austin C. Clarke was educated at Harrison College and became a schoolteacher before moving to Canada in 1955 to study at the University of Toronto. Beginning in 1959, Clarke worked as a freelance broadcaster for the CBC, for which he recorded a series of interviews and documentaries on racial issues in North America and Britain. This began a prolific period in Clarke's career, during which he wrote several short stories and the novels: *Survivors of the Crossing* (1964), *Amongst Thistles and Thorns* (1965), and *The Meeting Point* (1967); followed by the novel *Storm of Fortune* (1973) and a collection of short stories entitled *When He Was Free and Young and He Used to Wear Silks* (1973). In the mid-1980s Clarke published two collections of short stories, *When Women Rule* (1985) and *Nine Men Who Laughed* (1986), as well as the novel, *Proud Empires* (1986). Returning in the early 1990s to the short story form, Clarke published the collections, *In This City* (1992) and *There Are No Elders* (1993). In 1992, in response to a riot, Clarke produced the pamphlet, *Public Enemies: Police Violence and Black Youth*. Also in the 1990s, Clarke wrote *A Passage Back Home* (1994), a memoir of his friendship with the Trinidadian writer Sam Selvon, and *Pig tails 'n Breadfruit: The Rituals of Slave Food* (1999), a "food memoir" that combines recipes with memories of Clarke's formative years in Barbados. Clarke's 1997 novel, *The Origin of Waves*, won him the inaugural Rogers Communications Writers' Trust Fiction Prize in 1998. Clarke's memoir, *Growing Up Stupid Under the Union Jack* (1980), won the 1980 Casa de las Americas Prize for Literature. His novel, *The Polished Hoe*, won the 2003 Commonwealth Prize and the 2002 Giller Prize (Canada's most prestigious literary award). Over the course of his career, Clarke has held many political, professional, and academic positions, including: Cultural Attaché to the Barbadian Embassy in Washington, D.C.; General Manager of the Caribbean Broadcasting Corporation in Barbados; and visiting lecturer in creative writing and African American literature at Yale, Brandeis, Duke, the University of Texas, and the University of Western Ontario. He lives in Toronto.

ALSO BY AUSTIN CLARKE IN THE CLASSICS SERIES

Austin C. Clarke
Amongst Thistles and Thorns
Introduction: Aaron Kamugisha
ISBN: 9781845231477; pp. 188; 2011; £8.99

Milton Sobers is nine and on the run from beatings by his sadistic headmaster – and from his mother when he complains. His adventures over a day and night are nightmarish, sometimes comic but always painful in what they reveal of the constrictions of class and race. Yet we see enough of the boy's sharp intelligence and the power of his dreams to hope that one day he will make his escape. Set in Barbados in the early 1950s, this is an uncompromising portrayal of a world where poverty and blackness are despised, and children are used as whipping posts for adult self-contempt and frustration. It brings acerbic humour to its portrayal of how Milton's competing "fathers" begin his sexual education, and unmasks the way in which phrases such as "robbing the cradle" hide the reality of the sexual abuse of boys. First published in 1965, its anger still simmers but its portrayal of the attempted destruction of innocence and hope by colonialism and its institutions is coolly clearsighted. As the introduction by Aaron Kamugisha makes clear, the issues the novel focuses on are far from being distant history.

CARIBBEAN MODERN CLASSICS NOW AVAILABLE

Jan R. Carew
Black Midas
Introduction: Kwame Dawes
ISBN: 9781845230951; pp. 272; May 2009; £8.99

This is the bawdy, Eldoradean epic of the legendary 'Ocean Shark' who makes and loses fortunes as a pork-knocker in the gold and diamond fields of Guyana, discovering that there are sharks with far sharper teeth in the city. *Black Midas* was first published in 1958.

Jan R. Carew
The Wild Coast
Introduction: Jeremy Poynting
ISBN: 9781845231101; pp. 240; May 2009; £8.99

First published in 1958, this is the coming-of-age story of a sickly city child, sent away to the remote Berbice village of Tarlogie. Here he must find himself, make sense of Guyana's diverse cultural inheritances and come to terms with a wild nature disturbingly red in tooth and claw.

Neville Dawes
The Last Enchantment
Introduction: Kwame Dawes
ISBN: 9781845231170; pp. 332; April 2009; £9.99

This penetrating and often satirical exploration of the search for self in a world divided by colour and class is set in the context of the radical hopes of Jamaican nationalist politics in the early 1950s. First published in 1960, the novel asks many pertinent questions about the Jamaica of today.

Wilson Harris
Heartland
Introduction: Michael Mitchell
ISBN: 9781845230968; pp. 104; May 2009; £7.99

First published in 1964, this visionary narrative tracks one man's psychic disintegration in the aloneness of the forests of the Guyanese interior, making a powerful ecological statement about man's place in the 'invisible chain of being', in which nature is a no less active presence.

Edgar Mittelholzer
Corentyne Thunder
Introduction: Juanita Cox
ISBN: 9781845231118; pp. 242; April 2009; £8.99

This pioneering work of West Indian fiction, first published in 1941, is
not merely an acute portrayal of the rural Indo-Guyanese world, but a
work of literary ambition that creates a symphonic relationship between its characters and the vast openness of the Corentyne coast.

Andrew Salkey
Escape to an Autumn Pavement
Introduction: Thomas Glave
ISBN: 9781845230982; pp. 220; May 2009; £8.99

This brave and remarkable novel, set in London at the end of the 1950s,
and published in 1960, catches its 'brown' Jamaican narrator on the cusp
between black and white, between exiled Jamaican and an incipient
black Londoner, and between heterosexual and homosexual desires.

Denis Williams
Other Leopards
Introduction: Victor Ramraj
ISBN: 9781845230678; pp. 216; May 2009; £8.99

Lionel Froad is a Guyanese working on an archeological survey in the
mythical Jokhara in the horn of Africa. There he hopes to rediscover the
self he calls 'Lobo', his alter ego from 'ancestral times', which he thinks
slumbers behind his cultivated mask. First published in 1963, this is one
of the most important Caribbean novels of the past fifty years.

Denis Williams
The Third Temptation
Introduction: Victor Ramraj
ISBN: 9781845231163; pp. 108; May 2010; £8.99

A young man is killed in a traffic accident at a Welsh seaside resort.
Around this incident, Williams, drawing inspiration from the *Nouveau
Roman*, creates a reality that is both rich and problematic. Whilst he
brings to the novel a Caribbean eye, Williams makes an important
statement about refusing any restrictive boundaries for Caribbean
fiction. The novel was first published in 1968.

Edgar Mittelholzer
A Morning at the Office
Introduction: Raymond Ramcharitar
ISBN: 978184523; pp. 215; May 2010; £8.99

First published in 1950, this is one of the Caribbean's foundational novels in its bold attempt to portray a whole society in miniature. A genial satire on human follies and the pretensions of colour and class, this novel brings several ingenious touches to its mode of narration.

Edgar Mittelholzer
Shadows Move Among Them
Introduction: Rupert Roopnaraine
ISBN: 9781845230913; pp. 352; May 2010; £10.99

In part a satire on the Eldoradean dream, in part an exploration of the possibilities of escape from the discontents of civilisation, Mittelholzer's 1951 novel of the Reverend Harmston's attempt to set up a utopian commune dedicated to 'Hard work, frank love and wholesome play' has some eerie 'pre-echoes' of the fate of Jonestown in 1979.

Edgar Mittelholzer
The Life and Death of Sylvia
Introduction: Juanita Cox
ISBN: 9781845231200; pp. 362; May 2010, £10.99

In 1930s' Georgetown, a young woman on her own is vulnerable prey, and when Sylvia Russell finds she cannot square her struggle for economic survival and her integrity, she hurtles towards a wilfully early death. Mittelholzer's novel of 1953 is a richly inward portrayal of a woman who finds inner salvation through the act of writing.

George Lamming
Of Age and Innocence
Introduction: Jeremy Poynting
ISBN: 9781845231453; pp. 320; January 2011; £11.99

In one of the most insightful explorations of race and ethnicity in colonial and postcolonial societies, Lamming reaches far beneath the surface of ethnic difference into the very heart of the processes of perception, communication and coming to knowledge. In a novel that is tense and tragic in its denouement, Lamming has written one of the half dozen most important Caribbean novels of all time.

Wayne Brown
On the Coast and Other Poems
Introduction: Mervyn Morris
ISBN: 9781845231507; pp. 112; November 2010; £8.99

First published in 1972, *On the Coast* was a Poetry Book Society Recommendation in the UK, and established Brown as one of the finest young poets of the post-Walcott generation. This collection include all the poems of 1972, with those of *Voyages* published in 1988.

Una Marson
Selected Poems
Introduction: Alison Donnell
ISBN: 9781845231682; pp. 160; March 2011; £8.99

Alison Donnell aims for a representative selection that reveals the complexity of Marson's scope – from *Tropic Reveries* (1930) to unpublished work written in the 1950s: a range that establishes a significant poetic achievement.

Wilson Harris
The Eye of the Scarecrow
Introduction: Michael Mitchell
ISBN: 9781845231644; pp. 112; August 2011; £8.99

An unnamed narrator, in London in 1964, reflects on three periods of his life in Guyana which altered his understanding of the world. In 1948 he witnesses a march of workers protesting the killing of their comrades by police during a bitter strike and has the disconcerting momentary perception that his friend L. is an empty scarecrow of a man. That vision leaves the narrator with "a curious void of conventional everyday feeling". So begins a radical revision of Wordsworth's strategy of exploring imagination, memory and event in *The Prelude*.

Elma Napier
A Flying Fish Whispered
Introduction: Evelyn O'Callaghan
ISBN: 9781845231026; pp. 248; September 2010; £9.99

With one of the most delightfully feisty women characters in Caribbean fiction and prose that sings, Elma Napier's 1938 Dominican novel is a major rediscovery, not least for its imaginative exploration of different kinds of Caribbeans, in particular the polarity between plot and plantation that Napier sees in a distinctly gendered way.

Orlando Patterson
The Children of Sisyphus
Introduction: Kwame Dawes
ISBN: 9781845230944; pp. 288; November 2011; £9.99

This is a brutally poetic book that brings to the characters who live on Kingston's 'dungle' an intensity that invests them with tragic depth. In Patterson's existentialist novel, first published in 1964, dignity comes with a stoic awareness of the absurdity of life and the shedding of false illusions, whether of salvation or of a mythical African return.

V.S. Reid
New Day
Introduction: Norval Edwards
ISBN: 9781845230906, pp. 360; December 2011, £10.99

First published in 1949, this historical novel focuses on defining moments of Jamaica's nationhood, from the Morant Bay rebellion of 1865, to the dawn of self-government in 1944. *New Day* pioneers the creation of a distinctively Jamaican literary language of narration.

Garth St. Omer
A Room on the Hill
Introduction: Jeremy Poynting
ISBN: 9781845230937; pp. 210; September 2011; £8.99

A friend's suicide and his profound alienation in a St Lucia still slumbering in colonial mimicry and the straitjacket of a reactionary Catholic church drive John Lestrade into a state of internal exile. First published in 1968, St. Omer's meticulously crafted novel is a pioneering exploration of the inner Caribbean man.

Roger Mais
The Hills Were Joyful Together
Introduction: Norval Edwards
ISBN: 9781845231002; pp. 272; December 2011; £8.99

Unflinchingly realistic in its portrayal of the wretched lives of Kingston's urban poor, this is a novel of prophetic rage. First published in 1953, it is both a work of tragic vision and a major contribution to the evolution of an autonomous Caribbean literary aesthetic.

George Campbell
First Poems
Introduction: Kwame Dawes
ISBN: 9781845231491; pp. 172; September 2011; £9.99

A profound influence on Derek Walcott, George Campbell's *First Poems*, published in 1945, announced the arrival of modernism in Caribbean poetry. These poems of nationalist ferment in Jamaica celebrate blackness, the working class and the beauties of the Jamaican landscape.

Titles thereafter include...

O.R. Dathorne, *The Scholar Man*
O.R. Dathorne, *Dumplings in the Soup*
Neville Dawes, *Interim*
Michael Gilkes, *Couvade/A Pleasant Career*
Wilson Harris, *The Sleepers of Roraima*
Wilson Harris, *Tumatumari*
Wilson Harris, *Ascent to Omai*
Wilson Harris, *The Age of the Rainmakers*
Marion Patrick Jones, *Panbeat*
Marion Patrick Jones, *Jouvert Morning*
George Lamming, *Water With Berries*
Roger Mais, *Black Lightning*
Edgar Mittelholzer, *Children of Kaywana*
Edgar Mittelholzer, *The Harrowing of Hubertus*
Edgar Mittelholzer, *Kaywana Blood*
Edgar Mittelholzer, *My Bones and My Flute*
Edgar Mittelholzer, *A Swarthy Boy*
Orlando Patterson, *An Absence of Ruins*
V.S. Reid, *The Leopard* (North America only)
Garth St. Omer, *Shades of Grey*
Andrew Salkey, *The Late Emancipation of Jerry Stover*
and more...